Off Herring Cove Road
The Problem Being Blue

BOOK 3

OF THE HERRING COVE ROAD SERIES

MICHAEL KROFT

This is a work of fiction. The characters and incidents are products of the author's imagination, are used fictitiously and are not to be construed as real. Any resemblance to actual persons, living or deceased, is entirely coincidental.

Copyright © 2015 by Michael Kroft

Third Edition

All rights reserved. No part of this novel/book may be used or reproduced in any manner whatsoever, including by translation, without written permission, except in the case of brief quotation embodied in critical articles and reviews.

All adaptations of the Work for film, theatre, television and radio are strictly prohibited.

CHAPTER 1
Fifty Thousand Dollars, Please

Av Rosen stood blank-faced in line at a bank on Spring Garden Road, just two blocks up from what was once his main office for his once chain of drugstores.

In his black suit, which he felt was appropriate for a situation such as this, and between the almost waist-high, two-inch-thick cords, which guided its clients to the cashier's counter, he stood almost half a head over most of those in front of him, staring straight ahead through his protective introverted shell that for the last few months he had had almost no use for, except in a situation such as this.

He sniffed the air and smelled nothing out of the ordinary. He hoped to grab a smell of the always-fleeting scent of his wife's perfume. The scent that could on occasions such as this relax him, comfort him, and make him believe his wife was still looking out for him. Not smelling it, he thought perhaps she and he had differing opinions regarding this situation.

Alone in his world of anxiety, Av failed to notice the small senior directly in front of him release her frustration through a huff and then, with an impatient jitteriness, quickly look back to glance up at him. She looked forward again before spinning back and saying with some volume, "It's almost as cold in here as it is out there, eh?"

Av forced himself to look down at the woman, who appeared to be around his age, and ask in his monotone British voice that he seldom lowered and even more seldom raised, "I am sorry?"

"I say, it's as cold in here as it is out there. But then you're a man; you don't feel it like us fragile women, eh? My Dan was like that. He was hot when I was cold. We ended up sleeping in different rooms because of it, we did." With a laugh, she tapped Av's thin arm and added, "Oh, how people used to laugh at us when they visited, me snug in a heavy sweater and him sweating in a T-shirt."

Responding simply with, "Right," Av resumed looking forward.

From his desk on the other side of the counter and beside the vault's opened and overbearing square door, the bank manager, of such an average height, weight and look that he could have easily blended into the background, surveyed the growing line of customers and decided he was needed at the counter. As he stood up and fixed his suit jacket, his eyes focused on an older man standing out among the rest. It took the manager several seconds to recognize one of his more important customers. Not having seen the unusually introverted customer in over a year and with his thick black mustache gone and his wife not confidently standing next to him and holding his hand securely as a mother would hold a child's, he was almost unrecognizable.

"We might be here for another half-hour, I think," continued the woman.

Av continued looking forward.

She tapped his arm. "Talk, talk, talk, that's all they can do! No one can do their banking without updating the teller on their life, eh?"

Not paying attention to what the woman was saying, Av responded to the verbal question mark at the end her comment. "Right."

"No consideration for others!" she said, raising her voice. "And those damn immigrants, those chinks in front over there, they're the worst, the worst! They're going to keep us here till next week! They take so long trying to say what they want, we might as well've brought a lunch with us, eh?"

"Right," Av responded again to the verbal question mark,

before noticing several Asians further ahead turned around and staring coldly up at him.

Realizing what he had just agreed with and having only one place to escape to, Av decided to come back later that afternoon. He stiffly turned around to make his way shamefully through those between him and the exit.

"Mr. Rosen? Avriel Rosen?"

"Yes?" a startled and even more anxious Av answered as he turned toward the voice.

"Hi. I'm Mr. Harrison, the...the manager here. We met several times before. It's nice to see you again. Please, come with me." The bank manager forced a smile as he unclipped the cord from its chrome pole, stepped aside to allow his client to pass through and said, "Mrs. Kirkland, we're sorry for the delay. The wait shouldn't be much longer."

With a huff from the old woman, Av stepped out of the line, accompanied Mr. Harrison through an opening in the cashier's counter and then responding to the man's gesture, sat on a padded metal chair in front of the man's desk.

Awkwardly sitting behind it, Mr. Harrison adjusted his tie with noticeably shaking hands. "Sorry for your wait. I...I almost didn't recognize you without Ruth, without your wife...may she rest in peace." Normally the man would have started some small talk, but his customer's rigid presence forced him instead to say, "Please, next time you...you visit us, come and ask for me, or if you spot me...come right over."

"Right."

"It's been awhile since you've been here. I see Mr. Walker here almost weekly," said the manager, and then clearing his throat, he asked, "What...what's the pleasure of your visit? What can I do for you today?"

"I need to withdrawal fifty—"

"Fifty dollars? That's no problem. I can have that for you in a flash." The manager stood up and forced another smile. "I'll just need to step away for a sec to use one of those newfangled computers at the counter. I'll be right back."

Av forced out, "I am sorry, but...but I will require fifty *thousand* dollars."

Noticeably taken aback, Mr. Harrison lost his smile and his eyes widened. He continued to stand behind his desk for a moment before awkwardly sitting back down.

"Fifty? Fifty thousand? In cash?"

"That is correct."

"We...we normally don't keep that large of an amount on hand. If you'd...if you could give us a week, we could have it for you."

"I require it today."

With his face reddening and his forehead beginning to shine, Mr. Harrison adjusted his tie. "Mr. Rosen, that's quite a lot of...of money...of cash. I don't mean to pry, to stick my nose where it may not be appreciated, but I have to ask if there's something going on, something bigger I can help you with?"

"Yes, you can help me withdraw fifty thousand dollars in cash, today," Av said, his annoyance starting to drip through a crack in his introverted shell.

For a few of seconds Mr. Harrison just stared at the old man sitting across from him.

"Ok, right, I'll have to make a few phone calls to some of our...our other branches and send someone over to pick up what they can spare...but I expect I may be able to round up fifty...fifty thousand dollars in a couple of hours. Do you have anywhere to go, anything to do until then?" With a shake of the head from the old man, he added, "Ok then, perhaps, while you're waiting, I–we could pay for your lunch. If you would just bring us back the receipt, we'll be happy to reimburse you."

"That is not necessary," Av said, his expressionless face hiding his naive surprise with both the steps that would have to be taken and the offer of a free lunch.

Mr. Harrison glanced at his watch and cleared his throat. "Ok, well it's twelve forty now. Can we meet back here at...say three? We close at three thirty, but I'll be happy to wait for you if you're late getting back."

Av stood up. "Great. Thank you. At three then."

Under the watchful eye of Mrs. Kirkland, who was now

two people closer to the cashiers, Mr. Harrison stood up and walked Av to the bank's pair of glass doors, where they shook hands with Av failing to notice the man's sweaty palm -his was just as sweaty.

"Sorry again for the delay, Mr. Rosen, but we should have it here by the time you get back."

"Right. Thank you."

As Av headed down Spring Garden Road in the direction of the Halifax Public Gardens, Mr. Harrison shook his head as he returned to his desk, sat down and began turning his Rolodex wheel of contacts.

Where someone may have passed the time by shopping, Av would not, and where someone may have entered a restaurant for lunch, Av would not, but where someone may have entered the Halifax Public Gardens to feed the ducks, pigeons or squirrels, Av may have too, but only to watch curiously from a distance that someone feeding them.

With the Public Gardens closed for the season, he felt the need to keep moving and continued forward to nowhere in particular.

It was a chilly day but a bright one that required those passing him to wear sunglasses. After walking several blocks from downtown's retail area, Av began to take an uncommon interest in the various styles of sunglasses. It struck him as interesting that they came in all colors, sometimes multiple colors, and there seemed to be two extreme ranges from small, metal framed ones to large, plastic framed ones. There seemed to be lenses in every shape, including simple geometric shapes and oddly shaped ones like water drops falling straight down or inwards toward the nose. After a while of rating the glasses, it occurred to the old man that a much less flashy pair might be the perfect accessory for his introverted shell, though he did not think of it that way. He thought of it more as a mask he could easily and, perhaps, fashionably hide behind.

After twenty minutes of considering which style of sunglasses would best suit him, Av was surprised to find he was entering the area of Dalhousie University, only a twenty-minute walk from his home. Making a right onto Robbie

Street's several blocks of older detached houses lacking any substantial front lawns, he headed toward the retail section of Quinpool Road with most of its stores built into what were once also older detached houses lacking any substantial front lawns.

It had only taken him minutes to pick out a pair of black plastic-framed sunglasses with their overly large lenses somewhere between square and circular, and even with his habit of refusing help from a sales person, he was somehow still able to choose a pair that were popular that year.

Comfortably hidden behind his new sunglasses, which even without his mustache still made him look somewhat like a hip Groucho Marx, Av entered the bank. He spotted Mr. Harrison at his desk talking with a heavyset, balding customer squeezed into a three-piece suit and then was surprised to recognize him. Av took a deep breath and asked himself what his small friend would do. Finding his answer, he made his way to the counter where he loudly faked clearing his throat. Both men looked his way and both grew grins when they noticed the eccentric looking man whose face was covered by a large pair of women's sunglasses. Recognizing him, they mowed down their grins.

Meeting Av at the counter, Mr. Harrison forced a smile and extended his hand. "Welcome back, Mr. Rosen. Mr. Walker just dropped in for business. I–I say it's quite a coincidence, isn't it?"

Shaking the bank manager's hand, Av noticed the clammy touch and said, "I do not hold much belief in coincidences," and followed the man to his desk.

There, Mr. Walker also forced a smile and shook the hand of the stone-faced old man. "Mr. Rosen, How are you doing today?"

"As well as I can be," Av forced out as he released the man's hand.

"Great. I was just talking to Charles here, and he was telling me about a major withdrawal you'd requested. You could've just called me. I'd have picked it up for you. After all, that's part of what I'm paid for. Hey, it's quite the substantial withdrawal isn't it? Can I ask for its reason?"

Standing there feeling interrogated, Av's frustration trumped his anxious state. "Mr. Walker, excuse my candidness but you of all people should understand I am not a spontaneous individual and not prone to disclosing my reasons or reasoning except to those whom it may affect directly. And as I do not see it affecting you in any negative way, you will have to excuse me for keeping the reason to myself."

With all three continuing to stand while Mr. Harrison looked down at his desk as if he wished he was invisible, Mr. Walker said, "Right, uh...but Mr. Rosen, you must understand that I'm looking out for your best interests. With the buying and then the immediate reselling of Mrs. Dixon's home and then your recent rewriting of your will, you must appreciate my concern that you may be being taken advantage of."

Not appreciating the *right* followed by the *but*, which Av considered contradictive since the *but* automatically voided the *right*, Av stared coldly through his shades at his lawyer/money manager and said purposely slow so every word would be taken in, "I could appreciate your concern if it did not step in the way of my own, and I certainly do not appreciate your assumption regarding my naivety or the integrity of my friends' characters. I also do not appreciate the interference with this transaction. Based on your ignorance in the matter, it demonstrates, in my opinion, a high level of arrogance. Your job is to manage my investments, not manage my spending unless it threatens to exceed the other, which I am certain it does not." With Mr. Walker's face blushing and his eyes scattering about as if looking for a way out of the situation, Av continued, "With that said, I am finding myself forced to rethink my relationship with you." Av looked to the sweaty bank manager. "And with you also, Mr. Harrison, since I expect you must have called Mr. Walker here concerning my request." With the two men's discomfort exceeding his own, Av's comfort level rose, giving him the courage to take control of the situation. "Now, if we may return to the reason for my being here. Have you acted as we had discussed, acted as you said you would, Mr. Harrison?"

"Y–yes, sir," said the bank manager, who had forced his eyes up from his desk to look at Av in shame before nervously sitting in his chair. Picking up a pen and shakily pointing it at a couple of forms on his desk, he said, "If you could sign these two forms here, just right here and here, w–we can finalize it."

With Mr. Walker standing opened-mouthed, Av sat down across from the banker, took the pen from the man's shaking hand and quickly and messily signed his name on the two forms.

Mr. Harrison burst the copies from their carbon paper and handed over a copy of each. Then he whispered, "And here's the cash. Fifty thousand as requested," as he opened his desk drawer and handed the old man a small but thick rectangular canvas pouch. "It slipped my mind to ask you how you wanted it, so I...I put it in hundreds. Please keep the pouch, compliments of the bank. Would you like to have it counted again?"

To the banker's obvious relief, Av stood up. "No. There is no need," he said as he turned toward Mr. Walker. "Mr. Walker, since I expect you are charging me for your time here, I will need you to make better use of it by putting together for me a detailed and current breakdown of the value of all of my assets, including..." He glanced at Mr. Harrison. "...an up-to-date balance of my account here and any other investments I hold with this bank. I will expect it in three days from now, Monday morning at ten."

"But, Mr. Rosen, that deadline's almost impossible!" pleaded Mr. Walker.

"Mr. Walker, you were able to take this time out of your day without any advance notice, and I am now giving you advanced notice...but allow me to make it easier for you. You can deliver it a week from this coming Monday, at ten, but I will need you to add to my request an argument as to why I should keep you as both my lawyer *and* money manager."

Comfortably protected behind his new sunglasses, Av left the two stunned men without any handshaking or goodbyes and made his way to his black Cadillac parked along South

Park Street a few blocks up Spring Garden Road.

He had never expected that his wife giving Mr. Walker both their legal and financial responsibilities was a good idea, but then when his wife had made a decision, she would have given it much thought before committing to it, and up until her death, she had never been proven wrong with any of her decisions. Av wondered if this was the exception.

It was only after he had started the car that it dawned on him that the boys would be coming home almost at that moment, and it would be the first time he was not there to greet them. His initial concern, since Dwight usually forgot his house keys, was that they would have to wait outside the locked front door. Av relaxed when he remembered Blue never forgot his. The boy had been in the habit of carrying his house keys for years. Then a second concern struck the old man. Since he would not be there to meet them as he had always done for over the last month since they started at the new school, they would certainly wonder and ask where he was. As they were family, it would be much more difficult *not* to explain himself to the them than it was with Mr. Walker.

In the short drive home, Av would have to come up with a lie, one he felt was justified in a situation such as this.

CHAPTER 2
Thirty-Eight Days Earlier
September 5, 1977

To the boy, the hundred and forty-seven-year-old graystone building, which still looked like the nunnery it had once been, appeared much more prestigious than the recently-built public school he had attended the previous school year. Each weekday morning after walking up the wide steps of stone bricks, its funnel of students were swallowed by its main entrance's jaws of two three-meter-tall wooden doors built into the front of its two-story midsection, which stood prominently on three hectares of manicured grass. The building's only two modern additions of a gymnasium and a pool were hidden at the back of each of the school's two three-story wings laid perpendicular to the main entrance. The building still commanded respect, if not because of its size, design or age then by its air of elitism. Its student capacity was far beyond the three hundred-plus students it regurgitated each weekday at three thirty, each a little brighter in the mind but much brighter in the face, if only because it was the end of the school day.

His classroom appeared much like any other. It, like the boy's previous school, used the then modern laminated tables instead of desks (three rows of four with two students shoulder to shoulder,) and offsetting the young tables was an older wooden desk at the front of the room, just a few feet out from the blackboard taking up most of the wall. To the right of the boy was a heavy wooden door with its small window at adult height and beside it another blackboard. Where the back walls of the elementary classes would be taken up by a corkboard of the students' art, his was taken up by a corkboard of student poems, school notices, and inspirational posters. Lastly, to his left, the six tall but narrow wooden-framed windows starting just above his seated eye level and climbing to where they almost touched the four-meter high ceilings gave little opportunity for distraction.

Sitting next to a girl he was less nervous around because of his lack of attraction to her, the anxious, freckled-faced redhead sat seemingly patient and relaxed as Mr. Davidson, the first of five teachers the boy would meet that day, welcomed them back from summer break and then proceeded to do roll call. After two minutes, the man reached the R's and then after calling out a name, seeing the raised hand, and exchanging a few friendly words with the returning student, he called out, "Roy, Bartholomew."

The redhead put up his arm. "Here."

"Welcome to Saint Thomas Aquinas, Bartholomew. Is it Roy like Roy Rogers, or do you pronounce it in French as *rwah*?"

"English is fine, sir, but I go by Blue, not Bartholomew."

Snickers and giggles surrounded the boy. They quickly subsided with the raising of the teacher's hand.

"Blue? Not Bart...the shortened version? Or maybe Red because of your—"

"No, it's just Blue."

More snickers and giggles.

"Ok, Blue it is. Let me know if I mess-up your name. Where'd you go last year? Which school?"

"Rockingstone...Rockingstone Heights."

"Oh, a Spryfielder," smiled the teacher and then asked with an even larger one, "So...how—are—you—this—morn—ing?"

The classroom filled with laughter.

Blue glanced at his tablemate and found her laughing made her even less attractive. With his face almost matching his hair, he stared with disapproval at the teacher. "Fine...and

I've heard that one before, sir."

The teacher lost his smile and cleared his throat. "Right. Well, still, welcome to the school. I expect we're more than a bit ahead of Rockingstone, so if you feel you need extra help, feel free to come and ask. We can assign you a tutor to help with the adjustment, if need be."

Blue nodded and the teacher looked down at his list.

"Ok, where were we? Right. Sampson, Calvin?"

A taller boy two tables behind Blue raised his hand. "Here. And *it's* Cal, sir."

The class laughed again.

The teacher smiled. "Yes, I'm aware of that. I just say them as I read them."

**

Where Blue had to suffer from a frustrating repeat of the name game by a different teacher for each of his classes that day, Dwight's day had only gotten better with each of his. Where the new school had initially intimidated him, the little blond boy now found himself staring it down. Much of what each of his five teachers had taught that day he had either done before or had easily understood as it was explained. His sixth grade English Reading List included most of the novels he had already read on his own, so he only had to read most of them just once more, just as his aging friend had once advised him: *Before doing a book report, one should read the book once to take in the story and then a second time to take down the notes.* The only thing that caused him a bit of stress was the science project due in four weeks. He had never done one before and now he had to find a partner among the unfamiliar students, decide on a topic, research it and then decide on an interesting way to present it.

"Ok, everyone, one last thing. By the end of next week, I need the list of partners on the science projects and the subjects. That should give you enough time to pick both," said Mrs. Meagle leaning firmly on her cane at the front of the class.

Dwight was surprised when she threw him a knowing look, but then realized it was for the person behind him. He looked back to find a smaller black boy with straight black hair parted on the side looking forward at him.

The boy's eyes instantly lit up and he exposed his teeth through a large smile as he gave a small wave of his hand and said, "Hi!" to the new student in front of him.

Embarrassed for being caught looking, Dwight returned only the physical part of the salutation before looking forward again.

"Ok, and by Mr. Jones' note, I'm to remind you all to read the first five chapters of *Charlotte's Web* by Monday. That gives you a whole week, and don't for—"

The school's buzzer drowned out the teacher, and as she attempted to repeat herself after it had stopped, the noise of the students moving their chairs back, collecting their books and leaving the class also drowned her out.

Following the flow of the majority of his classmates, Dwight made his way to his yet unfamiliar locker on the main level. There, he pulled up his shirtsleeve, read his combination and then fiddled with the lock. After having to go through the motions twice before it snapped open, he pulled out his tanned leather schoolbag, placed several books and notebooks into it, zipped it up and placed its strap over the shoulder of his black blazer.

Closing the locker, Dwight was surprised to find the small black boy standing at the next locker over. The boy held his schoolbag by its handle while aiming a large smile at him.

"Hilockerneighbor.IsitrightbehindyouinScience.It'sstrange thatI'vegotalockerrightbesideyoutoo,right?"

Dwight tossed a confused look at the fast-talking boy. "Huh? What?"

The boy took a large breath. "Hi. I sit behind you in Science, and it turns out my locker is right beside yours. I'm Lyon, but my mom calls me Lee...my dad too. Everybody here calls me Lyon, but you can call me Lyon or Lee, whichever you'd like."

Not sure how to take his classmate's energetic forwardness, Dwight placed his lock on the closed locker door and snapped it shut. "Ok...I guess I'll...I'll call you Lyon," he said, not wanting to be a hypocrite. Since meeting Blue, he had come to despise his own 'wimpy' nickname and was uncomfortable using one, especially after going through the effort of repeatedly demanding that those who called him Dewey, including this narrator, to call him by his birth name instead. He continued to use the nicknames of Blue and Av for his two best buddies, but he had come to think of those as their birth names and they did not have any problem with it, even going as far as to prefer it.

"Ok, Lyon it is. And you're Dwight, right? That's what the teachers called you —Dwight Dixon, correct? Hey, you shouldn't wear your bag over your shoulder. It'll damage your blazer. My mom got mad at me when she figured out how I ruined my first one that way. I'm just telling you so you won't get into any trouble. No one likes getting into trouble, correct?"

"Right...correct...I guess."

"Doyouwanttohearsomethingstrange?" Lyon paused for a second. "Do you want to hear something strange?"

"Ok," said Dwight, curious as to what would be stranger than the boy's fluctuating speed of speech combined with his boldness.

"I live right next to you too! I'm behind you in class, my locker's next to yours, and we live right beside each other! It's like we're meant to be friends! It's like fate!"

"Right...fate. Ok, I have to...to go now. I'll see you tomorrow...I guess."

**

As his classmates skirted past him on their rush out of the classroom, some wished him a good day while making a point of calling him Blue Bartholomew. He did not appreciate the name and thought if it were to continue, an example would have to be made out of one of them, the biggest one, though he was well aware that that could only make the name go underground, never to be said directly to his face. Then he reminded himself he was not in Spryfield and picking a fight with the biggest boy just to make a point was not an option.

For the third time that day, he loosened his tie, but this

time, he was certain a teacher would not direct him to fix it. He stopped at his locker, quickly unlocked his combination lock, placed his homework into his schoolbag, flung it over his shoulder and relocked it. Turning around, he spotted the school's dean, Mrs. Colvin, standing down the hall from him by an opened classroom door. The middle-aged woman wore the same disapproving frown that she had on earlier that day, when her glaring eyes had first met his that morning on the second-floor in the other wing of the school. This time, her eyes seemed to look right into him as if searching for some mischievous plan hidden within the files of his mind. The plan he had yet to come up with but she was certain he would. Then, when a second grader gave a tug on the leg of the dean's pantsuit and excitedly said something to the woman, her eyes instantly sparkled and her frown flipped around to show her seemingly manicured pearly whites. Blue passed her as the second grader took off toward the stairs. Her smile vanished and her eyes tried to pierce him as he said through an exaggerated smile, "Hi, Dean Colvin. Bye, Dean Colvin."

Two floors down as students rushed past him to make their way to the exit at the end of the hall, he met up with Dwight who, having turned around to leave Lyon standing there, slammed his face into Blue's chest.

Trying to act as if nothing had happened, Dwight said, "Hey, Blue."

"Hey, how was your afternoon?" grinned Blue.

"Great. This school won't be as tough as I thought."

"Good to hear. Hey, look at that! You've already stained your tie! Even with Av getting us a bunch, you're going to need to borrow some of mine," said Blue, pretending to scold his smaller friend as he began to loosen his tie.

"Don't untie it or you'll have to do it up for me tomorrow too!"

"I'm just loosening it. Anyway, I'll still have to tie you another one. Lisa won't let you wear this one again until it's washed...or dry-cleaned...or whatever they do with ties. There, doesn't that feel better?"

"Yeah, I guess. How was your afternoon?"

"Tough. I already have lots of homework. We're doing stuff I never even heard of," said Blue, who then joked, "I'm still not sure if Shakespeare's someone or something Africans do."

"Excuse me for interrupting," said Lyon. "It's probably both, but the Shakespeare you're studying was a sixteenth-century playwright and poet. He composed thirty-eight plays that we know of and over a hundred and fifty sonnets. Many of his plays are still put on today. He's considered the greatest playwright ever."

Dwight used his eyes to signal to Blue that the kid was crazy. "Uh...Blue, this is Lyon. Lyon, this is Blue. Lyon's in my grade...my classes."

"Nice to meet you, sir," said Lyon, offering his hand to shake.

Blue glanced at a grinning Dwight before uncomfortably shaking the little boy's hand. "Hi, Lyon. Hey, it's Blue, not sir, ok?"

"Sorry...it's a...a habit," said Lyon turning his eyes toward the floor.

"No problem. So, you're a regular Encyclopedia Brow—" Blue stopped short when he realized it could come off sounding racist. "Uh...we should get going, Dw—"

All were surprised by a husky boy a couple of inches taller than Blue appearing out of the stream of students and grabbing Lyon by the collar of his blazer.

"Lyon, I'm your partner, right!? Right!?" the boy demanded as he pulled up on Lyon's collar, forcing the small boy against the lockers. "Right, Lyon!?'"

Blue brushed Dwight aside. "Hey! Why don't you pick on someone your own size, like me?"

The bully released his hold on Lyon, who stayed against the lockers and watched as his aggressor faced off against Blue.

With his fists hanging at his sides, the bully said, "Red, you're new here so I'll let you walk away this time."

"It's Blue, and I *am* new here, so I'll let you fall away this time," responded Blue, before quickly moving toward the bully, sliding a leg behind him and with both hands pushing him backward. The bully tripped, landed on his butt, and as he was picking himself up off the floor, Blue warned, "If you want pain, get up facing me. If you don't, turn around and go."

The bully twisted his body so his back was to the boys, stood up and disappeared into a wave of students.

Blue turned to a wide-eyed Lyon. "You get that a lot around here, racists coming after you like that?"

"He'snotaracist.He'sjustslowandwantstobemyscienceprojectpartnerforaneasyA."

"What?" Blue asked, glancing over to Dwight who wore a full smile and responded with an I-have-no-idea shrug.

Lyon took a couple of deep breaths. "Sorry, he's not a racist. I don't think there are any here. He just wants to be my partner for the science project."

"He's in our class?" asked Dwight.

Lyon nodded. "He sits at the back...in every class."

"Oh...ok," said Blue, who looked at his watch. "Hey, come on! We got to go! We kept Av waiting for five minutes already!" He started walking quickly down the then almost empty hall toward the far exit. Dwight and Lyon followed behind. "Still, Lyon, you know that guy was wrong to be so aggressive with you, right?"

"Right, but I might be as aggressive as him too if I was held back two grades. And I'd probably be jealous of me too for skipping two grades," Lyon informed the two as he struggled to keep up with them.

"He should be in Blue's grade, and you skipped two? You must be a genius, and he must be *really* stupid!" Dwight said in wonder of his first time meeting someone who had skipped grades and someone who had failed them. He had heard of such things but thought they were only tall tales.

"I don't think he's that. I think he just doesn't apply himself...and I'm not a genius. My parents force me to study, study all the time. Now, they have me studying calculus. They're always telling me it's fun, but it's not! I hate it!"

Looking ahead, Blue joked, "So what do they do to ground you? Send you outside to hang out with your friends?"

"No, I don't have any," Lyon said as he struggled to keep up.

Blue stopped to wait for two students no older than seven struggling with the heavy metal door in front of them.

Dwight looked at Lyon. "You don't have any friends?" he asked, before crashing into the back of Blue and then pretending nothing happened.

"How can I when everyone my age is two grades behind and those in my class are two years older? My mom says it's the reason I'm socially awkward."

Neither Blue nor Dwight knew how to respond to Lyon, but both found themselves liking him if only because they felt bad for him.

Blue reached out above the two small students' heads and pushed the door open for for them. As the students exited, Blue held the door open for Dwight and Lyon. "Are your folks picking you up?" he asked Lyon, if only to change the subject.

"No. They think I'm old enough to walk by myself now."

Outside, the boys found themselves to the right of the school's main doors where a line of cars was crawling along the semi-circle driveway picking up students. The two younger boys continued following behind Blue as he took the lead on the stone path to the main entrance of the building.

"Where do you live?" asked Blue.

"The house next to yours, on your house's left."

Blue looked back at Lyon. "What? The house next to our place? Really?"

Lyon smiled and nodded.

"Well, we're getting a drive. I'm sure Av will drive you too. What do you say, Dwight?"

"Sure...for sure, but maybe we can all walk to school together tomorrow instead of Av driving us," Dwight said with hopeful excitement. "It'll be the first time I get to walk with kids instead of an adult! That'll be so cool!"

Realizing his excitement may have made him appear even younger than Lyon, Dwight blushed but soon recovered from it when neither boy seemed to notice.

Blue said, "There's Av. Come on!"

Reaching the large, black Cadillac, which was making its third slow trip around the driveway, Blue opened the back door for Lyon and Dwight, closed it and then took the front seat.

"Hey!" exclaimed Dwight, who expected Blue to join them in the back and if not, then expected to share the front bench seat with him.

"Hello, boys," said Av still wearing his black suit from that morning when he had apprehensively expected to be escorting the boys into the school and only found out when they got there that the students were going in without their parents. Using the rear-view mirror, he looked back at the two smaller boys. "Dewey, I see you made a friend."

"It's Dwight!"

"Right, it is Dwight," Av grinned.

"Sorry to keep you waiting," Blue said.

"It is no problem at all."

"Lyon, this is Av. Av, this is Lyon," said Blue as he looked from one to the other.

"Hello, Lyon."

"Hello, sir."

"Av, he lives right next to us, and we thought you'd be ok driving him home instead of him walking."

"Of course."

"Hey, Av, is it ok if we walk to school with Lyon tomorrow morning...and back too?" Dwight asked.

"I cannot see why not, but you will have to ask your mother."

"Ok," Dwight said, confident that if Av thought it was ok his mother would too.

Breaking another grin, Av pulled an envelope from his suit pocket and handed it to Blue, who returned the grin as he took it, pulled out four bills, folded the envelope in half and placed it in his blazer's inside pocket. He then handed the loose bills to Dwight whose eyes lit up as he counted the money.

"Cool! Thanks, Blue! Av, how did he get you to give him money? I have twenty, so it must be...it must be forty altogether, right?"

Blue answered for the old man. "Right. We bet I'd speak extinctly for a mon—"

"I think you mean distinctly," Lyon cut in, causing Av's grin to grow to a full smile.

"Right, *distinctly*...for a month (no using my regular talk) so I'd fit in better at the school, and we bet that Spock here would have to shorten his words, his verbs."

"Do you mean contraction?" asked Lyon.

"Right, contraction," said Blue, becoming annoyed with the corrections. "But he lost right after the bet started."

Av added, "And if he uses his Maritime accent before the month ends, he returns the forty dollars to Spock and neither wins. In all fairness to me, I am an old man and changing my habits is almost impossible."

"So, that's why you were talking different today," said an enlightened Dwight. "Hey, wait a minute! Does that mean if you lose too, I have to give back the twenty dollars?"

"Hey, have I ever lost a bet, ever?" asked Blue.

"Nope," Dwight said, feeling more secure with his sudden windfall of cash.

Reaching their homes, Av dropped Lyon off first, and as soon as the little boy entered his home, his excitement showed his young age as he rapidly told his mother about his new classmate *and* friend and about his older, freckled-faced redheaded brother, whose name was Blue, not Red.

CHAPTER 3
Coping by Adjusting

That afternoon at home, Blue decided he would not do his homework after supper as he had always done, if he even did it, but he would do it immediately after getting home, as Dwight did.

With his bedroom door locked in order to keep out the distraction named Dwight, Blue sat at his adult-sized desk in his oversized bedroom struggling with his math homework due the next day. It was his most difficult subject, and for a flash, he regretted not being held back a year. His school marks were never that good, and that combined with missing almost a month's worth of school due to all that went on at the end of the last school year should have sealed his fate to repeat the grade. However, due to Dwight's mother's legitimate excuse of the recent extraordinary circumstances and her promise that Blue would apply himself going forward, the principal of Rockingstone Heights School agreed to move him ahead. Blue did not help his case by telling the principal, "Do whats yas gotta do. I really don't care." But back then his comment could be justified when one considered that his failing the school year would have been the least dramatic event of that spring.

Taking Av's advice, that afternoon Blue decided to read the instructions provided in his math book. Rather than going only on the teacher's instructions on how to solve the problems and then at home, trying to apply those to the chapter's questions, Blue read the chapter's instructions and found it helped him grasp the concepts better. He wondered why he had never done that before, and then it occurred to him that no one had ever mentioned it, and in fact, he had never even realized the instructions were there. His previous math teachers directed him to open the book to the questions on pages so and so, and that was exactly what he did, ignoring all other pages.

With a better understanding of the process, Blue would find out that evening that the combined time to read the instructions and do the questions would be faster and less mentally painful than just doing the questions based on what he was told in class. He would later think that maybe Av was right when he suggested that he might be better at being self-taught than being teacher taught. Perhaps he was smarter than he had thought. Maybe he could be book-smart too instead of just street-smart.

**

Dwight struggled through the boredom of rereading *Charlotte's Web* while taking notes for his book report. Not being able to take much more of it, he decided after finishing chapter three to stop for the night.

Surprised to find Blue's bedroom door locked when he tried to get in to hang out with him, and with nothing to do, or nothing that he wanted to do, Dwight sat up on his bed in jeans and a T-shirt rolling a badly scuffed baseball in his hands while thinking of his new friend. He found it puzzling that Lyon spoke like a boy much older than he actually was, a boy confident with his intelligence, that is when he was not speaking like an auctioneer. It puzzled him too that Lyon seemed cheerful, but how could he be when he had no close friends and no not-so-close friends, and why would his parents make him skip two grades, destroying any chance he might have of making some? Dwight could not imagine his mother doing such a mean thing, especially after he too had experienced alienation by age when he had lived on Gilmore Street for the first nine years of his life. There were no boys his age on the street, and he did not like playing with the younger boys and the older boys felt the same way. And then on top of that, Lyon's parents were forcing him to learn stuff beyond what was being taught in school. To Dwight, it seemed like they were trying hard to make their son very unhappy. Then he remembered that Lyon was black. It would be too cool to have a black friend!

Hearing Blue's bedroom doorknob unlock with a snap, Dwight let the baseball fall on his lap. "How's your homework going?" he called out.

"Much better than I thought," answered Blue as he walked into Dwight's bedroom with its many different-sized model jets hanging from the ceiling. He tapped the bowl of Dwight's goldfish, J.C. the Second, sitting on the dresser and watched the fish dash about. "I've only got a couple of scenes of *A Midsummer Night's Dream* left and then my homework's all done." He looked at his watch. "Hey, look at that, it's almost six. Let's go see what Av's up to."

Dwight gently picked up the purring orange tabby semi-sleeping across his shins. "Sorry, Sam, but I have to get up." Laying the cat down beside him, he stood up and asked, "Hey, are you staying in your school clothes?"

"Sure. I actually like them," said Blue, not wanting to admit he was too lazy to change clothes. "Sort of makes me feel smart. Dress smart to look smart, they say."

"You probably want to wear three sets then," Dwight joked and then got the expected light punch on the shoulder.

With Sam following behind, the two walked down the hallway to the floating staircase where Dwight gestured for a banister race. Getting a headshake from Blue, they descended the stairs and spotted Av through the two-level library's opened French doors on their left, halfway between the stairs and the marble-floored foyer's two large front doors.

In the library sparsely populated by books on its main floor and hanging over the boys was a metal-railed walkway following three walls of book shelves with the fourth taken up by a set of three twelve-foot, curtainless windows looking out at a large front yard surrounded by a cast-iron fence.

"What are you reading?" Blue asked the old man sitting in a brown leather chair with his back to them.

Startled, Av flung his head around. "You two surprised me. Blue, I have to get used to you speaking properly. I almost did not recognize your voice."

"It's not as hard as I thought. I was thinking of adding a British accent like yours, but I was scared I'd lose my contractions," quipped the redhead.

Dwight laughed just as the loud gong of the doorbell filled the foyer.

Removing his reading glasses, Av quickly reached into his pocket to pull out a crumpled twenty dollar bill. "That would be the Chinese food. We are celebrating the first day of school. Could one of you pay the man and bring the food into the kitchen?"

With the twenty in his hand and excited by the anticipation of his favorite meal, Dwight gave the delivery man the money and seeing the change of eight dollars and something cents, did as Av would do and gave the appreciative man back five dollars.

Av got up from the chair, and together Blue and he intercepted Dwight near the kitchen's entrance opposite the library and relieved the struggling boy of the large, heavy paper bag and the two-liter bottle of Sprite.

As Dwight and Blue prepared the dining room's antique table with dishes, cutlery and glasses, Av removed the containers of food, opened each and examined the contents. He would have preferred to order from what was their usual place until their recent move, but they did not deliver that far. Av's examination was interrupted by a second gong, and before he could ask the boys to answer it, both were passing through to the foyer.

"Yes?" Blue asked the two young men wearing shirts and ties under their opened spring jackets.

"Hi. Is your mommy or daddy home?" asked the black one.

"Mommy? Daddy? No mommies or daddies here —maybe a mother or father," Blue answered with condescension.

"Ok, can we speak to them, please?"

"Maybe. What's it about?"

"We'd like to talk about family."

"Really? You're Jehovah Witnesses, right?"

The two men nodded.

"Well, I can see why you'd want information from us, but there isn't much *you* can tell us about family."

The two men immediately stiffened up.

"Why is that?" asked the white Jehovah Witness.

"Well, let's see. You'd let a family member die rather than give them blood; you'd shun them if they don't follow your religion, and you don't even celebrate people's birthdays, their life. No, I think we should be teaching you about family."

As the men stood there confused trying to absorb what they had heard and who they had heard it from, Blue closed the door.

"We never got a chance to respond!" protested the black Jehovah Witness to the white one.

"No, we didn't, but we'll try again later, Blair,"

"Doesn't this frustrate you?" asked Blair.

"Not at all. You get used to it. At least it wasn't the door slamming right away."

On the other side of the door, Dwight asked Blue, "Who were they and how did you know all that?"

"Jehovah Witnesses. Don't you remember? I told you about that religion. They go door-to-door recruiting, but not so much in Spryfield. Remember when I was seeing Sally by the playground? She was a Jehovah Witness. She hated it but could never leave. That's why she had to break up with me; I wasn't a Witness. Someday she'll be going door-to-door too, and I hope she comes to ours. It'll be nice to see her again."

"Who was at the door?" Av asked the two as they entered the kitchen.

Before Dwight could answer, Blue said with a straight face, "Someone looking for directions to Halifax?"

"Halifax? You told them they were here, correct?"

"Sure, but they didn't believe me, so I sent them to Dartmouth."

Dwight laughed and then cut in before Av could respond. "Av, it was a couple of Jehovah Witnesses. Blue is starting to make your kind of jokes, but not as funny."

Av grinned. "That is quite the compliment, but perhaps I should rethink my *kind* of jokes. With my deadpanned face, if the joke were lost, it would appear I was lying...or crazy. For a long time, I may have been telling many lies without realizing it."

A few minutes later, after parking her small car beside Av's Cadillac, Lisa, a slender woman in a blouse and jeans, entered the house.

"I'm home! It smells like we're celebrating tonight!" she said as she kicked off her shoes, joined Av and the boys in the dining room and handed out hugs with kisses to the cheeks.

After all had served themselves, the two adults watched the boys devour their supper with passion.

"So...how was your first day at the school, guys?" Lisa asked, hoping the question would slow the boys down.

Blue was the first to swallow his food and answer that he liked the school but had not expected so much homework, but he felt he could handle it, especially if he used the method Av had recommended for doing his math.

Lisa smiled at Blue seeming to effortlessly drop his usual way of speaking and she joke that maybe their retired friend should study to be a teacher too.

With some food still in his mouth, Dwight told his mother about his classes and then told her about his new friend Lyon, impressing her with his new friend's intelligence. When he asked, she gave her permission for them to walk to and from school with him, "as long as you go straight to and straight back."

Av reluctantly and shamefully admitted that he had done little but read most of the day. He would have to adjust to the boys returning to school and to them staying there for lunch too. When he mentioned he may have to look into a hobby, a more productive hobby besides reading, Dwight insisted it could not be building model planes because that was what they did together, sometimes, and then joked that Av should take up knitting, which Blue seconded, adding he could never have enough socks. After the boys had stopped laughing at their teasing of their older friend, a smiling Lisa suggested to a blushing Av that he take up photography and turn one of the three guest rooms into a darkroom. Av like the idea and said he would look into it.

After Dwight had asked his mother how her school was going and after she had told him to swallow his food before speaking, he learned she had yet to talk to her classmates in her first week of university. Being at least ten years older than most of the other freshmen, she expected she was considered an old lady who should be avoided and perhaps discretely made fun of, surprising Dwight that the alienation by age applied to adults too. She found the courses interesting and the workload bearable, and she made a point of telling Av that that was mostly due to him watching the boys. Dwight was also surprised to learn his mother had only three classes on Monday, Wednesdays and Fridays and only two on Tuesdays and Thursdays, but she was at school all day. Between classes, she studied in the library so she would have more free time for them in the evenings.

**

The next morning, Blue and Dwight's alarm clocks went off just seconds apart, and seconds later each was turned off and the showers of their bedrooms' bathrooms could be heard. Blue liked waking up in the shower, and Dwight started doing it because if Blue did it, so should he.

Dwight found he liked showers too. They were much faster and, therefore, less boring if he had to take his twelve-inch G.I. Joe action figures out of the bath equation. He would still take a bath in the evening and secretly play with his G.I. Joes, which Blue thought were for infants, but that would only be once every two weeks at most.

As Mrs. Collins cleaned the downstairs bathroom, the boys entered the kitchen to have breakfast with Lisa in her pink bathrobe and Av in a polo shirt and pleated pants, which Lisa had gotten him and which over the last year and a bit, the old man had still not gotten used to their coarseness compared to his thirty-plus years attire of dress pants and dress shirts. With each washing of his relatively recent wardrobe of casual clothes, Av had hoped they would soften up, and when he found they finally were, they would disappear and new ones would spontaneously appear to take their place in his walk-in closet. After sitting at the kitchen's island eating their breakfast of eggs and burnt bacon, or super-duper crispy bacon as Av called it, the two boys took their lunches from off the kitchen counter and were about to say goodbye when the doorbell's gong filled the first floor.

Dwight was about to rush to the door when Blue held him back by his blazer.

"IT'S OPEN," Blue shouted, surprising all.

The doorknob could be heard turning several times.

"IT STICKS. YOU HAVE TO PUSH HARD," he advised the visitor, and then a second later, he added, "YOU HAVE TO THROW YOUR WEIGHT INTO IT."

All heard the sound of a thud against the door.

"YOU HAVE TO DO IT HAR—"

"Blue, stop it! The boy is going to hurt himself!" Lisa scolded.

"I just want to see how smart he really is," explained Blue as he left the kitchen with Dwight following behind.

There was another thud against the door before they released the deadbolt and found Lyon rubbing his shoulder with his schoolbag lying on the stone porch.

"Well, would you look at that! I guess it was locked," Blue grinned.

Lisa and Av soon joined the three at the door.

Being introduced to Dwight's new friend, Lisa was tickled to discover Lyon was black, amused to think her son's father would be rolling in his grave had he not been cremated, and proud that her son had not inherited any of his father's racism.

With boys following Lisa's request of walking directly to school, Lyon asked his new friends, since they looked nothing alike, if they had different fathers. He was not surprised to learn they did, but was surprised to learn they had different mothers too.

"So, you're friends. I assumed you were brothers with

different fathers...because of your different color hair. I saw you playing catch in the front of your house a few times and just assumed—"

"You shouldn't assume," said Blue, hoping the boy would drop the subject.

Lyon nodded his head. "Sure, we shouldn't assume something if we can verify it easily enough, and I just did, but we make assumptions all day. We expect things to be a certain way. We probably made a hundred of them since getting up. For instance, I assumed I'd wake up this morning, assumed my mom would make me breakfast, assumed that when I rang your doorbell, someone would answer it. I assumed too I'd wake up healthy, my parents would be up before me, water would come out of the sink, there'd be a clean uniform in the closet, and everything would be where I left it the night before. And now I'm assuming the school won't be burnt to the ground when we get there. I assume too—"

"I get it," said Blue shaking his head. "I *assumed* your problem was making friends, but now I know it's keeping them."

The conversation may have gone on longer if Blue knew the difference between *assume* and *presume*.

Having to hold back a laugh so as not to offend his new friend, Dwight proudly explained how he had met Blue, but as his mother had requested months ago, he skipped over the part about their friend Stevie and the drama that soon followed.

When Lyon inquired about Dwight's father and Blue's parents, Dwight explained his father's accidental death, and when he was about to tell his new friend about Blue's parents, Blue cut in and told Lyon that his mother had died and his father traveled a lot for business.

With Dwight looking up at him confused, Blue winked back at him before adding, "Lyon, keep that to yourself, ok?"

"Sure. But who would I tell? You two are my only friends, remember?"

Then Dwight proudly explained that Blue and he were more than just friends. They were best buddies, which were better than just friends and one could only have four best buddies, male or female, as per some law book that Av had claimed to have read.

"I'd like to be someone's best buddy too," Lyon hinted.

"You can. It just takes time to go from being a friend to a best buddy. Av says it can be weeks or months, or even years."

"So whose grandfather is he?"

"He's not," said Blue. "He's our best buddy too."

"Yup," agreed Dwight. "I met him first...before I knew Blue. He was my neighbor, a mean, scary neighbor at first, and then when I got to know him, he was nice and funny. He didn't like people. He was a pervert."

Lyon's eyes enlarged. "What?"

"An introvert. He means introvert," Blue calmed their new friend.

"Right, an introvert," said Dwight. "He still is, but not as much."

"Not with us, anyway," Blue added.

At school, as Blue went on his own way, Lyon flattered Dwight by continuing to stick to him. In each of their classes, he negotiated with Dwight's current table partner for their seat and once, to a teacher's amusement, even negotiated several people around until all were finally satisfied with their new placements.

Dwight would later learn that being Lyon's friend would cost him opportunities to make more of them, but he was content with that. He had learned the school year before that having a close friend was like having fifty not so close ones.

**

That second day at his new school, Blue tried to fit in with his classmates. He did not meet Dwight outside at recess as he did the day before but instead stayed in class and listened in on the exchange of jokes by his classmates. Then the next day's recess he did the same, but when the group began exchanging jokes, he volunteered some of his own, which he expected they had already heard but it turned out they didn't.

A couple of minutes before the bell signaled the end of that recess, Blue shocked his new classmates. He borrowed the heavy metal stapler from the teacher's desk, bent it back from its base as if he was going to staple something to the wall, and with his classmates watching closely, he held a two dollar bill to his forehead and stapled it there. After the astonished students, with some of them unable to control their wincing, had examined the staple in the bill attached to his forehead, Blue gave up the trick by showing that the stapler was empty of staples, showed the rolled up piece of tape on the other side of the bill and explained that he had earlier put a staple in it. After that, Blue was part of the group.

While explaining the trick to his friends, Blue almost failed to notice the frowning Dean Colvin staring coldly at him through the window of the classroom's closed door. When he did notice, she turned and walked down the hall.

Blue had Av to thank for the trick. That previous rainy Saturday while Lisa was studying in the library and the two boys played risk at the dining room table, a bored Av with a stapler in his hand joined a frustrated Blue and a delighted Dwight as they were finishing the game.

"I finally figured it out! I figured out how not to forget about my reminder notes, so I will not forget what I need to be reminded about!" proclaimed Av with a rare excitement. He then pulled a small piece of paper from his pocket and stapled it to his forehead. Both boys stared at him with opened mouths and wide eyes. They were so speechless that they never asked the old man the question he was hoping they would: how would that help you remember? So, he could not answer with his line, "Well, I would not forget about the note because people would be constantly reminding me about it, asking me why I have it stapled to my forehead." Instead, Av was forced to explain it was only a trick and then walk them through how he did it. Thinking it 'The coolest trick,' Dwight suggested it would be better to use paper money. Av took his friend's suggestion, flattened out a crunched up two dollar bill and then walked the two through the trick by putting the staples back into the stapler, stapling a staple into the center of the bill and then sticking a piece of Scotch tape folded over onto itself onto the back of the bill. Moving the base of the stapler back, he went through the motion of stapling the bill to his forehead. The old man's normally stoic face switched to surprise and then to pain as he removed the stapler to reveal two staples in the bill: the flat one he had stapled into it seconds before and a new one in almost perfect condition sticking almost all the way out. Luckily, the second staple only barely penetrated the old man's skull. Wincing, Av pulled the staple from his head and then told the boys he did it on purpose to show what would happen if they forgot to remove the staples before performing the trick. "The stuff I have to *purposely* do to myself to teach you boys something!" Av lied to save face. "I hope you appreciate it tomorrow when I show you how *not* to use a power saw."

It was difficult for the boys to feel bad for their friend when he wore a Spiderman Band-Aid on his forehead for the next three days.

**

On their lunch break of the third day of school, Blue informed his best buddy that he would be eating lunch with his classmates.

Dwight had been secretly disappointed that Blue was standing him up at recess, but he was vocal about being stood up for lunch too.

"What! Seriously? First recess and now lunch! Come on!"

"Dwight, we'll hang out to and from school, but I want to have lunch with the guys from my class."

"Fine," Dwight huffed, having never considered that the two years grade difference would affect their relationship at school. It was the first time the two had attended the same school.

With Blue not eating with them and Lyon being alienated by the students in the cafeteria to the point where Dwight and Lyon were unwelcome at several tables, the two opted for eating on the steps of the school's main entrance.

Expecting them to spend a lot of time together at school, Dwight decided to take their friendship to the next level by inviting Lyon to his house that evening.

Lyon's embarrassment was obvious.

"I can't...not tonight. I have...Ihaveballetpractice."

"Ballet?" asked Dwight who was beginning to make sense of his friends rapid speaking when he was nervous or excited.

"IwantedtodoTaekwondo,butmydadsaysIhavetodoballetbeforeIstartthat."

"Really? You've got to do ballet? You need to get a black belt or something in ballet first?"

Lyon took a deep breath. "No, there are no belts in ballet. My dad thinks it'll stretch and strengthen my legs before I start Taekwondo. I really want to learn Taekwondo."

"That's weird. I mean, isn't Ballet for girls? You have to wear a skirt too?"

"No, boys don't wear tutus! And there *are* boy ballet dancers!"

"Right...ok, what about tomorrow night?"

Slightly embarrassed by his own frustration, Lyon said, "Can't, I have piano practice."

"How about Friday night?"

"Sure! I have nothing then! I'll come over after supper!" Lyon said before a thought hit him. "Wait a second. My mother wants to meet you...so how about you come over to my place?"

"Cool," said Dwight. "Then let's do that!"

Dwight would later learn that Lyon had fencing lessons on Monday nights, French lessons on Tuesday nights and violin lessons on Sunday nights.

The little boy only wanted to learn Taekwondo.

CHAPTER 4
The Thirteenth Tribe

Beyond the dirty bar and just past the badly scratched pool table encircled by five bar tables in need of a wiping were three windows looking into what appeared to be a conference room covered in framed black and white photographs and various plaques. Beneath two of the smaller name-engraved plaques were two large-framed, almost identical weathered leather vests with three bold patches on the backs. The top patch of a thick, downward semi-circle had THIRTEENTH TRIBE stitched into it, the bottom, an upward semi-circle, had HALIFAX, and in between the two was a patch of two crossed tomahawks. In this strong body odor-scented room, which all referred to as church, was a cheap looking melamine conference table surrounded by ten chrome chairs. In every chair but two sat men, all white and all in jeans with T-shirts under their black leather vests patched identical to those on the wall.

"So, lastly, or I guess second last, what's been done with Leroy Mansing?" asked a man sporting a blond goatee at the far end of the table, and even though his was sitting, his five-two height was noticeable.

"He disappeareds," smiled a larger man sitting across from the windows. "No one'll find 'im. We—"

The goateed man barked, "We don't need to know what's done, do we? The less who knows, including me, the better. We just need to know if there's a chance he'll pop up again!"

"Nope, he won't," said a smaller man sitting next to the larger one. "And, Howard, if he does, who's gonna care abouts a dead drug-dealing blacky?"

"We don't want to find out!" said Howard with his voice rising. With the smaller man noticeably embarrassed, Howard took a moment to calm himself before turning to the larger one. "There going to be any blowback from the North End?"

"No. I talked to...to Mr. Blacky."

Some of those around the table laughed.

"He tells me all's good. Leroy was goin' inta the Fairview pubs on 'is own. He wasn't even sellin' their shit. They'd've dealt with 'im if we didn't beats 'em to it."

"So, Mr. Blac...Simon was ok with it? It's ours again and there won't be any fighting over it? What about the little shit, that little sissy he scared off, did ya replace him? You got someone else there?"

"Yeah. For now, we gots Bird managin' there. The small area will give'em some experience."

"Good," said Howard, who then seemed to flush red slightly. "And the last thing —the patch-over. Jack will be here early next week, and until he's done going through everything, I'm having everyone stay away from the clubhouse from next week on. It's a need-to-be-here basis only. That means only Numbers, Snap and myself will be here. We'll be busy here for a bit and then giving him a tour of the properties. We'll let everyone know when to come back. I'm betting there'll be church then...with Jack as the president and Snap here as the VP. Until then, it's business as usual. If you need to talk with someone, call or drop in on them, but stay away from here."

"So this is the end of your reign?" asked a man at the opposite end of the table.

"Yup, this could be the last time I sit here," Howard said forcing a grin. "You won't be getting rid of me altogether. I'll be semi-retiring by taking over Frank's weed distribution...and selling the other shit too. I'll easily triple that pussy's sales."

Breaking the moment of awkward silence caused by Howard referring to Frank as a pussy, the man at the opposite end of the table forced a smile and said, "Well then, I say we give ya a hell of a send-off. Tink, get behind the bar and start popping off the beer tops. And the beer better be cold!"

"Yeah, ok, but, Howard, what's gonna happen with us prospects, Bird and me?" asked Tink, the youngest and the cleanest shaven in the group.

"From what I understand, you'll remain prospects with the Headless. How's that top popping going?"

"I'm goin', I'm goin'," said the prospect as he got up and left the room. "I'll gives the bar a cleanin' up too."

Howard shouted back to him, "Don't bother. It'll just get dirty again." Then grinning with raised eyebrows, he said to those at the table, "Hey, let's get some women over here. Who's got some coke? Let's make this one of the best of what better be my many send-offs."

As the men left the room, Howard stood up and gestured to a man with a long, black ponytail.

"Any luck yet finding Frank's kid?" Howard whispered to the man.

"Nope, nots yet, but I wills...if 'e's still in Halifax. I checked six schools so fars and nothin'. I'm workin' me way outta Spryfield. I checked Rockingstone on Monday mornin', Central, Monday afternoon, B.C. Silver, Tuesday mor—"

"Yeah, yeah, yeah. Let's just hope he's here. Keep looking, but if you don't find him by next Friday, follow them home after he and the old man visits Frank on Sunday. They can't be more than two hours away if the boy's there every week, right? It'll be cool if we can find him before Jack and his old lady gets down here? They'll owe us one...and we can both use it."

As both men walked to the door, Howard grinned. "Hey, Snap, wouldn't it be ironic if he was in New Brunswick? Them coming down here and him going up there. Wouldn't Jack's old lady be pissed?"

CHAPTER 5
New Friends and a Hobby

That first week of school, Blue targeted a girl one grade lower for his affection, and after overhearing in the lunchroom that she was joining the next day's lunchtime Choir Club, Blue too was soon a member —for almost half an hour. It only took that long for the music teacher to realize the boy could not sing. After having the members practice several songs, something did not sound right to the woman, and it took several students individually singing the tonal scale before she came across the problem.

Trying to make his voice as high as most of the others in the group, Blue belted out, "Do, re, mi, fa, sol, la, ti, do."

The teacher stared at Blue for a moment and then with sympathetic eyes, asked, "Blue, would you mind if I asked you to leave?"

"Yes, of course I mind!" an embarrassed Blue responded. "But seeing how I'm not wanted, I'm not going to stay!" As he was leaving the room, he turned back and added, "Excuse me for thinking I'd be taught to sing and not expected to be a professional when I joined."

Blue soon found that being asked to leave the Choir Club was a good thing. Not only did he not want to be there for any other reason but to meet the young lady of his interest, but being asked to leave gained him some attention from her. After lunch, Karen, a thin blonde with large brown eyes, came up to Blue at his locker and gave her condolences, making a point of telling him that she thought asking someone to leave the club was selfish since it was only for the 'lazy teacher's benefit.'

Even with Karen approaching him first, Blue's confidence with the opposite sex still needed much boosting and each greeting from her as they passed in the halls would boost it further, making Blue think he could have enough courage to ask her out before the end of that month.

**

Taking up his classmate's invitation to their Thursday night hangout, Blue and Dwight followed the simple verbal directions Blue had been given earlier that day. The two walked the five minutes down Jubilee Road to Conrose Park, entered the open space of mowed grass and took a left toward the sounds of talking, shouting and laughter at the far corner amid a patch of pine and maple trees slowly fighting for dominance of the area.

"Hey! He showed up and brought a bodyguard!" yelled Blue's classmate.

All heads turned toward Blue and Dwight as they walked toward the dozen or so youths.

To Dwight's appreciation, Blue said, "Cal, this is my little brother, Dwight."

"Hey, Dwight," greeted Cal.

"Hey," Dwight parroted back.

"Guys, this is Blue and Dwight. These guys here are from our school. Well, all but John here. He's in *public* school," the boy named Cal said and then laughed.

The boy named John waved and then brushed his long brown bangs out of his face. "Hey, man, I do the public school thing because I can wear what I please. No damn rules for me! I dress, look and shit as I please!"

John's eyes sparkled when Cal informed him that both boys had been in public school the year before and he broke a large smile when Cal teased them about being Spryfielders.

As Cal introduced Blue and Dwight to the rest of the boys and each welcomed the other with nods of the heads, Blue was surprised to find some of the boys were as old as sixteen.

Brian, an older boy, grinned as he commented that they

normally do not allow 'little kiddies' into their group but would make the exception if he would smoke a cigarette.

"He doesn't have to smoke to be cool," Blue said in his automated protective manner.

Dwight cut in. "Sure, I will. It's not the first time I smoked." He took the offered cigarette, borrowed the lighter and added, "Not my usual kind, but it'll do."

He then impressed several of the boys by lighting it, sucking the smoke into his mouth and then inhaling it into his lungs just as he had done several times back when he, Blue and their friend Stevie smoked while each drank a beer, the beer that had given Blue the courage to approach a girl in their neighborhood. Dwight and Stevie had drunk with him because Blue said it was not cool to drink alone, and all smoked because Blue said it was cool to smoke when drinking. Dwight hid his dizziness from the group of older boys and felt no urge to puke like he did the first time he had smoked.

Then, Brian offered one to Blue.

"No, thanks. He's cool enough for the two of us," said Blue, shooting a glare at Dwight, who threw a Cheshire Cat smile back at him.

Cal interrupted the two *brothers*. "Cool! Glen's here! Hey, Blue, we charge a buck fifty for the beer pool, but seeing how you're new, it's free this week. Glen, your brother came through for us again!"

"Yup," said Glen as he struggled with two arms to carry a case of twenty-four bottles of beer. "I'm thinking we should start drinking hard liquor. It's easier to carry and less obvious." He placed the case on the ground and as he opened the top of the cardboard case, several of the boys left their spot on the grass to join him. "It's warm, but warm beer is better than no beer, right?"

Cal introduced Blue and Dwight to Glen and then offered them each a beer. Blue accepted and Dwight, keeping up with his attempt to be cool, took one too and waited for the opener to come around.

With beers being drunk by most, Blue discovered he preferred cold beer over warm, and Dwight found he appreciated warm over cold —it went down easier. Dwight and Blue listened as the others talked about their teachers, the girls they were interested in and other boys they disliked. About half an hour into it and as both boys relaxed, the group began trading Newfoundlander jokes, before they segued into 'dirty' ones. Dwight failed to understand even one dirty joke and when he asked if someone could explain one, Cal was about to when Blue, finding himself having to focus harder to talk distinctly, cut in, "Dwight, I'll tell you later, like two years later," causing some of the older boys to laugh and tease a disappointed and embarrassed Dwight about his age.

An hour later and after a second beer each, the two light-headed boys took twenty minutes to make the five-minute trip home.

As they walked while occasionally looking down at their feet to make sure they were doing as expected, Dwight said, "Here's something that has me stumped. You wanna hear it?"

"Sure."

"Ok, a classmate's someone in your class. An inmate's someone in prison. A bunkmate's someone who shares a bunk bed, like you and I before we moved here, but what's a checkmate? Lyon was teaching me chess yesterday, and each time he won, he'd say, 'checkmate.' So, what's a checkmate mean? I get it means he won, but what's the word really mean? I didn't want to ask him and look stupid."

Blue laughed. "I hate to be the one to tell you, but you probably looked stupid losing each time," and then catching himself from stumbling over, added, "You sound more like you smoked weed than drank beer."

"What's the difference?"

"One's all *philersophical*, and the other's all lovey-dovey...sometimes."

"Weed's what Frank sold, right?"

"Right," said Blue. "One time when he was smoking it, he went to the washroom and ten minutes later came back all confused. When I asked him what was the matter, he told me he went to the bathroom but couldn't remember why he went there."

Dwight nodded his head.

"Get it? There're really only two things you'd go to the bathroom for, regular like, and he forgot which one it was when he should have felt the urge. Get it? It makes you stupid."

"Yeah, you told me it makes people stupid," Dwight said still not getting the joke.

"Right...anyway, a checkmate is the one who pays the bill. When you get a checkmate, the other guy pays the check, pays for whatever: the drinks, the dinner, whatever. You probably owe Lyon a lot of drinks and stuff now."

"Seriously?"

Blue laughed again. "No. I'll answer where I can and lie where I can't. That's one of the few things I remember about my granddad, Frank's dad. He used to say that...and he called ketchup cat-shit. I never understood that one. Why would you want to put something on your food that you call cat-shit? I'd think it'd be a turn-off."

"Yeah, me too. Ok, I'll ask Av later. He's sure to know."

"Oh, no you won't! He'll smell the beer and wonder what's going on. When we get to the house, don't spend too much time with them...better yet, don't spend any time with them. They might figure out what we did and ground us. We'll just go to your room and play Trouble or something."

"Fine. I'll ask him tomorrow, then," Dwight said. "Hey, you know what?"

"What?"

"I liked that you told them I was your brother. You're just like I imagined an older brother being."

Blue smiled and placed his arm over his smaller friends shoulder.

"There you go. Now you sound like you drank two beers. You know, you're like a brother to me, and everyone else assumes you are, so why explain the real story? It's too long, anyway. You're even better than a brother: I wouldn't get mad at you for insulting my mother."

Dwight placed his arm around Blue's back too. "I know how you feel about your mom, so that's not saying much."

Blue started laughing, and then Dwight started laughing. Then they broke their holds on each another and staggered down the sidewalk roaring with laughter.

Blue was the first to calm down. "Damn, everything is funnier when you're buzzing."

Dwight stopped laughing. "Blue, you hung out with Stevie and me, but did you ever hang out with kids your own age, like tonight?"

"Sure...sure, I did, but they always wanted to steal or get in a fight, sometimes with each other. They were jerks. That's why I hung out with Stevie. He didn't like that shit. He may have been a fighter, but he only did it when he had to. He only fought for a reason, and he didn't steal. And that's why I liked you. I knew right away you didn't like doing either, and I knew you'd stand your ground when you had to. I saw you do it. Remember, the two triplets wanting to steal your bike?"

Dwight nodded his head. "Yeah, that was the first time I had to, ever."

"See, it was natural for you."

"So, you're going to go back next week?"

"Sure, I think so. You?"

"No. I didn't feel right. I felt like a little kid."

"That's because you are."

"Hey!"

"You're younger than all the rest by at least two years. They see you as a little kid. You get it, right?"

"Yeah, I guess, but that means I won't hang out with you on Thursday nights either. First, it's recess, then lunch and now, Thursday nights! I miss you, best buddy!" Realizing what he had just admitted, Dwight paused for a second, before adding, "I don't really like beer. It makes me say stuff I wouldn't normally say."

With his arm again around Dwight's shoulders, Blue said, "That's what big and little brothers do. We have different friends but we still get our time together. We can't be around each other twenty-four hours a day. I'll have my friends and you'll have Lyon, and who knows who else. You get it, right?"

"I get it, but I don't like it," said Dwight as he placed his hand on Blue's far shoulder. "Ok, let's try this. Let's walk with separate legs. Outside legs first, inside legs next. No! You're left and my right. Ok, now the other leg. Yeah, that's it!"

Continuing to cling to each other and walk as Dwight had insisted, the boys closed in on their home.

Blue asked, "Hey, you're not going to say anything about what we did tonight, right? We should keep it a secret, like the graveyard by Stevie's."

"I'm not going to say anything. You?"

"No. Hey, you know what? Talking ext...distinctly is hard when you drink. It's almost as hard as walking like this. Hey, you want to know something else?"

"Yeah, what?"

"I'm glad I got you. I miss Stevie, but it doesn't hurt as much with you around."

**

Like the previous summer break, Av may have spent the boys' first week of school coming up with pranks to pull on them, but that summer, he was forced to stop. Together, the boys were able to spot most of his pranks and putting their minds together, they were able to come up with some great ones that Av never saw coming. With the pranks becoming too one-sided, Av became overly cautious with everything from opening a door to putting on his clothes. Eventually, the stress forced him to surrender.

That Wednesday morning with little to do but look forward to the weekend when the boys would be home, he left Mrs. Collins to clean the Library and forced himself downtown.

At a photography store, Av was overwhelmed by the variety of equipment available, and refusing help from the store's staff when it was offered, he decided to play it safe by first buying a book on the subject. He chose a small book entitled *Photography for Beginners* and when he realized it was written for middle school, he was more than pleased with his choice. In the recently cleaned library, he read the book and was amazed at all that was needed to take and develop black and white photographs, not even colored ones. A thirty-five millimeter camera with a flash and several optional lenses would be needed, but he would also have to make one of the guest rooms lightproof. Since he needed a water source, he would have to develop the negatives in the guestroom's bathroom, would have to run string from wall to wall to hang the drying negative strips and would have to purchase a timer, the chemicals, several plastic jars to develop the rolls of negatives, and some other minor accessories. To develop the prints, he would have to purchase a couple of basic tables, an enlarger, a focus finder, a red lighting system, some chemicals and trays, and after all that, he would have to stretch string from wall to wall in the bedroom to hang the drying prints. Besides having to obtain and set up the equipment to make a proper photo lab, the steps required to develop the negatives and the prints were beyond Av's appreciation for the art, more so when it was all for taking and developing of merely black and white photos.

With his new knowledge on the subject and with a greater respect for photographers as artists, the old man backed away from photography. Before then, he had always considered photography an art of percentages. There were certainly many photographs that one could call art, but he had felt that if ten children were each given a loaded camera, an easy five percent of their photos would be considered art by the most critical of critics, as long as it was never revealed that they were taken by children excited to take pictures of anything.

Having decided against photography as a hobby, he decided to avoid anything that was considered art. He reasoned that if he had had any interest in art as a hobby, he would have been doing it earlier in his life.

Just before one in the afternoon, Av decided to make his way to his and Dwight's regular hobby store.

As he stood in his driveway fishing out his key from his back pocket, two young men wearing spring jackets over their white shirts and black ties surprised him.

"Hello, sir," said the young black man.

"Hello," replied Av as he tensed up.

"I'm Blair, and this here is Will. What's your name?"

"Mr. Rosen."

"Great. Mr. Rosen, we've come by to see if you follow the word of Christ."

"I do, but only the message, not the man," said Av remaining tense.

"Ok, then we'd like to give you some information on his love for us," said Will holding out a pamphlet.

Leaving the young man's offer hanging, Av asked, "Right. What religion do you follow?"

"We're Jehovah Witnesses."

"Right. By my religion, I am not permitted to say the first part of your religion."

"How's that?" asked Blair.

"I am Jewish."

"Oh, yeah? We're Christians. Let me ask you this: what do you call Him when you pray?"

Av cleared his throat. "Well...He commanded us not to call Him by His name...and if I am to pray, I would expect that His name is not required. It should be obvious to Him that I am speaking to Him, considering who...what he is."

"So you don't follow the word of Christ?" asked Blair, seemingly ignoring what Av had said.

"I am Jewish...so, no, not officially."

"Well, perhaps you'd like to read some information on his message?" Will asked, holding out the pamphlet again.

Becoming annoyed, Av asked, "Do you know much about the Jewish religion, about the Mormons, Catholics, or Muslims? The reason I ask is that you seem to ignore my religion and continue on with your religious sales pitch, making me believe you do not."

"It's not a sales pitch," said Blair. "We're not selling anything."

"Well, that may be so, but your persistence in informing me of your religion comes across as trying to sell me on it. You have even brought marketing brochures. If you were selling Fords then I would expect you to have strong knowledge of the competitions' cars in order to better be able to sell me on yours. If I were selling brushes door-to-door, I would certainly know every detail about my competitors' brushes. How else could I convince someone to switch from their current one?"

"We're not selling anything," Blair insisted a second time. "We're just spreading the word."

"Right, well, it still comes across as selling to me, not a product but a belief system," said Av, who paused before adding, "Now I must go. Have a good day, gentlemen."

As Av unlocked the door and opened it, Will pushed, "Sir, Mr. Rosen, maybe you could answer me this: do you think the world would be a better place without evil in it?"

Av released his growing annoyance with a sigh. "I am not sure. We could certainly do with less, but I am not sure if it would be a good thing to have none. How then would we appreciate the good in the world? If we never felt sorrow, how could we appreciate happiness? We would need something to contrast it against, I believe. And, I expect, the only way to decrease the amount of evil is for everyone to share the same perspective."

Blair's eyes lit up. "Really? We don't all view it the same, really? What about the holocaust? You're Jewish. You must view that as evil!" he challenged.

Av felt he should just leave, but, instead, he said, "I certainly do, but Hitler obviously did not, and, I expect, the majority of the Nazi party did not. There were groups in other countries during that time who also shared Hitler's view. Even today there are groups that share it. Now, gentlemen, we will have to continue this conversation at another time."

With the two men at a loss for words, Av got into the car, and before closing the door, said, "Please watch yourselves as I back up. I can hardly see. I can hardly hear, and I can hardly walk. Thank goodness I can still drive."

With the two Jehovah Witnesses stepping further away than necessary, Av put the car in reverse and backed out to the end of the driveway.

He regretted inviting them to continue the conversation at another time and expected they would. Then he found, because of their visit, he had a greater appreciation for the car's tranquility.

At the hobby store, Av ignored the plastic model airplanes and jets, which would normally interest him and Dwight, and he ignored the model train accessories, which interested mainly Dwight. Instead, he focused his attention on the more complicated hobbies, like the powered model airplanes and powered model rockets.

Being at that store some thirty-plus times, he was comfortable with asking for assistance from the proprietor, and after talking with the familiar man for several minutes, he decided the powered plane was the better option. He could spend some time putting it together and then his family could fly it together.

Av left the store with a top-of-the-line remote control system and a simpler single-winged model airplane kit. At home, he would set up an area in a guest room to build it, and over the next ten days, he would spend much of each putting the plane together, finding it an exercise in taming his impatience with the tedious tasks of using his large, awkward hands to cut the many small pieces from the balsa wood and then glue them together to make the skeleton of the main wing, tail wings and body. He would have to follow the directions carefully to wire the moving parts, like the rudders, ailerons and elevators, to their control mechanism, which he had mounted in the plane's body. He would then mount the engine and its gas tank into the plane's body. And lastly, he would cover the plane with tissue paper and install its propeller. He would decide to put off painting the plane to ensure it was ready on time for its premier flight.

**

Since their second day at school, Lyon stuck to Dwight's side so often that without his new friend beside him, Dwight began to feel out of place at school, even when he went to the bathroom.

That Friday morning of the first week of school, and continuing throughout the day, Dwight found it strange that Lyon was constantly approached by their classmates asking, "Where's it at now?" Each time one approached, Lyon responded with a number and the classmate usually responded with a larger one before leaving. Usually, it was a different classmate, but sometimes it was a repeat of another asking the same question.

Then at the end of the school day and just before meeting up with Blue, Graham, who had accosted Lyon four days before, met the two at their lockers. "Where's it now?" he demanded. "One-ten," responded Lyon, causing Graham to huff and leave, complaining, "Too much! That's too much!"

Dwight guessed it was some sort of game being played and did not want to seem nosey by asking. He was certain that either he would soon figure it out or Lyon would tell him what was going on.

That Friday evening after supper and with his mother's permission, Dwight made his way to Lyon's house. He rang the doorbell, which chimed instead of gonged as his did, and waited for a response. He was about to press it again when the door opened and a small Asian woman with a rather large stomach greeted him and asked in what sounded to the boy like a Chinese accent if he was Dwight.

"Yes, ma'am," he said, assuming the woman was Lyon's equivalent to Mrs. Collins.

"Wonderful. I'm Lee's mother. It's nice to meet you. I've heard wonderful things about you. Lee is up in his room studying. Let me show you the way, but first, could you take your shoes off here, please?" the woman asked, pointing to a short row of shelves holding several pairs of shoes.

Confused by the word *mother*, Dwight removed his shoes, placed them on a shelf and then followed the woman slowly making her way up a set of stairs, where she kept one arm on her stomach and the other on the railing, and then down a short hall.

Knocking on a door, the woman said, "Lee, Dwight is here."

"Cool!" Lyon said from somewhere behind the door and then opened it to reveal his grinning face. "Thanks, mom. Come on in, Dwight."

"Lee, that wasn't the proper use of the word *cool*. Now quickly, what should you use?" demanded his mother.

"That's great?" asked Lyon, his dark skin turning darker.

"That's correct. Now you boys have fun, and if you need anything, I'm just downstairs."

"Thanks, Mom. That's...that's great."

Dwight entered his friend's bedroom and watched him rush to clean up the books and papers scattered over his adult-sized desk.

"Your mom's Chinese?"

"No, she's Korean, South Korean. My parents met there during the war or 'policing action' as my dad calls it. He was a doctor over there and over here he's a surgeon at the Queen Elizabeth the Second Hospital."

"That's too cool! You're not just black but Korean too!" Dwight said, thinking how great it was going to be to have a friend who was both black and Korean, whatever Korean was.

Finishing tidying up his desk by placing his loose-leaf notes into his calculus textbook, Lyon said, "I'm a cross-culture child. That's what my mom calls it. She doesn't like the term mixed race."

Dwight missed what Lyon had said. He was more preoccupied with the boy's room. It looked nothing like his. There was not one poster on the walls and not one model jet hanging from the ceiling, and on each side of his bed, there were two stained pine boxes that looked like toy chests acting as nightstands. Resting on one of the boxes was a large model plane with a remote control next to it. And like Dwight, Lyon had lots of books, but instead of being on two shelves as Dwight's were, they filled two bookcases almost as tall as him.

"Hey, what's the funny writing on those books there?" asked Dwight.

"Those are Korean books."

"You can read that? And you're learning French, too?"

"I was brought up with Korean and English. Korean's a lot easier. Here look at this one," Lyon said as he pulled a book from the bookcase. "The writing looks like Chinese symbols, but it's letters put together to form little blocks. You read the top letters from left to right and then read the bottom letters. Sometimes, there're only two letters so they stretch them to make it look like a block, sort of. It's quite ingenious. When it's a single letter to make a vowel sound in a syllable, they add the *ng* sound, like in *ing,* to the beginning just to give it shape. See this oval here with the line next to it. That's the *ng* symbol. You can't pronounce it at the beginning so Koreans ignore it and just pronounce the single letter. Look, the smaller space between the blocks is a new syllable and the bigger space there between them means a new word. It's phonetic, so it's easy to pronounce, except the B's and P's and the G's and K's sounds can be confusing at first because they use the same letters. It has almost the same consonants, but a lot more vowels. They consider things like *wa*, *we* and *wu* as vowels. It's so easy to pronounce the written words that every Korean adult, every single one can read Korean. It's that simple. It just looks super complicated."

To press his point, Lyon used his finger to point out what he was pronouncing and then told Dwight what it meant in English.

"That's pretty...uh...cool," said Dwight, who had lost interest after hearing it looked like it Chinese but wasn't. "Hey, let's see your toys!"

"I don't have many. One of those boxes is full of Lego and the other's full of Meccano pieces," Lyon said shyly.

"Seriously? Full of Lego? That's a lot of Lego's! I only got a shoebox full. Hey, where's your G.I. Joes?"

"I'm not allowed to have any. Not allowed war toys."

"Yeah? Maybe you can come over to my place tomorrow and play with mine?"

"Sure, but I'll have to ask mom. But let's not tell her about the G.I. Joes, ok?"

"Sure, sure," agreed Dwight. "How about we build something with the Lego pieces. We can play with the Meccano pieces but it takes a lot more time screwing all those pieces together. I only got a couple of hours."

"Ok, let's do that," said Lyon, who dragged the box without the plane sitting on it closer to a spot where they could work.

Then the two sat on the floor and after discussing what they would build together, decided to build a helicopter with Lyon working on the tail end while Dwight worked on the cockpit. It was the first time either had used Lego with a partner who was not an adult, and both were pleased with how well they worked together, with the only argument being over what color bricks to use for certain parts of the vehicle.

As they worked away, Dwight asked about the remote-controlled airplane resting on the box that must have contained his friend's Meccano pieces. "Did you make that yourself?"

"No, my dad bought it already built. We just had to snap the wings on."

"Av's making one from a kit. He has to cut pieces from wood and then glue them together."

"That's the hobby type plane. Mine's more of a toy. Hey, maybe I can see his when I come over tomorrow."

"Sure, but I don't know how far he's got, but he's been working on it a lot day and night."

By the time Dwight had to leave, the two had only the landing skids left to build on the helicopter. They exchanged phone numbers, and Lyon agreed to call Dwight the next morning to set a time to get together later that day.

That Saturday morning Dwight yelled out that he had got the phone, yelled louder that it was for him, and then he talked with more volume than necessary to ensure that anybody within a short distance could hear his side of the short conversation. With a huge smile, he placed the receiver back on its base, and when he turned around, Blue was standing at the kitchen's entrance with an unusually large smile. "Now I know what to get you for your Birthday."

"What?"

"A phone call," laughed Blue.

"Come on! It was my first one, first one ever!"

Blue walked into the kitchen and placed his hand on his friend's shoulder. "That's cool. They say you'll always remember your first."

Not getting the reference, Dwight said, "Hey, I got your birthday present early, and here it is," and then punched Blue's shoulder.

Blue snickered, "That's early by ten months. Hey, that was Lyon?"

"Yeah, he's coming over at one. What are you doing today?"

"I was going to see if you wanted to go fly a kite (seriously, I found your kite in the basement) but seeing how Lisa said it's going to rain and you're with Lyon, I may just bug Av to leave his plane and go do a matinee or something."

"Not a movie! You guys can't go without me!" Dwight protested.

At one o'clock, the door bell rang.

Dwight, who was anxiously waiting on the other side of the door for almost five minutes, excitedly opened it to find an awkward looking Lyon holding his mother's hand.

"Hi, Lyon! Hi, Misses...Misses..." Dwight's face reddened when he realized he did not know Lyon's last name, or if he had known it, he had forgotten it. "Hi, Lyon's mother."

"Hi, Dwight," said the two.

"Dwight, you can call me Mrs. Johnson. Is your mother home?"

"Sure...sure, she is. Please, come in and I'll get her."

Relieved that Mrs. Johnson was not going to join him and Lyon as they played, Dwight closed the door behind them and then startled them when he shouted, "MOM, YOU HAVE A VISITOR!"

Curious, Lisa left the desk in her room to join the group in the foyer.

"Hi, Lyon. And hi, you must be Lyon's mother. I'm Lisa Dixon."

As the two ladies shook hands, Mrs. Johnson said, "Hello, I'm Min-hee Johnson. I thought I would come over and welcome you to the neighborhood. My, what a big home you have!"

"Yes, it's large, maybe too large. We're still getting used

to it. I'm finding when I misplace something here, it's pretty much gone. It can be a real bother trying to find it," Lisa joked. "Dwight, why don't you show Lyon your room? Min-hee, would you like a coffee or tea?"

"Yes, tea please."

"How far along are you?"

Hearing Lyon's mother say, "Six months," Dwight clued in that she did not have a weight problem.

With Lyon following Dwight up the stairs, Lyon's mother followed Lisa past the stairs and down a hall to the right toward the living room. The two boys could hear Lisa saying, "This is so great to finally meet a neighbor. In Spryfield, our houses were so close together you couldn't help but meet them. I miss that."

It took several minutes for Lyon to get over the embarrassment of having his mother join him, and it took the two several more before they were sitting on the floor playing with Dwight's G.I. Joes.

Lyon was fascinated by the realistic looking action figures, which Dwight corrected his friend on when he referred to them as dolls. Not being able to control his fascination, Lyon grabbed one and rubbed his fingers over the short, fuzzy hair on its head and then played with its rubber *kung fu action grip* hands. He was surprised to learn that one was Av's, who had bought it on Dwight's recommendation when Dwight told his elderly friend two summers back that they needed two to play together so he should get one for himself.

When Lyon's initial fascination with the action figures wore off, he asked Dwight if he had any board games. Dwight brought out Trouble and then watched Lyon set it up on the bed and move some pegs around as if a game was in play. With a smirk on his face, Lyon went and locked the bedroom door. As he sat back down on the floor, he told Dwight that if his mother came in, they were to hide the action figures and pretend they were playing Trouble. Then with an understanding of why his friend had done what he did and impressed with his cleverness, Dwight excited Lyon with his G.I. Joe helicopter, which was large enough to seat one of the twelve-inch action figures inside. Lyon surprised Dwight when he acted like the eight-year-old he was by calling dibs on the helicopter and excitedly placing the black G.I. Joe into it.

As the mothers talked in the living room, the boys played for almost half an hour before someone rattled the doorknob and then knocked on the door.

Both fearful, Dwight and Lyon looked to each other before Lyon quickly scooped up the G.I. Joes and the helicopter and slid them all under the bed.

"Who is it?" asked Dwight.

"It's the big bad wolf," answered Blue.

Dwight opened the door.

"What are you guys doing?" asked Blue, and then to Dwight's embarrassment, he saw Lyon with a G.I. Joe back in his hands. "Oh, playing with dolls...or are the dolls playing Trouble?"

"Uh, no...uh...we—"

"Would you like to play too?" Lyon asked as he held up the action figure. "They're called action figures, not dolls."

"No, I'm too young to play with them. Thanks anyway," Blue smirked.

For a second, Lyon's face formed a question mark. "Oh, that's sarcasm. You're being sarcastic."

"I like to think I'm the king of sarcasm."

"That's not much to be proud of," Lyon said nonchalantly, and then turned darker as he regretted saying it.

"Oh, yeah? How's that?" Blue challenged and then regretted it, fearing the explanation would be much like the boy's explanation of assumptions.

"It'seasy,tooeasyandnotverynice." Lyon took a deep breath. "It's too easy. All you have to do is say the opposite of what you mean and in a tone that says you're being sarcastic. That's how it's defined in the dictionary. It's so easy that if a monkey could talk, it could be sarcastic too. And then sarcasm involves insulting someone or something, indirectly. Like if you asked me if I liked ice cream when I was eating some, I would say, 'No, I hate it,' which is really saying I like it and the question is stupid. Sarcasm is misunderstood too. A lot of people confuse any witty comment for sarcasm, but it's not. It's a specific type."

"Right...ok," said Blue, holding back his urge to use sarcasm. "I'm going to check to see how Av is coming along with the plane. I've never seen a person sweat so much doing something so simple. Hey, let me know which G.I. Joe wins at Trouble."

As Blue left, Lyon said to Dwight, "See, that wasn't sarcasm, more sardonic, but some people would think it was."

"People use sarcasm on you a lot, don't they?" asked Dwight.

"Too much," nodded Lyon as he looked down at the floor.

An hour later when Mrs. Johnson was leaving, Lisa showed her to Dwight's room where Lisa was surprised to find Dwight had locked his door to keep Blue out. Mrs. Johnson was pleased to see the boys playing a board game, though she was curious about the little plastic machine gun lying on the floor. And Dwight was delighted that Lyon's mother had allowed her son to have a sleepover that night and even more pleased since that meant his new friend would join them for both supper and their Saturday night movie.

Later in the afternoon, Av and Blue returned from the hobby store with two model building kits for Dwight's model train set, and all four were soon in the basement building them, with Dwight and Lyon working on one and Av and Blue working on the other. After completing the buildings and debating on where they should place them on the train set spread out over a piece of plywood resting on Lisa's old melamine kitchen table, they glued the buildings down.

That evening, the five watched *Star Wars: Episode IV - A New Hope* at the Highland Cinema just across from the Armdale Rotary, which separated the main section of the city from its more rural areas. It was Lyon's first time watching the movie and the fourth time for everyone else. He enjoyed it but found it annoying when Dwight, Blue, and even Av said parts of the dialogue along with the characters.

With Lyon sharing Dwight's double bed, the two were

asleep half an hour after returning from the movie, and in the morning, both were left thinking sleepovers were not such a big deal.

CHAPTER 6
Problems of the Father

Inside the painted white walls of cement blocks sat a man previously acclimatized to his surroundings by two past tours with Canada's Correctional Services. Sitting on the plain metal-framed bed in his required clothing of a tan, buttoned shirt and matching pants with a black stripe down the side of their legs, he passed the time skimming the pages of a paperback novel trying to decide if he wanted to read it. After a hundred and thirty pages, he still was not sure. He sat the book down, stood his slim but muscular body up and leaned backward, cracking his back. Walking to the window beside the white porcelain sink standing beside the coverless white porcelain toilet, he peered out at the grounds of the institution. His side of the wing, one of four in the X-shaped building, looked out onto the restricted space between the three other buildings identical to his. There was nothing of interest to see except the slow growing weeds in the distance being cut down by a ride-on mower. He tapped on the window's plastic pane, not to get the driver's attention but just to tap on it. Sitting back down on the bed, he pulled out a pack of cigarettes from his pants' pocket and placed one between his thin lips. Tearing a match from a small book of them, he lit it.

Sitting on the bed, he was amusing himself by making donuts of smoke and then watching them softly collide with the cement ceiling when a rap of knuckles against his opened door of metal bars distracted him.

"You should've given me advance warning. I'd have cleaned up the place and had coffee ready," he joked in his French accent.

A heavyset man wearing the same standard clothing but with several sweat stains on the shirt entered the cell, accepted a cigarette and with his own book of matches, lit the end.

"Frank, I wish I could says this 'ere's a friendly visit, but they needs their money."

"I hear you. I expected this sooner. The extra stuff they gave me came due. How did it work out? Did they get their numbers up? Are they patching over?"

Bringing his body odor closer to his fellow inmate, the visitor set himself down on the bed,

"Not yet, but it's in the works. They tells me nothin' abouts that stuff. I just hears the rumors. I thinks when I gets out, if they're patched over, they'll makes me a prospect again," the man said before raising his voice. "I ain't doin' another year or two of that bullshit! If that happens, I'm dones with 'em!" He took a puff from his cigarette and calmed down. "They tells me nothin', except ta tells ya yer due. And even then, it's only through that jackass Kenny. I told 'im that I wants a meetin' with em' next Sunday myself. Enough of this Kenny callin bullshit. I can do that shit myself. I ain't Kenny's bitch! I'm supposed ta pass on the message and I doesn't even knows the amount!" He flicked his ashes into his palm. "Hey, I hopes it's not much...fer yers and my sakes. If I gots ta hurt someone in 'ere, I'd rather it be Kenny. You knows what I'm sayin'?"

Frank nodded and then displayed his new skill of flicking the butt into the toilet several feet away.

"An extra brick of weed, the brick they gave me on consignment to shoot their numbers up for the Headless. So, I'm looking at thirty-two hundred. It shouldn't be a problem. I've a stash of cash hidden. The stash the cops never found."

"Good. How's yer boy? Comin' to visit today?"

"Fine, and he is. Did they tell you to find out where he is too?"

"Yeah, but I don't gets why. Why yer keepin' it a secret

and why they wanna knows. They tells me nothin', ya know!"

"They'll want to be ready if they need to use him as a threat. They can't use him if they don't know where he is, right? He's gone through too much to have to deal with this shit too."

"Yeah, sure, too much."

"I don't even know where he's living. I mean, I told him not to tell me so if his mother ever asked, ever decided to act like a mother, I can tell her I don't know and not be lying," lied Frank. "Demp, do me a solid. Could ya tell them I don't even know?"

"Right, sure, gots it."

Frank pulled out another cigarette and lit it, reminding himself that that was four so far that day. He was two cigarettes away from his self-imposed quota, and the afternoon had yet to arrive. Cigarettes were then his currency, and he didn't want to watch them go up in smoke by his own hand.

"So five weeks ta go, eh?" asked Demp.

"Just over five. It'll be a short trial. They'll probably do the sentencing then too. They found the weed and a lot of the cash. They also found dad's Lugar, and I'm sure they'll try to attach that to the dealing. I've been told the best I can hope for is a shorter sentence."

"So we're together untils I get outs fer good behavior," the fellow convict laughed. His laugh grew louder and was soon joined by Frank's chuckle. Calming himself down, Demp added, "If one of us is the Boy Scout, it's ya. It's a shame they don't gives less sentence for just sellin' weed."

"Oh, well," Frank said and then took a long drag from his cigarette to help hold back his heart from beginning to race. "I knew that going into it, going into it three times —shame on me."

"Makes ya wish ya selleds the hard stuff now, doesn't it? Doin' the same time and all anyways. Ya'd have a lot more cash stashed away by now."

"No. I was never good with that. I may be doing the time, but I'll be sleeping well at night. I never sold the stuff that'll kill anyone."

"Right," the other inmate said through the half-smoked cigarette hanging from his mouth. Getting to his feet, he emptied his palm of ashes into the toilette, wiped his hands together and then rubbed them against his pants. He removed the cigarette from his mouth and flicked the burnt end into the toilet. Placing the remaining portion into his shirt pocket, he said, "Well, gotta go. I mights see ya after visitin' hours. Hey, let me know abouts the cash and hows they're goin' ta get it, eh? We knows how impatient they ares with that shit. I'd hate fer are relationship ta takes a more intimates turn after all these years. I won't likes that. Even if they likes ya, they won't be lettin' nobody outta their debt, esp'cialy now with the patch-over."

"Got it and will do," Frank promised.

"Hey," said Demp stopping at the opened wall of bars, "I bet ya wishes ya joined the tribe now. This owin' money thing wouldn't exist. Twice they offers and twice ya refuses. Ya wouldn't've even had ta spends no time as a prospect."

"Yeah, maybe," said Frank, wishing he could open the window to air out the cell. "But I just needed to sell pot, not give my life to it."

With Demp gone, Frank allowed himself to be covered in the guilt of involving his son in his problems. He thought again about how he came to be there, and again he blamed his onetime best friend. And again, Frank caught himself and removed the blame. He could only blame himself for his situation. He could only hate himself for it, and he did. There were many times when he had planned on quitting, but then each time, he set his savings goal a little higher and continued. He tried to give himself the excuse that he was doing it for his son's future, but he knew that was not it. He was doing it because he was good at it, making it easy money.

**

Each time he took the route, it grew a little duller than the last. The initial tranquil feeling of hiking along a wide, paved path through a dense forest of thin but very tall trees had worn off. Now, the blur of trees a half-dozen meters away occasionally made him feel like he was driving through their living room of light brown wainscoting on dark green paint. It felt like a Freudian thing, but his was not a sexual desire; it was a comfort desire. He would rather have been sitting in his recliner while watching television than sitting in the car while watching the road.

The car seemed as anxious to have the drive over with too. With nothing except the speedometer to keep him aware of the car's speed, Av had to check it routinely, occasionally restraining the car from doing more than the posted hundred kilometers an hour.

As was then the norm while Av drove the route, Blue slept while leaning against the passenger door. Av was content with that. During the weekly hour and a half drive, he never knew what to say to the boy. He was not one to start a conversation for the sake of conversation, and Blue was never in the mood to start one on the way to or on the way back from the Springhill Institution, which the boy thought was only given that name because it sounded slightly better —*My dad's in an institution* sounded a bit less dramatic than *my dad's in prison*.

About an hour and fifteen minutes into the drive, Av took the exit marked Springhill and drove down the single-lane highway toward what was once a mining town. After counting the six signs warning against picking up hitchhikers, Av called out to Blue, telling him they were almost there.

Blue woke to the familiar site of the razor wire fenced in facility with most of its several single and two-story structures scattered about as if dropped from above without any thought to their placement. Directly in the middle was the only place that seemed to have any order to it, the two by two X-shaped inmate residential buildings.

With Av parking as close to the front entrance as possible. The two made their way to a square single-story structure breaking the fence's line. They went to the front counter and after the guard who was familiar with them had checked that their names were still on the inmate's visitor list, gave them their visitor badges and unnecessarily directed them to the screening area, they walked through a metal detector and were waved into the visiting area where they would wait for the inmates to enter from a door on the opposite side.

In the room of painted gray walls of cement blocks, much like the same gray the unpainted cement blocks originally were, Blue selected the same table he had selected since their first visit. There the two waited patiently while discretely glancing at and listening to the other visitors around them. Some were as old as Av and some as young as a month. Some, when in a large pack to see the same inmate, stood against the walls, giving the others in their group the first chance to sit at the table that allowed a maximum of three visitors at a time, more if the visitors placed children on their laps.

They only had to wait ten minutes before the inmates entered through the opposing door.

Av picked up his chair and placed it against the wall next to the visitor's door just feet away from the uniformed officer standing guard. He opened his novel and began reading. The situation may have warranted bringing his protective shell if not for his many visits developing a familiarity with the place, and with that familiarity came a strange sort of comfort.

"Hey, Blue," said Frank, sitting down across from his son.

Hearing his friend's name, Av looked up and gave a short wave of his hand.

Frank nodded his head toward the old man and mouthed, "Hello."

"Hey, Frank," Blue greeted his father with a weak smile.

"Blue, you're looking good. You started your new school, right?"

"That's right. The school's great. I'm actually getting into this whole learning thing. You're looking good too, except for your hair. It's getting long."

"Yeah, they only give haircuts every six weeks here. No more bi-weekly haircuts for me. How's Lisa and Dwight? Hey, I forgot to ask you last week, did Lisa start university yet? That's what she was planning, right?"

"She did. Started two weeks ago and likes it. Dwight's Dwight. He's as good as ever. He's made a friend, a little black, Asian kid. The kid lives next-door to us and is some kind of genius or something."

"That's good, really good to hear."

"Yeah, everyone's fine."

"That's what's different about you! You dropped your gutter talk! You decided to fit into the new area, right?"

Blue blushed slightly. "Sort of. Av thought I'd fit in better at school if I dropped it. We made a bet he'd start contracting his words and I'd start speaking proper like. It's a lot easier than I thought. But he lost right away."

"I guess he hasn't learned not to bet against you. I'm sure he'll figure it out soon enough. I really like that old man. He lives to help, no?" Frank switched to whispering. "He's even paying for my lawyer. After I signed the guardian papers for you, I have two suits show up with one telling me the other is now my lawyer. He wouldn't say who was paying, but I'm certain it's Mr. Rosen, just like he paid for Stevie's funeral. He thinks we don't know about that, but it's hard to keep a secret in Spryfield, right?" Frank sighed and looked down at the table. "Sorry. You already know all that. You know, sometimes I get so hungry for conversation and with the excitement of seeing you, I just start rambling on about the same stuff. Sometimes, I wonder if I'm losing it."

Blue's eyes saddened. "It's cool. Hey, anything new and exciting going on in here?"

"No, nothing new and exciting, and I don't want there to be anything. If it's exciting in here, someone's getting hurt. I pretty much keep to myself to avoid the drama."

"Makes sense, I guess. So, any word about your trial? Have you heard from the lawyer?"

"Nothing recently. It's going to be a long thirty-six days," Frank informed his son. "I'm so anxious to get it over with; I'm counting down the days. I'm sure it's going to be quick, and I'm sure there are years coming. I'm pleading guilty, after all. I was caught red-handed, right?" Frank noticed his son's eyes glossing over. "Hey, things could be a lot worse. You might *not* be with Lisa. You have no idea how much of a relief that is to me. I was just telling Demp...you know Dempsey...the big guy with the Thirteenth...the guy who's always sweating." Blue nodded his head. "He was locked up in here about two weeks ago for murder, but they'll probably press for manslaughter since it'll be easier to prove. Well, anyway, I was just telling him the best the lawyer can do is to get my sentence reduced, and with my time already in here and good behavior, who knows how soon I could be out? But let's not kid ourselves, ok? I'm getting five to ten."

"Right," said Blue sounding defeated.

"Right," Frank agreed and then confused Blue when he whispered in French. *"Listen, How'd it go with our stuff? Did you get a chance to grab the...the other stuff?"*

Blue's face reddened as he answered in French, *"We...we moved it all out last Sunday. Most of it's in a corner of the basement. We threw out the cut-up mattresses, sofa and loveseat and put the TV and stereo in my room. But...but I couldn't get a chance to look for the other stuff without anyone noticing. I never had a chance to be alone. After we moved the stuff, Lisa had us clean the place. It's a lot cleaner than when we moved in. I'm...I'm sure I can get it before the end of the month."*

Frank nodded. *"Ok. That's so strange about the furniture being ripped up. No one told me the cops had come back to search again. Anyway, do you still have the keys to the apartment?"*

Blue nodded. *"We have to give them back to what's his name at the end of the month."*

"Good. You know, I really don't want to involve you in my problems, but I've no choice. There's no one I can trust more than you. I probably should've said something about this before last week. I didn't...don't want to put pressure on you, but the thing is I owe them money and got to pay them. Just this morning, Demp came around asking about it. That's why I've got to bug you to pick it up as soon as you can. Do you think you can get down there sometime this week?"

"Sure, I guess. How much do they want?"

"It's just thirty-two hundred. You give them that, and then you hide the rest for yourself, for university."

Amused by his father's assumption that he would go to university, Blue smiled. *"Ok, who do I give it to?"*

"It's Howard. You never met him, I don't think. He's the president of the Tribe while it's still the Tribe. Listen, I don't want you talking to the guy, just give him the money. After you get it, I'll figure out how we'll get it to them. Either you'll drop it off somewhere for them to pick up or meet them somewhere crowded to hand it over. No talking to them. You just give it to them and get out of there."

"Ok. It's no problem," Blue said in English, expecting the topic to be finished and tired of having to put an effort into comprehending and speaking a language he almost never practices.

"Good. I was thinking of having Howard pick it up and be done with it, but I'm sure he'd take it all. There's like fourteen thousand there." With Blue's face showing his shock, Frank continued, *"I probably should have told you that earlier too. I considered giving the rest to Mr. Rosen, but I know...and you know he'd never take it, so you hold on to it. I'm sure you can figure out a place to hide it. Blue, listen to me, don't tell anyone about it. We don't know how they'll feel about the money. It could just make things worse in every way."* Frank glanced down at the surface of the table and took a long, deep breath. *"Blue, this is the only time I'll ask you to lie to Lisa and Mr. Rosen. Now, you might think by saying nothing it's not lying, but it is. We both know it is. I don't want to put this on you, but I haven't got any other choice...seeing how I'm here and not there. These guys could make life difficult for me in here and you out there."*

Blue nodded. "Ok, I'll deal with it and we'll talk about it next week."

Frank switched to English. "Ok, I guess that's it, that's all then.

Relieved, Blue grinned. "Hey, I could have a girlfriend soon if I can find the courage to ask her out."

"A girlfriend? Do tell!"

Blue told his father how he had come across Karen, whom he thought was the prettiest girl in school, and how he was kicked out of Choir Club, which his father told him was his side of the family's fault since they could not carry a note.

Blue told his father about the school, his enlightenment with doing math homework, and then lastly, he told his father about hanging out with his new classmates.

"You know this is the longest we've talked in a long time," said Frank and then laughed as he added, "Usually, we just stare at each other and trade sentences, right? Ok, so I'll see you next week and I expect to hear more about Karen. And listen, tell Mr. Rosen I said thank you and to have a safe drive back, ok?"

As they both got up to leave the table, Frank said, "Good luck with Karen. I can't give you any more advice than I already have. Hey, speaking of girlfriends, is Lisa dating anyone?"

"Not that I know of, but if you're still interested, you have some serious making up to do to win her back," Blue smirked.

"That's true. Thanks for coming and, again, let Mr. Rosen know I said thanks. Blue, be careful, ok?"

"Will do, and you too."

The drive home was much like the drive to the prison, except Blue could not sleep. Instead, he stared at the road ahead for the entire trip, sometimes reflecting on his father's situation and at other times reflecting on his own. At one point, Blue was so motionless that Av thought he had fallen asleep with his eyes open.

Later that night after lying that he was going to study with a classmate, Blue wheeled his ten-speed bike out of the house. With Dwight's small backpack strapped on his back, he pedaled to Quinpool Road and followed it to the Armdale Rotary. Thankful for the quiet streets —it had been a while since he had ridden his bike— and being supplied with extra energy from his emotional cocktail of frustration and anxiety, Blue rode counter-clockwise around half of the rotary before taking the Herring Cove Road exit. It was then that the little man realized how out of shape he was. It was uphill for a bit and then up a much steeper hill for another bit.

Once he made it to the top of the steepest hill, reaching the intersection at the Cowie Hill subdivision, he was finally on even ground. Being more comfortable on the bike, Blue put it in its tenth gear and flew by the hill of townhouses on his right. With his destination another two miles away, he ignored all he passed. Nothing interested him on Herring Cove Road, and he had not been away long enough to feel nostalgic about it. He soon made the green lights at the intersection where the Spryfield Mall was to the right and where he could coast down the twisting road if he chose to. He chose not to. Continuing in tenth gear, Blue tore down the road, overtaking several Sunday night drivers and ignoring the few shouts of "Hey, Blue!" from kids recognizing him as they walked in the opposite direction. Ignoring the red lights, he flew through several small intersections before coming to Autumn Drive.

With the bike ride diluting much of his emotional cocktail, Blue created a cloud of dust as he skidded to a stop at the three-story apartment building where the gravel road ended at the forest line. Retrieving his apartment keys from his pocket, he carried the bike in through the building's outside glass door, unlocked the inside glass door and carried the bike down the dirty metal stairs to the ground floor. The unpleasant smells and the mix of noises coming from the ground floor apartments had not changed since he had moved out.

Unlocking and opening the apartment's door, Blue wheeled in his bike and laid it up against the wall. He closed the door with more force than necessary and filled the empty apartment with the echoing slam. Looking around, the apartment had a strange effect on the boy. There was no sign of him ever having lived there. It seemed like that part of his life had been erased —he and his dad had never existed.

A loud knock echoed through the apartment.

Blue froze for a moment before deciding he better answer it since the door was unlocked. "Yes?" he asked as he opened the door to see an overweight, middle-aged neighbor in his usual state of inebriation.

"He–hey, Blue. How are ya? I–I heards someone and w-wanted ta make sssure thhhere'sss no f-funny ssstuff goin' on."

Blue had to hold himself back from rolling his eyes. "Hey, Max. No funny stuff here. Just me getting some things. In a bit of a rush, so—"

"He-hey, how's yeeer old man? Gettin' out sssoon, eh?"

"No. Got to go, Max."

"Ok, well—"

Blue closed and locked the door.

Walking the few steps down the hall to what was once his father's bedroom, he turned on the light, closed the door and knelt down by the section of baseboard with the door stop attached. The small piece of baseboard was slightly out from the wall and Blue wondered why his father would not have taken the time to put it back in place. Then he looked about the room and noticed for the first time that some of the other sections of baseboard were sticking out a bit from their wall. He had never noticed that when they had moved their stuff out the Sunday before, but then his mind was not on them at the time. It must have happened when the apartment was searched a second time, he thought. That more thorough search that ended up destroying their furniture and forcing him and Av to screw the covers back on the television and eight-track stereo.

Blue easily removed the loose baseboard to reveal a small, rectangular hole about six inches wide and three inches high. He knelt down to get a better look but could see nothing in its blackness. Sticking his right arm into it, he felt around to the left of the hole. There was nothing. He pushed it further along until his fingers touched the stud. Changing arms, he could feel nothing to the right of the hole either, so he stretched his arm until he could feel the stud at the other end too.

Blue sat up and tried to make sense of finding nothing, and then it hit him that maybe he had mixed up what his father had said. Maybe that was his old hiding place. Maybe his father had hidden the cash in his room. That would be a better hiding place since few would think of checking a kid's room.

In his room, the longer piece of baseboard with the door stop attached was on tight, and he had to use his house keys to get an end of the board off the wall enough to grip it with his fingers. As Blue pulled at it, the two long nails whose job it was to keep the baseboard snug against the wall moaned as they started to give, forcing a bit of paint to come off the wall with the board. With more effort, the board gave way, leaving Blue to stare at the thin section of unpainted drywall. There was no hole.

Shit!

On the slow bike ride home, Blue's mind raced. Either the Thirteenth Tribe got their money or they got revenge. Sometimes the revenge was temporary and sometimes permanent, deadly permanent. Frank was in a bad situation and Blue could not yet see a solution. Knowing Demp was in prison with his father, he knew who would have to do the terrible deed, no matter how much of a friend his father was to him. That was Demp's job on the outside, an enforcer. He collected the past due money for the Tribe and handed...fisted out punishments when due.

Blue considered selling what he had, but there was not much besides his father's television and stereo. He even considered stealing the money, but from where and how? He could break into houses and steal things. He could try to hold up a corner store or hold up a person on the street. But then even if he had the tools, the courage and the know-how to do each swiftly, he would not be able to. It takes a certain type of person to cause other people problems in order to solve his own, and Blue was not that type of person. Then he considered asking Av for help, but then his old friend had done more than enough for the boy and asking for his help, which he was certain Av would do, seemed even more wrong than stealing it. He did not want to bring him into the situation, did not want to involve him with the biker gang.

Blue tried to calm down by telling himself he should not worry until he had talked to Frank, and there was the hope too that in the coming week he could find a solution himself. With every problem he had faced before this, a solution either came to him before hand or turned up at the last minute, and he hoped this was not an exception.

That night when Blue handed Av the apartment keys to be handed over to the landlord before the month's end, Av said nothing to the boy about his stoic demeanor. The old man assumed it was due to the ending of that part of the boy's life, forcing an absolute acceptance of his father not having an active part in it going forward, and he hoped the troubled boy would come to him when he felt the need to talk about it. There was nothing he expected he could say to make things right, and he had discovered before then, through his relationship with Lisa and Dwight, that people with problems needed to be listened to more than talked to, and they needed to be the ones to instigate the conversation.

CHAPTER 7
An Estranged Mother

It was normal for Blue to be unusually quiet Sunday nights and it usually continued on to the next morning, but that Monday morning the second week of school, Blue had an additional reason to be quiet. Due to his worries, he was also tired from the lack of sleep the night before. For Blue, being tired meant being grumpy, and knowing he was grumpy, he made a point of keeping his comments in check and said nothing when Lyon proudly declared on their way to school that he had decided on a subject for his science project.

"Seriously? A hovercraft? That is so cool!" said Dwight, before his tone became placid. "I guess you've found a science partner?"

"No, not yet," Lyon informed him. "I have some bids, though."

"Bids?"

"Right. I take bids on who'll be my partner. They don't have to do anything for an easy A. So instead of picking someone, I take offers. The last science project made me eighty-five dollars," Lyon said with pride.

"Eighty-five! Seriously?"

"Seriously. That's why Graham was so aggressive with me last week. He's never won a bid. I don't think his parents give him much money, probably because he does so poorly in school."

Dwight asked, "Won't you get in trouble if you get

caught? You can't be allowed to do that."

"I probably shouldn't, but there's no rule against it. And the teachers know, but they say nothing. Really, if I didn't do well on the projects, no one would want to be my partner anyway...because I'm...I'm *socially awkward*. They probably shouldn't let me, but they know I'm doing all the work, so why not make my partner pay? Besides, what can they do to stop me? Dean Colvin tells me I'm her model student, and she wouldn't want to suspend or expel her model student, right?"

"I guess."

"Really, what I'm doing is what they'd be doing if they were me. People change when they get older. They get stupid. All they worry about is getting more of what they have...and then they get afraid of other people. They get stupid. It's grownups who start all the wars, get all afraid of other races and that sort of thing. We don't think so much about that unless our parents tell us to. It's almost got me afraid to grow up. So...anyway, I'm just doing something they can relate to."

"Oh...ok," Dwight said, exchanging looks with Blue.

Neither had any idea what to say to the boy's short diatribe and neither wanted him to continue.

Lyon asked, "Have you decided on a subject, yet?"

"Nope, I haven't even thought about it."

"Why not make a hovercraft?" grinned Lyon.

"I can't...I can't do that. You're already doing it."

"We can do it together."

Blue cut in with bitterness. "Dwight doesn't have that kind of money either...unless you give him a monthly payment plan for the next decade."

Ignoring Blue, Lyon said, "I won't charge you. You're my friend, right? Friends don't charge friends. I even figured out how to do it, and I know you'll help me build it. It'll be like us making the Lego helicopter, and it'll be my first time actually *working* with a partner too. It'll be fun!" Lyon's voice then took a serious tone. "But if anyone asks, you paid one hundred and thirty, ok?"

With an excitement that belittled his guilt for costing his friend the opportunity to make so much money at one time,

Dwight accepted both the offer and the condition.

While the other two continued walking on while discussing how they could build the hovercraft, Blue stopped to tie his shoe. Finished, he got to his feet and noticed for the first time that both boys swaggered slightly as they strained to carry their schoolbags in their hand.

"Hey, is there a reason you guys don't wear your bags over your shoulder?"

Both stopped to turn around, only then realizing they had left Blue behind.

"Yes," answered Lyon, as they waited for Blue to catch up.

"Well?" asked Blue.

"Well what?" asked Lyon.

"What's the reason?" asked Blue as he joined the two.

"Oh," said Lyon, "You only asked if there was a reason, which I thought was a strange question since everything has a reason, but you wanted to know it too?"

Fighting off the urge to tell their new friend where to go, Blue said, "You know, Lyon, I liked you better when I didn't know you. Ok, so...so what is it? Why would you two rather strain your arms?"

"The strap hurts the blazer," Dwight informed him.

"It chafes the material," added Lyon.

Blue took his schoolbag from off of his shoulder and examined that part of his blazer. "Damn, it's only been a week and I can see it starting."

Blue too switched to carrying his schoolbag by hand, and all walked with a slight swagger.

"Dwight, give me your bag. I'll walk better with one in each hand. Cool, that's perfect," said Blue, before looking over at little Lyon with his schoolbag in hand. "Uh...this is too light. Lyon, hand me yours too."

With only Blue slightly swaggering as he carried three schoolbags, none of the boys noticed the light-brown pickup truck standing out among the Volvos, Mercedes-Benzes and BMWs dropping off students. Not noticing the truck, they did not notice the grinning ponytailed man noticing them from its driver's seat.

That day at school, Blue found he had to force himself even harder to pay attention in class, and when he hung around with his classmates at recess and lunch, he found he had little to say. Even when Karen cheerfully greeted him the several times their paths quickly crossed, Blue could only mumble, "Hey." He wanted to say more but lacked the motivation.

Blue was quiet on the walk home that Monday afternoon too, but neither Dwight nor Lyon noticed. With Blue carrying the three bags, the two younger boys spent the walk discussing what they would need to build their hovercraft, and by the time they reached their homes, it was agreed that Dwight would get the thin sheets of balsa wood for the craft's body and they would use his model train's control box for controlling the electric motor, which would spin the horizontal fan. Lyon would get the motor, glue and a small piece of aluminum to make into a fan, and together the two would begin building the body of the hovercraft the following week.

With Blue finding their conversation distracting him from his father's problems, he listened with interest and failed to notice the pickup truck passing them several times on their walk home.

**

After Thursday's supper and with his melancholic state continuing, Blue made his way to his new hangout. Looking forward to the beer, he entered the park where he could easily hear his new friends, but because there was so much excited conversation, it was impossible to understand any of it. As he got closer, some of the conversations turned to whispers while the rest stopped abruptly.

"Hey, here's Blue!" Cal called out. "Here's our hero!"

Walking into a wall of apprehension, Blue shook off what he could and tried to ignore what he couldn't.

"Hey, guys," he mumbled.

"Hey, man, we were just talking about you," said John sitting cross-legged on the grass. "Well, more like arguing. Some of us figure you're *that* Bartholomew, *that* Bartholomew

Roy. The one with the Kid Killer."

"Not me. I get that a lot though," said Blue, hoping to brush off the topic.

"Ok," challenged John, "Then show us your shoulder. I heard you...he was shot in the shoulder."

"What? Ya–you some kind of perv or something?" Blue growled.

"If there's no scar, then you're not the guy, right?"

"Ok, you perv, if you insist," said Blue taking off his spring jacket and pulling his right arm out of his T-shirt. Lifting the side of his shirt up over his right shoulder, Blue challenged back, "You see any scar?"

"Nope," John said. "I guess you're not him, then."

"Show us the other one," another boy demanded.

"That wasn't enough for your kicks?" said Blue, moving a few steps to his left to stand in the shade of a tree. "Fine." He put his right arm back into the T-shirt, removed his left and lifted the T-shirt over that shoulder. "Any scar?"

"Nope," said John again.

Cal walked up to Blue and examined his shoulder. "I'll be!" He spun the reluctant Blue around. "It went straight through! There's a scar on his back too! Shit, that must have hurt! Did it hurt?"

"No, I didn't feel it. It knocked me out cold. I felt nothing until I woke up."

The rest of the amazed boys began to gather around a much irritated Blue.

"Hey, look with your eyes not your fingers! Ok, that's enough Show-and-Tell. Hey, I said don't touch! I don't know where your fingers have been! Take a picture —it'll last longer! All right, all right, the shows over. The next one's in an hour. Hey, what part of don't touch don't you get?" said Blue, pushing away a boy and then sliding his arm back into his T-shirt. "Damn pervs, all of you!" he declared as he picked up his jacket and put it on.

"So tell us about it. How'd it happen?" asked one of the boys.

"First, give me a beer," Blue demanded as he reached into

his pocket for a dollar-fifty.

Cal handed one to him. "Your money's no good today. Your story's payment."

Blue nodded his head and then guzzled down the beer. After a long burp, which caused some to laugh, he handed Cal the empty bottle and demanded another.

Grinning, Cal opened a second and handed it to Blue, who immediately drank down half of it.

With most of the boys sitting in front of him, Blue released another burp, sat down on the grass and said, "You probably aren't going to get your dollar fifty's worth. It's really a short story. I got shot by a cop...a detective. The Kid Killer was going to kill my friend, so when I was about to hit him with the butt of a rifle, I got shot and was out cold. Well, it was really a pellet rifle...otherwise, I would have shot him myself, right? So, I didn't feel or hear a thing. I just know what I heard later: I flew into the air and was out cold. See, not much to tell, right?"

"You were shot by a cop?" someone asked. "That's incredible!"

"He wasn't trying to hit me. He missed the killer, and I was pretty close to him."

"How'd you find the killer?" asked Cal.

"I didn't. He found me, just like he found his other victims. Ok, I've really had enough of this shit. That's all that's to it. You can all just wait for the movie."

"There's going to be a movie?" ask John.

"What? No! Can we move on to something else, please? I got shot, blah, blah, blah. That's the whole story!"

"Sure, sure," said Cal. "Hey, I heard Karen Hickey likes you. What a last name, eh? Hickey? Is that her name or what she makes?"

All but Blue laughed.

Blue was flattered by the info, flattered she had told somebody; though, before that night, he was almost certain she shared his interest. Then he felt bad about his cold responses to her greetings that week.

"Can we move on to something besides me? Seriously, I

don't...I don't know any Karen Hickey," Blue begged.

After another minute of teasing Blue about Karen, the conversation turned to which girls the other boys liked, who had dated whom, and who had got shot down before even getting to first base.

As the boys were drinking and sharing recent rumors, none noticed the middle-aged, mustached police officer approach from the other side of the field.

"Excuse me, gentlemen. Do you folks happen to know who's causing the litter at this corner of the park?" asked the officer, causing the surprised boys to hide their cigarettes behind their hand and their bottles of beer with their jackets.

"Uh...no officer...no idea," said Cal.

"We've had complaints about the litter here. The litter here that should go in that can there."

"Oh...well, we can clean it up before we leave."

"Good, and maybe you could also clean it up each time you leave."

"Right, we can do that. Is there a problem with us being here?"

"No, but there is a problem if you're smoking underage...or drinking underage. Whose case of beer is that?"

"Mine," Glen reluctantly admitted, surprising the others with his honesty.

"Are you nineteen? Are any of you old enough to drink?" the officer asked, with his expression changing slightly when he made eye contact with Blue.

"Sure, sure," said Cal, trying to discretely butt out his cigarette. "Some of us go to Dalhousie."

"Really? You don't say? What are you studying?"

For a second all were silent until a tipsy Blue said, "Arithmetic," causing some of the older boys to restrain their chuckles and the officer to smile.

"Well, young man, I think they call it Mathematics in university, or something along that line. Ok, everyone who has a cigarette going, put it out, and anyone hiding a beer should pour it out now or you'll get a ticket, a ride home and we'll have a talk with your parents."

As the kids reluctantly began pouring their beer to the ground, the officer walked over to the case of remaining full bottles and tapped it with his foot. "We'll be confiscating this beer," he said, and then pointed at Blue. "You, PhD. in Arithmetic, round up the empties and place them in the case, then follow me to the car with it. The rest of you clean up the mess, including the butts."

Picking up the box, Blue went around to his friends and had them place their drained bottles in the case, and then while the other boys began picking up the litter, he followed the officer to the far side of the park, through the fence's gate and onto the sidewalk.

The officer said nothing as he opened the police car's trunk and relieved Blue of the case.

With the trunk closed, Blue asked with a sarcastic tone, "So, what are you going to do, give it to charity?"

"No...well, sort of. It'll be donated to the officer's party. We have an awards ceremony coming up. Every year the Department gives out a few awards to the officers, and afterward, we have a small celebration. You know, Blue, they have a special Citizen's Award for Bravery too and I heard Greene...Detective Greene submitted yours and the other boy's name (Dewey right?) for consideration...oh, and the old man's too."

Blue was jolted out of his beer buzz by the officer's use of his name rather than by the news of the award.

"You seem to be adjusting well after the incident," the officer said with such a casual and familiar manner that it forced Blue to try to recall if he had met him in the past. "But take my advice, it's best to stay away from the booze...or drugs for that matter. A lot of folks, even some officers take to them to deal with what they went through or seen. I'd hate for you to go that way. I've seen it firsthand. There was one officer, I knew, who let the stuff take over his life. We, he and I, came across a gruesome biker torture, so gruesome that they removed the victim's limbs, and did it so he wouldn't bleed out right away. The message they were sending was so horrible that the officer lost it, not right away but over time. It was really how he looked at it. You see, every time he talked about it, and he did it a lot, he would put himself in the victim's place. I looked at it objectively, and he looked at it subjectively. His was the wrong way to look at it. He started drinking to deal with it, and when that stopped helping, he turned to drugs. Anyway, what I'm trying to say is you shouldn't try finding escape in booze or drugs...if that's what you're doing."

Blue shook his head. "I'm not."

"Good. Do you want a drive home?"

"Uh, no. I'll walk, but thanks anyway. I just live over on Jubilee."

"Ok. Well, hang in there. Maybe I'll see you at the awards ceremony. You'll get an invitation if they accept Detective Greene's nominations"

"Ok...right...thanks," Blue said as he turned to walk back to his friends.

"No problem," said the officer as he went to get into the car. Halfway in, he paused for a second before calling out to Blue, "It's Strange, I was transferred from Spryfield to here and then I meet up with you again. Only this time, you're conscious, eh? Or mostly."

Blue did not respond and could hear the officer laugh as he closed the door and started the ignition.

When alone in his room, Blue would wonder about the officer and his story. He wouldn't be able to place him anywhere in his past, besides when he was shot, and would wonder if he was on the take with the Thirteenth Tribe, as he had heard some were. With an understanding that he may be being a bit paranoid, he would replay several times the officer's story, trying to decide if there was another more discreet warning to it besides the obvious one about drugs and booze. Was the officer trying to warn him about messing with the Tribe? Blue would not be able to decide one way or the other, but then, if there were a second more subtle point, it would be wasted on him. He did not need it. He had heard stories about the Tribe's violence, some with much more detail than what the officer had briefly described.

**

As Lyon left his friends to walk the remaining short distance home that second Friday afternoon of the school year, Dwight and Blue walked up the long driveway to their house. Both noticed the blue Mustang parked behind Av's Cadillac and both notice the New Brunswick plate on its back bumper.

"Whose car's that?" asked Dwight.

"No idea, but it's cool," answered Blue.

With Dwight nodding, the two took the branch of the driveway that led to the front doors.

"Hey, Av," the boys called to their friend sitting on the wooden steps with Sam contently lying over his long, thin thighs.

"Hello," responded Av, setting Sam on the steps and standing up. He did not look too glad to see them. "Dew...Dwight, your mother needs you in the kitchen."

"Uh...ok," Dwight said as he walked past his old friend and into the house, thinking something was wrong and hoping he was not in trouble because of it, though he could not think of anything he did recently that was so bad.

"Blue, you...you have a visitor waiting in the library."

"Ok," Blue said, becoming as apprehensive as Dwight. By Av's tone, it did not seem to be a welcomed visitor.

As he followed Av through the foyer toward the library, he tried to guess who it would be. Did his grandparents on his mother's side finally remember he existed? Were they waiting to see him after who knows how many years? Did his grandfather on Frank's side finally leave his shack in the woods to come to visit? That would explain the New Brunswick license plates but not the model of the car. As Av entered the library and stood to the side to let his young friend pass, Sam sat guard just outside the entrance and looked in with caution. There with her back to Blue as she sat in one of the leather armchairs facing a wall of books was a redheaded woman. She turned her head, smiled and then stood, revealing her thin five-foot frame in a low-cut blouse and a short, denim skirt.

"There's my Bart. God, I missed you so much!"

Every part of Blue froze, except for his jaw that had dropped and his eyes that had enlarged as he stared at the woman holding out her arms.

"Come to your mother."

"What the...what the hell?" Blue asked. With betrayed eyes, he looked to Av. "What the hell?"

"Come here."

"What? The hells I will!"

The woman walked toward him. "It's been too long."

"What the hell?" Blue protested as he stepped back and held out the palm of his hand. "Don't come near me! My mother? Ya calls yerself my mother? Why'd ya ever thinks yer my mother?"

Av had planned to leave the two alone, but Blue's reaction forced him to stay in place.

"Cause...cause I *am* your mother," the woman stammered as she stood a few feet from her son.

"No! No, ya ain't...ya ain't! A mother doesn't leaves 'er kid, doesn't do it without a word. Ya didn't even leave a note when I came home ta an empty apartment! What mother does that shit? Get the hells away from me! Get the hells outta 'ere!"

"Bart, I know my showing up is a shock, but I'm your mother...and I had my reasons for leaving like I did. I only found out where you were yesterday, and I've come to take you home."

Blue's voice rose to almost a shout. "My names not Bart! It's Blue! Ya don't even knows my name! We only moved here last month, so ya should've knew where I was before here! Ya could've showed up then, but, no, ya shows up 'ere after...after seven years and expects me ta calls ya mother! Ya ain'ts my mother! Yer the lady who...who popped me out! That's it, that's all!" said Blue with tears building in his eyes.

"Bart...Blue, I'm back now. We can be a family again. Frank's going to be away for a long time. I'm all you have. I'm your family." She then looked to Av and her expression went cold. "Can we be alone, please?"

Av, whose heart was pumping hard and whose breathing was becoming rapid, forced a shake of the head.

Blue grabbed Av's arm tight. "He can stay. Av's family — my family. He's been more of a family than ya ever was! Lisa's more a mother than ya ever was! I should be callin' her mom, not *you*! Ya should be takin' lessons from 'er. I'll never calls ya mom, ever! I won't even calls ya by yer name! To me, you're just...just the...the bitch!"

Shocked and then moved by Blue's words, Av's heart beat even faster. He felt the urge to sit but continued standing as Blue gripped his arm even tighter.

The woman shook her reddening head. "I should've known you'd be as stubborn as ever! I'm your mother! I have the right to have you with me!"

"No, ya doesn't! Ya gave that ups when ya screwed off with Jack. I knows ya did! Ya was only too happy ta sign those papers. Frank tolds me, and unlike ya, he never lies ta me! Hey, Jack didn't want no kid, did he? No, with me around, he wouldn't take ya, right?"

"Bart...Blue, that's in the past!"

As much as Blue tried to hold them off, more tears built up in his eyes pushing the first ones down his cheeks.

"The past? What? Yas expects me ta forgets that shit? Yas expect me ta forgets the last seven years? And ya wants me ta forgives ya too? Or maybe ya don't! Maybe, ya think ya dids nothin' wrong to needs it! This is my family, not *you*! I won't be goin' anywheres with ya, anywheres! Go back ta yer *wonderful* Jack and forget abouts me!"

"Blue, you're only twelve, you don't have a choice," his mother hissed.

Struggling to fight back a more intense wave of tears, Blue forced out, "I'm thirteen, fer Christ sakes!"

Av forced himself to cut in. "Miss, I think it is time for you to leave. You only mentioned you wanted to visit Blue, not to take him with you."

"I will not be going without my son!"

Av's heart beat even harder. "We...Mrs. Dixon is his temporary *legal* guardian. From what I understand from

François Roy, you had signed away all rights to the boy...to Blue here. If you want to take this to court, I will...we will certainly meet the challenge. Seeing as you have arrived unannounced...and misinformed us of your intentions, I feel your deceit warrants being asked to...to leave this house. You can either leave on your own...or we can have the police do it."

The woman glared at Av and then at Blue, who had wiped his eyes and was giving an insincere goodbye by wiggling his fingers at her.

"Fine! We'll deal with this later. Here's my husband's card, and, maybe, Blue here can tell you who my husband is. Maybe then, you'll think twice about going to court!"

Av stretched out his free arm and took the card. Holding it some distance away so he could make out some of the writing, he noticed a handwritten, local number on it.

Not realizing he was still holding on to Av's arm, Blue took the old man with him as he stepped to the side to let his mother pass.

"This is not over by a long shot. Until later, then," the woman said as she left the room.

As she passed Sam, he hissed and swatted the woman's nylons, causing them to tear, her to scream and a teary-eyed Blue to grin.

As she walked to the door as quickly as she could in her loudly clicking high-heeled shoes, Blue finally released his hold on Av and yelled, "How the hell'd ya knows where I was?"

The woman yelled back, "Howard told me. Goodbye, Blue."

As the door slammed, Av noticed Blue's shock to his mother's response, and as both remained where they were, listening to her growling car leave, he placed his hand firmly but gently on the boy's shoulder.

With the car gone, Av cleared his throat. "Well, that was a...a short visit...but not short enough. I am going to dip my feet in the pool. Would you like to join me?"

Drained of emotion, Blue asked in a monotone voice, "You filled it with water? I thought you were going to wait until next spring."

"No, I did not fill it, but will it not be great when I can say it and mean it?"

As he followed Av out of the library and toward the back of the house, Blue wiped his eyes with his fingertips and dried them on his dress pants. The two walked past the floating stairs and past the hall on the right to enter the solarium. Sliding the glass door open, they entered the backyard where Av grabbed two lawn chairs, set them on the walkway around the empty pool and the two sat down.

"It will be great when we fill it up, no?" asked Av, his heart calming down.

"Sure," Blue said, still shocked by the visitor.

For a while, neither said a word.

Both stared at the empty inground pool with its cover stretched over it, making it look more like an inground trampoline.

Occasionally the two looked to each other, and after the third time, Blue asked, "So, were you serious?"

"About what?" asked Av, glad that the boy was the first to speak.

"About going to court."

"Absolutely. Just as we are family to you, you are family to us. We will do anything to keep you with us, to keep us all together."

"We?"

"Lisa and I, of course. Oh, and I am sure Dewey will demand it also."

Blue grinned as his eyes became moist yet again. "It's Dwight!" he joked, trying to imitate his friend's scolding voice, but his own cracking voice made it a poor attempt.

Av smiled. "Yes, yes it is."

After another moment of silence, Blue informed Av, "I owe you forty bucks."

"No, I do not believe you do. The bet allowed for extraordinary situations, and I would say that that was one huge extraordinary situation, one where you would be allowed to speak as you did, even allowing a few curse words if you deemed them necessary to make your point."

"That *was* one huge situation...and sorry for the swearing."

"It was deemed necessary."

"I...I never expected to see her again. I never realized how much I needed to be with you guys until I almost had to leave. Even if I don't fit in, I don't want to leave."

"You do not fit in?" asked Av with his dark, bushy eyebrows raised. "You do not feel you fit in?"

"I think everyone feels that way...even Dean Colvin."

"Dean Colvin? She told you this?" asked Av with his eyebrows then turned in.

"No, not in words, in her look. She stares at me with this giant frown. At first, I thought it was all in my head, but now, I'm sure of it. It's like she's waiting for me to screw up. I know I'm not as smart as you guys, not as...as good...as wholesome...I guess that's the word. I mean, you had a good life before me. Lisa did and Dwight definitely did. There was no sh...badness until you met me. Maybe, I just spread bad luck."

"Yes, that is you, Bad Luck Blue."

Blue looked over at a grinning Av.

"You don't agree? How can't you?"

Looking toward the pool, Av said, "First, you are smart. It is obvious you are intelligent, but you have never truly applied yourself in school...until now. And second, before we met, there were things going on in our lives that were not good. For instance, before meeting Lisa and Dewey...Dwight, (that is taking some effort to get used to) I had kept myself shut up inside my head. Ruthy, my wife (she would have liked you) had led me through life. If not for her, I may have ended up in an asylum, or even worse." The awkwardness of the disclosure forced him to pause, and then with Blue's curious eyes looking over at him, he continued. "I was pretty much living to breathe, nothing more. Dwight pretty much broke me of that. He has a way of getting through to me. After Dwight had cracked my shell, it was my spending time with you that finally crumbled it completely...or as much as it will crumble. Recently, I had wondered that if Ruthy and I had adopted a child (we could not have children, you see), if that child would have snapped me out of my...my walking coma. But, if we did and it did not, it would have been harder on her having to look after *two* infants by herself."

"I didn't know that," Blue admitted.

"Now you do, and does that make you feel better about your place in the family?" Av asked as he finally looked at Blue.

"Not really. I mean, it should, but my dad's a criminal. What does that say about me?"

"Nothing, nothing at all. You are not your father, and I think your father is actually a rather good man who has made bad decisions. To me, he is a good man...if only because of you, his son. Anyway, it is irrelevant what or who your father is. He is not who you are." Av paused for a couple of seconds to allow Blue to take in what he had said. "Now, I will tell you a secret, a secret between you and me, but first, let me ask you this, knowing Dwight the way you do, would you think his father was a racist?"

"No, definitely not."

"Well, here's part of the secret, (a secret Dwight does not know and should never know) his father was very much a racist. He was an alcoholic to boot. But much worse than that, he was a sociopath who tried to kill someone, someone who certainly did not deserve to die, I think. And he went and got himself killed trying to do it."

"Dwight's dad tried to kill someone?" asked Blue, floored by the information.

"That is correct. Now do you feel that should reflect on Dwight, and do you feel he has any of those traits?"

"No!" Blue said with conviction.

"Right, then why should your father's actions reflect on you? You decide what course your life takes. You make the decisions in your life. Mind you, you are quite mature for your age, but you should still reflect on the advice of those..." Av cleared his throat. "...those a bit more experienced than yourself, and whom you can trust to have your best interest in mind. Did you catch how I added that extra piece in there for

Lisa and me?"

Blue smirked.

"So, as to your fitting in, I think you fit in rather well with this...this less than wholesome family. We are not bad people, just people who have experienced bad situations through no fault of our own. I would say your presence in this family makes it stronger, greater than the sum of its parts. You and I have it rather lucky. Most do not get to choose the family they belong to, but we do. I have to say that Dwight has grown from your presence...and so have I." Blue's facial expression questioned the statement. "You have an interesting way of looking at things, and sometimes, when I find myself being indecisive, I ask myself what you would do and then do what comes to mind...if I agree with it."

With the surprised and then flattered look in the boy's eyes, Av did not know where to go from there, so he stood up.

"We should go in and see how Lisa and Dwight are. I am certain they are...were as worked up as we were."

Changing his mind, he sat back down.

"One more thing. Blue, secrets are never a positive thing, but sometimes they are necessary. Some people consider secrets to be lying: if you do not disclose them then you are lying by default. But I tend to think of them as simply not full disclosures that are sometimes necessary."

"I guess that makes sense," agreed Blue. "In certain situations."

"Right," said Av, who then reached into his pocket and pulled out the card, which Blue's mother had given him. Holding it out to read, he squinted and said, "If I am being too nosey, let me know, but who is Jack? You mentioned Jack as your mother's husband, but it says here, Patrick Stewart."

"Pat's Jack. Jack's his nickname. He used to jack cars, steal cars before he joined the Headless Norsemen."

"The Headless Norsemen? The biker gang? The big one?" asked Av.

Blue nodded his head.

"Oh...ok. It says here he runs a salvage yard."

"I think that's just for moving Headless' cash. The

Headless have lots of businesses for that sort of thing. He's down here to patch over the Thirteenth Tribe to the Headless Norsemen. Frank says he'll be the president when it's patched over." Seeing the confusion on Av's face, Blue added, "The Tribe is going to be part of the Headless."

"Right," said Av, trying to hide his shock with hearing about the biker gangs. "And Howard? Your mother had said a Howard had told her where you were."

"Howard (I guess that's his real name,) he's the president of the Tribe...for now."

"Right, ok," Av said as he stood up again while Blue did the same. "All this reminds me of a story, a story far back, far back when I was in my mid-twenties. My nephew's birthday was coming up, and at the time, he was often going on about parrots. So, as his birthday gift, I bought him a parrot with the cage and all. Let me tell you, he loved the bird when he saw it, but after a week, he started complaining about its singing *When the Saints Go Marching In.* Every night, the parrot sang that same song over and over. So, after six weeks and many of my nephew's requests to take the bird back to where I had bought it, I finally decided the bird was not going to change its ways and picked it and its cage up. Now, what do you expect I heard coming from the parrot the whole six-block walk back to the pet store?"

"It sang *When the Saints Go Marching In?*"

"No, but that is a good guess. All the way back to the store, the parrot repeated, 'My uncle is an idiot! My uncle is an idiot! My uncle is an idiot!'" Av said in an angry parrot's voice.

Blue laughed, and as the two walked into the solarium, he asked, "Av, what does that have to do with our talk?"

"Nothing at all, but it is a funny story, no?"

Blue smiled and nodded his head.

**

Sitting at the kitchen's island, Lisa and Dwight had heard most, if not all, of Blue's forced confrontation and were still recovering from it. Their eyes were still red, but their noses were no longer running. The earlier shock of potentially losing

Blue had sent Dwight into the arms of his mother, and it was only after the two had talked about what they had heard when Dwight finally calmed down. For the first time, Lisa did not try to protect her son from bad news. She told him there was a chance they could lose Blue, but they would fight it to the end, just as they had heard Av tell the woman. They would not back down unless Blue decided he wanted to be with his mother.

With Dwight pacified for the moment, an thought hit him and he shot up from his stool to remind his mother that Lyon was coming over for another sleepover and they should probably cancel it. He was pacified again when Lisa told him she had done that earlier and Lyon would be visiting tomorrow morning instead.

Both mother and son were comforted by Blue's laugh as he entered the house and comforted more when he and Av entered the kitchen together with upbeat faces. Dwight's mood was uplifted when Av declared he was ordering Chinese for supper. And when Lisa protested that they should not be eating it so often, dropping Dwight's mood, Av changed her mind by asking, "Why? The Chinese eat it every day, no?" and then he amused Dwight and Blue by adding, "Which makes me wonder, what do they call Chinese food in China? Just food? How boring would that sound, *eh*?"

With the four pretending they had forgotten about that afternoon's unexpected visitor, nothing was said about it during supper as all searched for things to say to take their minds from it.

Av asked some questions:

"Mississippi is a big word. Who knows how to spell *it*?"

Dwight was the first to jump in. "M–I–S–S–I—"

"Wrong," Blue cut in. "It's I–T."

"Some months have up to thirty days, others up to thirty-one. How many have twenty-eight?"

"ONE!" Dwight yelled out.

"Wrong again," said Blue. "All of them."

After almost twenty questions, Dwight hid his embarrassment of getting all but two of them wrong by telling, to his mother's disgust, *Mommy! Mommy!* jokes, which were popular at the time:

Mommy, Mommy! Why do I have to keep walking in circles? Shut up or I'll nail your other foot to the floor!

Mommy, Mommy! Why are we pushing the car off the cliff? Shut up or you'll wake up your father!

Mommy, Mommy! Daddy fell in the fire. Shut up and get the marshmallows!

And then after a dozen of those and to Lisa's further disgust, Blue finished off supper with *Dead Baby* jokes, which were also popular at the time:

What's the difference between a truckload of dead babies and a truckload of bowling balls? With bowling balls, you can't use pitchforks to unload them.

What is red and white and squirms in the corner? A dead baby playing with razor blades.

What is red, white and green and sits in a corner? Same baby three weeks later.

"Ok, ok," said Lisa. "Supper's finished. The joke tellers can clean off the table."

"Ok, but just one more," pleaded Blue. "How do you make a dead baby float? Fill a glass with Root Beer and add two scoops of baby!"

"Or," laughed Dwight, "Take your foot off its head!"

With the grinning boys clearing the table, Lisa asked Av, "Where do they hear such horrible jokes?"

"I prefer to blame it on our education system."

Later that night as the boys were preparing for bed, Dwight hauled his sheets, blankets and pillows into Blue's room and informed his best buddy they were having a sleepover. Hearing the boys talking and laughing, Av decided he wanted to be part of the fun too, so he also brought his bedding into Blue's room. As Lisa walked up the stairs, she heard from down the hall opposite her bedroom the boy's laughing at their older best buddy making himself comfortable on Blue's floor, and she too joined them. Blue felt it was wrong to be the only one having a bed, and after no one accepted his offer of it, he pushed the bed a couple of feet to make more room, removed his bedding and took the spot on the floor next to Lisa.

"I'm glad Mrs. Collin's doesn't come over on Saturday mornings," Lisa said. "She might think we're crazy sleeping all in one room."

"We could always tell her we had watched a scary movie," said Av. "That is to say, if she did work Saturday mornings, which...which she does not."

With Sam stretched out over his legs, Av told himself he would have to call Mrs. Collin's early the next morning to cancel her plans to clean that day. Earlier that week, she had changed her Friday morning cleaning to that Saturday, and since no one mentioned her absence that morning, Av had forgotten to mention her change of schedule.

For almost the next hour, the four shared jokes in the dark, until Dwight asked, "Hey, why's an oven like a woman?"

Not giving the question any thought, Av asked, "Why?"

"You have to get them both hot before putting in the meat."

Lisa gasped. Av's eyes tried to escape from his head, and Blue roared with laughter.

Lisa sat up. "Dewey...Dwight, do you know what that means?"

"No, but Blue's friends find it funny, and Blue won't tell me why! Mom, why's it funny?"

Blue roared again.

"And with that, it's time for bed," said Lisa, trying to sound angry. "Av, stop your grinning. I can't see it, but I can hear it."

Returning to the floor, Lisa gave into a grin but successfully fought off her urge to laugh.

Almost ten minutes later, with the two boys moaning about Av's nonstop snoring, Lisa got up and went to her room and returned with three sets of earplugs, which she had bought in bulk since her room was across from Av's. The boys were more than happy to have them.

The next morning, Blue woke up and discreetly dealt with

his rush of anxiety while thinking it strange how the evening before he had temporarily forgotten about his other more pressing problem.

Dwight woke up groggy. Every time he had fallen asleep, he was soon awakened by a bad dream. The theme of the dreams was the same: he would lose Blue, one way or another. One way was Blue being swallowed by a whale, another was Blue vaporized by the blast of a laser gun, another was Blue abducted by aliens and another, which was the only one that did not make any sense to the boy, was Blue being carried away by a giant stork. The last was Dwight falling from a cliff, which was really more about Blue losing him, but, in Dwight's mind, still worked out to the same thing.

As she was preparing breakfast while everyone was showering, Lisa was greeted by Mrs. Collins.

Seeing the surprised look on the young mother's face, the older woman, wearing what looked like yellow hospital scrubs, said, "Dear, didn't Mr. Rosen tell you I had switched Friday for Saturday this week? My brother came in from Calgary."

"No, but that's ok. Uh...we all slept in Blue's room last night so don't bother cleaning there. We'll make the beds ourselves." To Mrs. Collin's puzzled eyes, Lisa added, "We...we watched a scary movie last night."

"Oh well, dear, it is really no fuss. I have to make them anyway. They make those scary movies so much scarier now, don't you think? They used to be all about ghosts and all that, and now, well, now they're about murder and all that awful stuff. Was it that sort, dear?"

"Oh, for sure. Lots of evil mothers and dead babies in this one."

"Those would be the worst. No one wants to sleep alone after watching one of those."

**

Later that Saturday morning after ensuring for the third time that all the parts of the plane were functioning, Av announced they would be taking it on its first test flight. Lyon arrived half an hour later and after assuring them that the day's light wind would be fine for flying, they headed to the field at the top of the Cowie Hill subdivision.

At the elevated field of freshly mowed grass, surrounded on three sides by forest with the fourth looking out past the top of a school, and beyond that, the top half of a cement high-rise apartment building, Av carried a small container of fuel, the unpainted plane and its remote control out to the center of the field.

With the plane's power turned on and the little propeller spun to get the gas-powered engine started, all watched as Av did as he had read and moved the throttle on the control box to full. Sounding like a tiny motorcycle, the plane's engine sped up as it began to taxi across the grass. As it picked up speed, Avriel pulled up on one of the control's two joysticks and all watched with fascination as the plane took flight. As it was leaving the large field's airspace, Av lowered its speed to almost half, evened it out and, with the small joystick on the right side, caused it to make large circles above them.

"To steer the plane, you just have to use this lever on the right. It controls the up and down and left and right. But if you want to turn sharp, you will have to turn the plane on its side using this controller on the left here and then pull back on the right lever as if you were climbing up but instead climbing to the side," Av proudly told the group. "And to straighten out again, you just have to release the right controller and use the left one to even out the plane."

For several minutes, Av steered the small, buzzing plane around the field. Getting bored of that, he disappointed Dwight by handing the controls to Blue standing next to him. Blue took the plane up higher and turned it sharply as Av had instructed, flying it up and down the field. After a few passes of the small plane, Blue also disappointed Dwight by handing the controls to Lisa, who then delighted Dwight by immediately offering them to him. Dwight scared everyone when he put the plane into a dive and when it was just feet from the ground, pulled it up into a steep climb. Then he too flew it back and forth across the field's airspace. Several times, the boy had to restrain himself from trying stunts he lacked the experience for.

After a few minutes, Dwight forced himself to hand over the controls to Lyon, who took them and seemed to do as Dwight had initially done. He flew the plane sharply toward the ground and then sent it back into the air. After evening it out and turning it back toward them, the little boy did what no one had done: pushed the throttle to full power and as the plane gained speed, pulled up on the right joystick, sending the plane straight up into the air and back around, completing its first loop-the-loop. He repeated it several times, keeping the plane just above the group and impressing all except Dwight, who said, "I forgot he has one at home." Then Lyon evened out the plane, made it roll over several times before turning it back toward them and flying it in a large figure-eight.

As he looked up at the plane, Av could not avoid experiencing subtle flashbacks to the planes he had witnessed overhead during the war. The loop-the-loop brought back one memory and the plane's rolling over brought back several others. Then when Lyon guided the plane straight toward them before pulling it up toward the sky, Av flashed back to a very rough memory and had to control his sudden urge to pick up Dwight and Lyon and command the others to run for safety. Av found himself needing to wipe his forehead several times that cool mid-September afternoon.

"Wouldn't it be cool to put a video camera on it and record what it sees?" asked Lyon as he performed several more loop-the-loops.

"Sure, but that'd be way too heavy," said Blue. "They'd invent a time machine before they'd invent a video camera small enough to fit on a model plane."

"Hey, here's a question," said Dwight. "Why try to make a time machine to go back years? Why not make one go back only a minute or so? It'd be easier, wouldn't it? Going back a minute, instead of years. Must be a lot easier to do, right?"

All stared at Dwight, with Lyon even taking his eyes from the plane for a moment.

"Uh...right, even going back a second would be pretty...pretty hard to do...I guess," admitted Dwight. "It's going back, not just how far that's the problem, right?"

With all nodding their heads, Lyon went back to focusing on the plane.

As a finale, Lyon spun the plane upside down and performed three more loop-the-loops. Saying, "I think the fuel is getting low," he evened it out, placed the throttle back to the half position and handed the controls to Av.

Figuring he could land the plane as well as he had sent it into the air (adopting Dwight's way of thinking that it would be easier to bring it down than to send it up,) Av accepted the controls and flew the plane in a couple more circles before he had it slowly coming down toward them. With slightly shaking hands, he did as he had read and cut the speed more and lowered the plane until it was a dozen feet from the ground. Then, as he had read, Av cut the speed even more and pulled back on the horizontal stick so the plane's nose was turned up slightly as it descended.

"I think you're coming in too slow, sir," advised Lyon — too late.

The plane stalled and fell toward them. It hit the ground and flipped over several times, sending parts flying off as it passed the large-eyed, open-mouthed group.

Dwight and Lyon were the first to shake off their shock and the first to go after the pieces.

"Sir, I think it's beyond repair," Lyon informed Av when he, Blue and Lisa joined the two.

"Yes, it appears I did an outstanding job destroying it. I suppose we should keep what is left as extra parts, in case I...I decide to build another," said a disappointed Av.

All silently nodded in agreement.

Ashamed, Lyon looked up at the old man. "I'm really sorry. I thought you had flown before...landed before. I didn't know this was your first time flying. If I knew, I'd have offered to land it. You took off so well, I thought you were experienced with model planes."

Av tapped Lyon's shoulder. "It's not your fault at all. I should have asked you to land it. I was rather over confident, I believe."

It was at that moment, Av decided remote controlled airplanes would not be a sustainable hobby. If he had to spend forty or so hours putting it together only to destroy it on its first flight, the payoff was not worth the investment of time.

Av looked to a sympathetically speechless Dwight. "On the bright side, I never wasted any time painting it. Perhaps, this is a sign that model rockets are more for me. They look much simpler to build, and we just launch them in the air and wait for them to fall to the ground." Then trying to make light of the situation, he said, "Perhaps, we should vote on it. Everyone who feels I should try model rockets put up their hand. Anyone who does not, walk around like a duck and quack."

With grins on their faces, all raised a hand, including Lyon who had neither made nor launched a model rocket but wanted to.

"Everyone? Well, I was hoping to see at least one person quacking and waddling about," said Av, feigning disappointment.

CHAPTER 8
An Estranged Stepfather

On the back of his black leather vest were three bold patches. On the thick bottom patch curving upward was the word FREDERICTON. The center patch was a pair of large, bold Viking battle axes. And on the top thick, downward curving patch were the words HEADLESS NORSEMEN. The patches were the first things visitors would be drawn to. That was all anyone could see of the muscle-bound man on the other side of the window as he hunched over the boardroom table.

Examining a page of a hardbound ledger, the Headless Norseman picked up an opened stubby bottle of beer beside a pile of more hardbound ledgers, put the brown glass bottle to his mouth and emptied it before calling out loud enough to be heard at the bar on the other side of the windowed wall behind him, "Hey, Numbers, come here for a sec."

"Well, I'm bein' beckoned," said the small, potbellied man to Snap and Howard sitting with him at the messy bar opposite the church. "Let's see whats 'is majesty needs now."

The two nodded their heads as Numbers wiped the sweat from his semi-bald head and stood up.

Standing over the Headless Norseman as if comparing their vests' back patches, Numbers asked, "What's up, Jack?"

"In this here payment ledger, there're names, actual

names, written next to the amounts."

"Yup."

"Why do it this way?"

"It's always been done that way. We know at a glance who's getting what, right?"

"Ok, tell me what would happen if this here book got into the wrong hands?" demanded Jack.

"Whose wrong hands?"

"Hell, I don't know. Let's just say...hmmm...THE COPS!" Jack almost shouted.

"I...I guess...I guess there'd be hell ta pay."

"Yeah, lots of people would be screwed at a glance! This is *not* how we do it!" Jack took a deep breath and said in a calmer tone, "We use a book like this too, but we keep a smaller book for the names. Then the two are matched up by a code, like C2 for a cop. This way, if a book's stolen or found in a raid, they mean little without the other. So...I need you to put the names in a separate book and give each a code. Then, black out the names in this one and use the codes instead. This is damn careless, man. That's what kills a club. The other books, these older ones should go somewhere safe. You can't keep them here. It's the first place they'll look. Hey, you got pretty much no need to look at these old ones, so let's store them somewhere else. Actually, you know what? We don't need these with the patch-over. Some of them are what...eleven, twelve years old? We don't need the risk. Let's just burn them, just to be safe. Take them outside and burn them all except for the last five years worth. Do it now so you don't forget. And on your way out, have Howard bring me another beer when he comes in. Hey, burn the ones from the very beginning of the club too?" Shaking his head, he released an exasperated sigh. "And after that, let's black the names out on the ones that are left and set up the code system. Looks like we have some work ahead of us, eh?"

"Ok...right," said Numbers as he made second pile of ledgers from the first and picked it up. On his way out he asked, "Ya said ya wants ta see Howard?"

"Yeah, and have him bring me a beer when he comes,"

Jack said with bitterness.

A couple of minutes later, after setting two opened bottles of beer on the table and then sitting his short body in a seat beside Jack, Howard asked, "How's it all going?"

Jack picked up one of the full bottles of beer and turned his seat toward Howard.

"Good, but there's some stuff to fix up on the bookkeeping side, some careless, sloppy shit. But it's fixable in a few days, I think. Hey, is it always this quiet here?"

"No, I told everyone to stay away for a few weeks to give you some quiet time while you examine the books and stuff. They're continuing doing as they do, but nothing new unless they call me to get the go ahead from you."

"I appreciate that, but I'd like to see some of the guys soon. It's been a while. Maybe we can do a dinner with them next week. How about I give you the names and you make it happen?"

"Sure," said Howard, picking up his bottle of beer and taking a drink.

"So, tell me, are you still planning on retiring when the Tribe's patched over?"

"Yeah, nothing's changed. I ain't going back to being a regular member. I've never heard of a president sticking around as a regular patch after he's stepped down. Mind you, I never heard of a president ever stepping down. If we go, it's usually in a box, eh?"

"Yeah, that's true. You know it's not personal, right? They just want someone who knows their system, their way of doing things. I can do without the job, but seeing how I was a member here, I suppose I'm the best person for the patch-over and don't have much of a choice. Hey, the offer is still there as VP."

"I know, but going from Pres. to VP is just as bad to me as going back to a regular patch again. Leave Snap as the VP. He's good at it...well, he takes orders well. The guy doesn't get ideas, so he has nothing to conflict with yours."

Frank took a drink. "I'm just not sure Snap is right for me. Give it some thought and we'll discuss it in a couple of weeks.

Now with all the other stuff, we should probably work out a schedule. You'll need to walk me through the operations. I'll have to tour all the Tribe's buildings, including the grow houses and put a value on them. Then there are the businesses. I'll have to see their *other* sets of books, see how much more we can push through there. With the increased business, we may just have to open a couple more to handle the extra cash." Seeing Howard's lack of enthusiasm, he added, "Hey, you should come off sitting pretty in the end. You're going to get a cash payout for your years, and, maybe, I'll be able to work some kind of monthly dividend for you. It's not unusual to keep someone on the payroll after they retire, eh? You should do great too taking over Frank's business, especially when you include the full menu. He did pretty well with just the weed. You should do great with selling everything." Jack took a drink and paused for a second. "Anyway, you should do well all considering." He turned his head to the many photos covering the walls. Laughing a low laugh, he pointed toward one. "Hey, do ya remember when that photo was taken of Hurtin' there? The next morning, he almost drowned in his own vomit! Dodds only saved him cause he heard the bubbles coming from him passed out face down in it." Jack laughed again. "I miss that guy. He was funny without trying to be. It's a shame what happened to him, but it had to be done. What was his name? I knew him so long as Hurtin', I can't even think of it."

"Alex...Alex O'Connell. Yeah, it's a shame, but it was his choice. He knew the penalty, and still..."

"Yup, you had to do what you had to do, but, I miss him. Still, I'm glad you left his photo on the wall. Good memories, eh? Hey, how's Lense doing? I'd like to see him at the dinner."

"Dead...by a van. That's his vest there," Howard said, pointing to one of the framed vests on the wall.

"Shit. I never heard. And the driver of the van?"

Howard grinned. "Never got a scratch, but soon after, he had the strangest accident and will never walk again."

"Got to love those spontaneous *accidents*," Jack said as he matched Howard's grin.

"Yup. So, I guess all the photos will be coming down too, be retired too?" asked Howard.

"Yeah. It'll be a new chapter for the chapter," said Jack, obviously proud of his play on words. "Hey, one last thing and then I'll have to leave you guys alone in an hour; I promised to take Cindy out to dinner tonight. She's still pretty upset over that whole Bart shit yesterday. Anyway, I need you to clean up the past dues. There's only three, but one's Frank's. If he's still the man I knew, I'm sure he has the cash set aside somewhere."

"I'm sure he does too. Speaking of Frank, you ever talk to him?"

"No. We parted ways when I parted with Cindy."

"Right. Ok, I'll talk to Snap about the accounts and get them cleared up ASAP."

Both men stood up, shook hands and then embraced as bikers do. After a second, they broke their embrace and Howard left as Jack went back to examining a ledger.

With his half-bottle of beer in hand, Howard joined Snap at the bar.

"Where's Numbers?"

"He mumbled somethin' abouts collectin' some books and burnin' 'em. I think' 'e's out back."

"Good," Howard said and then whispered, "Hey, we need to settle those three accounts, the last of the consignment shit. Send another message to Fish, and have some guys rough up Gary. That should get his attention. I think he uses more than he sells. For Frank's, I'll get the thirty-two hundred from the stash and you can get Numbers to apply it, but don't let on to Demp it's clean. We'll keep Frank thinking he owes us."

"Ok, but I don't gets it. Why leave Frank thinkin' he still owes us? Didn't we gets enough out of 'im? We got his customers...and his stash. What a dumbass, puttin' it behind a baseboard! How predictable, eh?" Snap whispered back.

"Ok, just shut up about that. Yeah, we *were* going to forget about it, but I have an idea, a big plan, and you'll probably want to go along with it, especially now that Jack-*ass* in there mightn't keep you as VP. You might want to just work with me when I'm out the door."

"What? He saids that?"

"Pretty much, yup."

The words could be seen bouncing around in Snap's head for a second before he said in a fiercely controlled voice, "But, we broughts the offer ta...ta the church, and this...this is are thanks? They...they cans just sit on it and...and rotate!"

"Yeah, you go tell him that to his face while I stay here and cheer you on," Howard dared him, and then forcing a smile, he added in a gentle tone, "Look, let's just make the best of what we got before then, alright?"

CHAPTER 9
An Estranging Father

"*Gone?*" Frank asked through a whisper in French. "*If it was the cops, it was most likely Greene. Hey, you told me you guys cleaned the apartment. Who cleaned my bedroom?*"

"Lisa," Blue answered in English, "But there's no way it's her!"

Hearing Blue's voice from across the room, Av looked up from his novel.

"*Lower your voice,*" demanded an anxious Frank. He tapped his knuckles on the table. "*It's all...it's all good. It's not good news, but not as bad as it seems. I'll work out something with Howard. So...so, what else is...is new?*"

Seeing his father having to force back his panic when he hardly ever panicked, worried Blue, and though he wanted to believe his father would be able to work something out with Howard, Blue was not confident he could. It seemed his father was just saying what he was saying so as not to worry him.

With his father trying to hide how worked up he was over the missing money, he did not want to add to the man's stress, but he could not leave him in the dark. Switching to English, he reluctantly told him about his mother's visit and who had told her where he lived.

Frank's eyes gave away his shock, the double shock with the extra news that the Tribe had been searching for Blue.

With his intense eyes making Blue feel they were burning through him, Frank asked in an unusual cold tone, "How do you feel about living with your mother?"

"You may as well be asking me how I feel about living with someone I hate," said Blue softly, hoping his father would do the same.

Continuing with his tone, Frank said in French, *"Hey, when we're done, have Mr. Rosen come talk with me, ok?"* Blue nodded his head. *"Listen, Lisa's got custody of you and nothing can change that, except, maybe, if Jack can afford...wants to pay to go to court to fight to get her rights to you back. I can't expect that'll work out too well for them. It's been seven years, and Jack's a member of the Headless too. Neither can be good. Now here's the other thing that's bothering me. Howard loves to take advantage of a situation and he will if he can. I could be being paranoid, but if he went through the effort to find you, then he's probably planning something. If he approaches you to help me with the debt, to do something about it, you don't. There's no reason for you to get involved."* Frank paused for a moment to calm down. *"Look, Jack is taking over the club and he won't let you get involved in this, not when he's with Cindy. She's got to have some motherly instincts in her."* Frank shook his head and then wiped the perspiration from his forehead. *"This shit is just so messed up. So tell me, what do you do if Howard approaches you to do something to make up for the money?"*

"Nothing," Blue said sheepishly.

Frank stared at his son who seemed unable to look him in the eye. *"Has he approached you?"*

"No," Blue answered in English. "Why would you ask that? I'd have said something."

"Well, you look like the cat that swallowed the canary."

Blue's voice grew in defense. "It's you! Your eyes are burning through me and your tone is super serious. It's like I did something wrong!"

"Sorry, I'm sorry. It's not you. It's...it's the Cindy and Howard shit. I guess it wound me up."

Frank reached out and affectionately took hold of Blue's

hand, only to immediately have to release it when a guard shouted, "Roy, no touching! You know better! Show me your palms!"

Frank raised his open hands in the air and then putting them down, said, "Listen, I should probably talk to Mr. Rosen. Blue, I need you to be strong and not get involved. Remember, if they approach you, you're not to get involved. Nothing good can come from it, nothing."

Still uncomfortable with his father's tone, Blue said only, "Ok," and stood up. He then noticed and traded a nod with Demp, who was hunched over the table whispering with a visitor whom Blue failed to recognize but may have if he had worn the Tribe's vest of patches.

Seeing Blue walking toward him, Av placed the bookmark in his novel and stood up.

"Av, Frank wants to see you," Blue informed him and then set himself in Av's chair.

"Right...right," said Av, whose heart started beating hard as he walked over to Frank's table and rigidly sat his thin body across from him.

"Hi, Mr. Rosen."

"Hello, François," Av said stiffly.

"I wanted to ask if Blue's behaving himself?"

"He is behaving himself very well. All considering, I would say extremely well."

"Good. That's good to hear. Listen...Mr. Rosen, I want to thank you, thank you for all you've done for Blue...and me. Will you tell Lisa I said thank you too?" Av nodded his head. "I'll never be able to repay you guys, but you know that," Frank said before taking in a deep breath and missed Av doing the same. "But this thing Blue told me about my ex, Blue's mother, worries me, and I'm sure it's stressing Lisa and you. I know Blue has no interest in being with his mother, but if she takes it to court, there is a slight chance she could win...I'm guessing." Seeing no change in the old man's stone face, Frank continued. "Look, I don't know if this'll help, but I can always do up a will. I don't have much, but I do have Blue, which is everything to me, and maybe, if Lisa's up for it, I can leave her

Blue...for adoption I mean. At least, if it goes to court, you can show the will with my intent for Blue to go to Lisa when I'm gone, and, maybe, that's just enough ammunition to counter any chance his mother has. I don't know if Blue's old enough to have a say in court, so the will could be enough ammunition if he's not."

Av's stiff expression continued as he said, "Yes, that could possibly work, but you should only do that if you truly wish it."

"I do. Don't get me wrong. I'm not suggesting I'm going to die in here. Hell, I've been here twice before now and I'm still around. I'm just saying if for some reason something happens to me, Blue is taken care of, if Lisa wants it...if you want it. And the sooner we deal with this the better."

"Right," Av said. "I will talk to Lisa and then my lawyer to ensure it's legal. With her consent, I can have him speed it along. He may have to visit you once or twice in the next couple of weeks to finalize it."

"Good. Here's the other thing I've got to ask. I think this seeing me each week is tough on Blue for several reasons, but one is that seeing each other weekly, we have little to talk about. You two spend more time traveling than actually visiting. Maybe we can make the visit every four or five weeks. Let the news pile up so we make more out of the visits. Besides, I can always call when needed."

"Is Blue fine with that?"

Frank's face reddened. "I...I haven't told him. I'm hoping you will. Call me a coward, but right now, I just can't handle it if he gets upset. I know these visits are taking a lot out of him, having a bad effect on him, and just for a short break from my monotony. And I think it's hardly worth it for you too."

"I am fine with the journey," Av informed the father.

"But I'm not. I think once every month or so is more reasonable for everyone. By then, the next time he visits, I'll have news about my trial. It would be a...a more substantial visit."

Av did not say it, but he agreed with the effect the visits were having on Blue. Fewer visits would probably mean Blue would not be so melancholic every week. It bothered Av to see it but it bothered him more that there was little to nothing he could do to bring the boy out of the state.

Driving home, Av broke the normal silence by informing Blue of Frank's decision. He was relieved to hear Blue also agreed with the idea.

Blue did not say it, but he felt taking almost four hours out of Av's day each Sunday for only a visit of twenty minutes at most seemed too unfair to his old friend. Blue could have taken the time to make the visits longer, but to do so would mean informing his father about all the good things happening in his life, and he did not want his father thinking he was better off without him. Blue never told his father about what he and his new family did together since he moved in with them: their visiting Montreal, Disney World, and London, England, where pedestrians seemed to be moving targets for the drivers, which Dwight narrowly avoided twice. He had never even given his father any details of the oversized home they recently moved into. Up until the previous visit, the father and son's discussion were mostly about how each was handling the change, with the discussions digressing to their past life together, where it was obvious Frank was pining for it and less obvious that Blue was pretending to.

CHAPTER 10
Like Father, Like Son

"We can put the engine on top with the fan inside that large hole. See, we can secure it with balsa wood," Lyon informed Dwight the Monday morning of their third week of school. Holding up the piece of paper with his hand drawn design, he pointed to the electric motor. "We'll solder a couple of wires to it and connect them to your train's controller. I have a soldering iron at home we can use."

"Cool. But you want to start Wednesday night? Don't you have ballet then?"

"Yes, but I can get out of it for the science project, and I'd much rather do the project over ballet. That's why I chose Wednesday night," said Lyon with an exaggerated wink. "Here, take the design and look at it tonight."

"Ok," said Dwight, folding up the paper, placing it in the inside pocket of his blazer and not understanding what more he would see on the paper later that night that he had not already seen then.

"So, you guys are all set, but, Dwight, you still have to get Av to get the balsa wood," said Blue as he swaggered slightly. "And the stores close at five or five-thirty today and tomorrow."

"Yeah, I'll see if he can do it today after school."
**

That Monday morning after the boys had left for school and as Mrs. Collins cleaned the kitchen, Av sat in the library and read a small book he had recently found in a used bookstore. He liked used bookstores. Besides enjoying the smell of millions of yellowing pages filling the place, when he was not sure what to read from current writers whom he was not up to date on, he would peruse the titles in the used bookstores and be confident that any title he came across multiple times in the store was a bestseller. Not finding anything to tempt him in his regular sections of the store, he tried the Religion section, and in that smaller section, he found a book regarding the Jehovah Witnesses. It was not their version of the bible, but their book of responses to potential questions posed by non-Jehovah Witnesses. Thinking it might give him a quick study on their religious position, Av bought it.

After reading a good portion of the book, he decided he needed something else to do. Standing up and looking out to the front yard through the tall windows of the library, he got an idea. He would cut the lawn. Av had hired a man to do it, who would be paid whether or not he cut it, but it would give him something to do and he may even enjoy riding the lawn mower the previous owners had left with the house.

After familiarizing himself with the parts of the mower, Av was happy to find the tank was three-quarters full, the oil appeared fine and the machine started on the fourth try. With an almost childish joy, he drove the mower to the front of the house, put the cutter in gear and while hugging the fence on the left, drove toward Jubilee. After going the full length, he looked back and found he had not cut the lawn. He rode back up to where he had started, made sure to lower the blade, and again followed along the fence. Satisfied the grass was cut that time, Av drove the mower around the yard, working his way from outside in, until after twenty minutes and having cut a fair portion of the grass, the mower died.

Having checked that there was still gas in its tank, Av examined the machine's engine. Understanding little of what he was looking at, he heard, "Hello again, Mr. Rosen," and looked up to see the two familiar Jehovah Witnesses walking toward him.

"Hello, sir. Nice to see you again," greeted Blair, the black Jehovah Witness.

"Hello," said Av, mentally hurrying to put on his protective shell. Closing the hood, he sat back on the machine, looking as if he was about to continue cutting the lawn.

"Last time we talked, you had mentioned we'd continue our last conversation. We happen to be in the area and thought we'd drop by," Will, the white Jehovah Witness, informed the old man.

"So I see. Do you folks work?" asked a curious Av.

"No, we're Dalhousie students."

"Right. That's good to hear. I–I do not have much time to talk, maybe five minutes. I must finish this lawn."

"No problem, sir. We'll only be five minutes."

"Right. But before we talk, I really should be upfront with you gentlemen. I am not very fond of cults."

"We're not a cult," Will said matter-of-factly, making Av believe they must have been used to the comment.

"No," agreed Blair. "By the dictionary's definition, a cult is a religious group controlled by one leader. We don't have one leader...unless you count Jesus."

Recognizing the response from a portion of the book he had begun reading, Av felt confident saying, "The dictionary is not the place one should refer to the definition of a cult. If one leader were the definition, then the Catholic religion would be considered a cult. They have only one pope, I believe. The definition should be pulled from an encyclopedia. Much like...let us say the word *zen*. If one would look it up in several dictionaries, one would find the answers lacking. It is much too complicated to be defined by a couple of sentences. To me, the definition of *cult* depends on the degree of extreme religious practices, not the number of leaders. It should also be based on the amount of distance the group attempts to place between it and society, and also, the level to which it denies its members their individuality."

"But we're not extreme and we don't separate ourselves

from the government," said Will.

"And we're ok with our members' individuality," added Blair.

"Why would you think that?" asked Will.

"Well, I read in your book *Reasoning* that you consider paying taxes the same as giving to charity. That's your response to the question of whether or not you give to charities, correct? You only believe in the Kingdom of God, not the government, so paying taxes is the same, to your group, as giving to charity, correct?"

"Where did you get the book?" asked Blair with a confrontational tone.

"I found it in a used bookstore."

"You shouldn't have that book! That's only for Jehovah Witnesses!"

"I did not know that. I bought it legally. I have a receipt. I do not know how it found its way to a used bookstore, but I found it when it did. Now returning to what I had read, would that be correct?"

"No, we give to charities, like...like...," said Blair, pausing to look at Will.

Will said, "We help out those in need with...with food drives...and...and hot meals. But let's go back to the cult question, what do we do that's extreme? Extreme for who?"

Not buying into their response to the charity question and deciding to ignore Will's question, Av glanced at his watch that he could not make out without his reading glasses. "Gentlemen, it is about time I go back to work. It has been...uh...interesting talking with you two."

Reaching down to shake the gentlemen's hands, Will tried to place a brochure in it, and after having it refused this time too, both Witnesses walked to the opened gate at the end of the driveway.

With Blair and Will out of sight, Av considered closing and chaining the gate. Realizing he would be locking out the boys too, he stepped down from the mower and once again opened its hood to try to figure out the machine's problem.

With an oval of longer grass in the center of their front lawn, that afternoon Av and Dwight would rush downtown to the hobby store and return home with a plastic bag full of balsa wood of various thicknesses and, to Dwight's excitement, three boxes: one three-foot long box containing a three-staged model rocket needing assembly and two smaller boxes containing a launch pad and a plastic case large enough to hold an oversized lantern battery to power the ignition switch.

Av would return later that week for the required large battery, a pack of several rocket engines, a pack of several igniters, and a roll of wire —all that he had missed in their rush to leave the store as it closed.

**

Blue was amused to find the school's dress code had a cycle. It was strictly enforced at the beginning of each school year, but as the days passed, the boys' ties loosened and their top shirt buttons came undone, and the girls' blouses opened by a button or two and their plaid skirts began to shorten with the help of safety pins. Instead of wearing their skirts four inches below the knees, more and more girls began wearing them four inches above. And as more girls began following the unofficial policy, the older boys began hanging out at the four stairwells' first and second landings. They hung out there every morning, recess and lunch, but never after school. Nothing could distract them from leaving. The boys' hangout would be short-lived. When the majority of the dresses became short enough to catch the attention of the school's administration, the teachers would again enforce the dress code. And after few days of it being followed, the enforcement would again slacken, the skirts would begin to shorten and the boys would return to the stairwells, looking up through the eight-inch gap between the steps.

It was at a landing of a stairwell during Monday's recess that Blue first heard about the legend of Pantiless Patty. The story went back between three to twenty years depending on the boy telling the story of Patty discovering why the boys hung out in the stairwell. Angered by the boys sneaking peeks at the girls' panties, Patty decided to get back at them by not wearing any. Patty went pantiless briefly or for the rest of the school year, depending on the boy telling the story.

Most girls seemed oblivious as to why the boys hung out at the stairwell, but one girl was definitely not. Karen, who never pinned up her skirt, knew exactly why the boys were there, and it was there she knew she could find Blue with his friends. That Monday at recess she found him there and pulled him aside.

Thinking she was going to scold him for his *group activity*, Blue prepared himself with the weak defense that he was only there because his friends were.

"Hi, Karen. What's up?" Blue asked in a shy manner that was unusual for him.

"Blue," said Karen, looking everywhere but at him, "do you want to have lunch with me? I–I brought enough for two and I thought...well, I thought we could have lunch together outside."

Blue's anxiety with what he thought she was going to say was then replaced by surprise. He tried not to stammer as he said, "Sure...sure, that sounds...sounds great. Then I'll...I'll meet you by your locker...at lunch?"

Karen's large eyes lit up and a smile covered her face. "Great! Ok, I'll see you then!"

With Karen leaving down the hall at an excited speed, Blue returned to his friends, and after Cal had pumped him for she wanted, he admitted that Karen had asked him to lunch. With all the teasing he then got from the group, Blue was, for the first time, thankful that recess was only for fifteen minutes.

In the seclusion at the far side of the school's running track, the two shared Karen's ham and cheese sandwiches. Karen did most of the talking, and as he had once been advised by his father, Blue did most of the listening. As he sat listening to the one who could possibly become his girlfriend, he found it cute the way her giggle scrunched up her nose and caused her eyes to squint. He found it cute too that when she sneezed, it was a loud *ahhh* but a soft *chooo*. He also enjoyed watching her force food to one cheek so it would be out of the way while she talked, and coincidently, out of the way when she sneezed.

After she finished telling Blue about herself, Karen asked Blue about his family and was surprised to discover he lived with his cousin, Dwight —it had only then occurred to the redhead that being cousins made more sense and did not require much, if any, explanation— and she learned too that his father was away for work and his mother had passed away.

Just before lunch ended, Karen asked if they could meet there for lunch again the next day, and without giving it any thought, Blue agreed and offered to bring lunch for the two of them.

It was only later that night when he realized he had no idea what to make that he reluctantly asked Lisa for help. Thinking it was the cutest thing, Lisa jumped at the chance to help him impress his new girlfriend and put together a garden salad, devilled eggs, small, crustless devilled ham sandwiches, a large bottle of apple juice and two plastic glasses. Increasing Blue's magnitude of awkwardness, Lisa arranged to have the lunch delivered cold by Av, who was honored to do so and offered to learn to play the violin by lunch the next day.

Blue impressed Karen with the lunch, which Lisa had made for them and Av had delivered, but after learning she disliked devilled eggs and apple juice, the two decided they would bring their own lunches from then on, except on special occasions like a birthday, where one would bring the food for the other with the menu agreed on beforehand.

It was after their second lunch together, when the two shared a quick and discreet kiss, that Blue felt his life was looking up.

**

As the boys walked home from school Wednesday, a light-brown pickup truck stopped beside them. None paid any attention to it until the passenger called out from the rolled down window, "Hey, Blue. How's it going? Hey, how's your old man?"

Blue turned pale as a sudden wave of dizziness engulfed him. "Good. He's...he's good," he forced out.

"Good to hear. Listen, I'm Howard, your dad's friend. We should do some quick catching up."

Feeling like he was about to faint, Blue said, "Ok...right," laid down the boys' school bags, and turned to Dwight. "You...you guys head home, I–I'll be there in a bit."

"We'll stay with you and wait," said Dwight, noticing Blue's unusual lack of composure.

"No. It's...it's Frank's friend. It's fine...really. Take your bags and I'll see you in a bit. Well, what are you waiting for? Get going and I'll see you in a bit!"

"Ok, *fine*," said a defeated Dwight as both boys picked up their school bags. He huffed and swaggered away, saying, "You don't have to tell me twice!"

"Yes, he did," corrected Lyon.

"Huh? What?"

"He had to tell you twice. You only left after he told you a second time."

Dwight huffed again.

After waiting for the boys to be some distance away, Blue turned to Howard, "What's...what's going on?"

With an exaggerated smile, Howard opened the door and stepped out of the truck. Gesturing for Blue to get in, he joked, "Come into my office."

Blue thought it better to go along with him.

Squeezing Blue between him and the driver of the pickup, Howard said, "Blue, this is Snap. He's the VP of the Tribe."

Blue forced his right hand to the left of him and shook the man's hand. "I think I saw you at the prison talking to Demp."

"Yeah, you and me mets a couple times before. Sometimes I'd visits Frank. I would'a been drivin' the bike and wearin' my colors then. I lets my hair grow longer too," he said, swinging his head to expose his ponytail.

"That's probably...probably it. Without your colors, it's like trying to recognize you guys when you're naked," Blue tried to joke as the color began to return to his face.

Snap's face went cold, causing Blue's heart to skip a beat or two. "Ya sayin' without are colors we're nothin', kid?"

"No...no, it's nothin'...nothin' like that. It's like...like if someone's always wearin' a...a suit, and then...and then one days ya...ya sees 'im in jeans and a T-shirt, it can be hard ta recog—"

"Look, Blue, this isn't a social visit," Howard cut in. "We got a problem...or I should say Frank's got a problem, and we're going to give you a chance to fix her."

With his face trying to match the color of his hair, Blue's lips became dry and his heart pounded in his chest as he forced out, "What...what do ya wants me ta do? What cans I do? Frank...Frank tolds me ta stay outta it. He tolds me if ya comes lookin' fer my help, fer me not ta."

"Calm down kid, just relax. Yeah, I can see where your old man's coming from. Frank doesn't want you involved. I get it. But your dad owes over three grand and we want it back, and he can't do that from inside now can he? Now, we could have Demp hurt him, but that doesn't get us the money, does it? Doesn't do shit for us except to send a message to the others, eh?" Howard's tone and face then feigned empathy. "Listen, we could avoid all the nasty stuff by you just doing some simple selling to earn back the money he owes. We give you some stuff and you just sell it at school. You'd have the thirty-two hundred (let's just make it an even three grand) paid back in no time." Seeing the boy's panic continuing, Howard grinned. "Now, you can do as your dad wants and stay out of it...and he suffers, or you can help him out and everyone is fine." Howard picked up a small backpack from down at his feet and dropped it on Blue's lap. "This would be your first stuff to get sell."

Under the cold stare from Snap, Blue tried to compose himself as he unzipped the bag and looked through it. "W– what's this?" he asked as he pulled out a transparent plastic bag of pink pills and dozens of individually wrapped powders.

"The pills are acid and the powder's heroin. You can start selling coke and LSD next time we meet."

Blue's nervous state seemed to suddenly vanish.

"What? No, I won't sells 'em! Frank wouldn't and neither wills I! No way! That ain't goin' ta happen!"

Howard's nostrils flared as he stared at Blue for a second.

"Fine, give them to me," he said as he grabbed the bag of pills and powders and placed it in the glove compartment. "So, you'll just sell the weed. That's...that's fine. It'll take you longer to pay off the debt, but if you're good with that, then so are we. The rest is just the weed. It's wrapped tight, so make sure you got a garbage bag to put it in when you open her up. It's really good for hiding the smell of the stuff too. Now, I don't expect any of the kids to be able to order any large quantities, so to make it easier for you, I figure you'd sell them by the joint. There's a sample one somewhere in the backpack there. You roll them like so and charge a couple of bucks for them. You got a dozen packs of rolling papers in there too to hold you over til next Wednesday. Ok, now this is what we'll do. We'll meet at that there park by your place every Wednesday at seven. You give us the cash and we'll give you more weed and papers if you need them. Hey, if you can find some other guys to sell at other schools, or even someone to sell the harder stuff at your school, that'll lower Frank's debt too. We'll talk about it when it happens, ok?"

"I didn't say I'd do it! Yer assumin' I'm goin' ta! I told yas, Frank doesn't wants me ta!" Blue protested.

Howard shook his head in frustration. "Kid...Blue, do you want your dad messed up? Do you want him eating from a straw? That's what'll happen. We can't be letting him out of his debt. It wouldn't be good for business. Imagine what our other dealers would do if they found out we went easy on someone who owes us money. We'd lose their respect, and no one wouldn't care about paying us back our money. It's either you help us or Frank eats from a straw...or worse."

With the threat sinking in, Blue fought to control his panic. "Jack's good with this, with me sellin'? Cindy's good with it too, is she?"

Howard's face flushed. "What? Yeah, whatever. Don't worry about them. We're still the Tribe, and I'm still the president. Jack doesn't have a say."

"Ok. So, I just gotta sell three thousand worth or fifteen hundred joints and we're done, right?"

The two men laughed.

"No. That there stuff's not free. You have to pay that back too, but any profits you make go against the debt of Frank's weed. That there's about thirty-six hundred bucks (the price went up since your old man got some) and it'll get you about twenty-five hundred thin joints. Look, seeing how you pretty much got to do this, I'll make this stuff an even three grand. See that? Right there you just saved another six hundred bucks off the debt. That makes six grand altogether you owe. Remember, the more you sell, the faster you can stop."

"Ok," said Blue getting control of himself. "I'll do it. I'll do it, but you can't tell Frank. If you tell him, if he finds out, I'm done with it, for sure done with it."

"Sure, you don't want him to know. It's our secret. In fact, outside of the three of us, no one has to know, right?"

Blue nodded. "Ok, but just so you really get it, no telling Frank or it's over."

"I get it," said Howard, who looked past Blue to Snap. "You get it too, right?"

"I gets it," confirmed Snap.

"Look, I...I have to get going now. If I'm too far behind those two, I might get some questions thrown at me, and I'm not much of a liar."

"Ok," said Howard, who opened the door, stepped out of the truck and helped Blue put on the backpack. Handing the boy his schoolbag, he said, "So, we'll see you next Wednesday at seven. Don't be late...and good selling. Hey, remember, when you open up that there bundle, make sure you have it in a garbage bag first. The stuff's wrapped so tight, it's going to explode as soon as you slice her open. Hey, and you need to cut up the buds with scissors or something to make the pieces small enough to roll." Howard patted Blue on the shoulder. "Ok, now go make me proud, kid."

"Hey," said Blue as the thought hit him. "Maybe we should tell Frank his debt is cleared up. Maybe tell him you removed it because of his loyalty or something like that. That way, he can relax about the whole thing. Just don't tell him anything about this."

"Ok, kid, that's what we'll do then. We'll tell him it's because of his loyalty, his not saying nothing to the cops about us supplying him with the stuff. We'll do that this week. Ok, so we'll see you a week from tonight, at seven."

"Ok," said Blue.

He removed the backpack, and with it in one hand and the schoolbag in the other, turned and walked away.

Seconds later the truck passed with a quick honk of its horn.

Watching the road, a frowning Snap said to Howard, "I don't feel rights about all this. We gots like fourteen grand from Frank, which I got none of by the way. Shouldn't we just leave it alone? I mean, we paids for that weed with Frank's money and now we're havin' 'is kid buy it from us? This is just gettin' so messed up."

"Shut the hell up!" growled Howard. "That's business, man. You're not seeing the potential. This here's the start of something big. That fourteen grand is our start-up money and that kid's our way into the schools. Imagine all that there cash we can make if we're selling into *all* the schools. This is just the beginning, man! We'll be rolling in it! We won't need to be part of the Headless. We'll be independent!"

That evening after lying to Dwight that he and Howard were catching up on events and then lying that the backpack was full of Frank's stuff that had been left at Howard's, Blue began rolling the joints. After sneaking a garbage bag from the kitchen, he had opened the sealed package of marijuana inside of it, and as Howard had warned him, the package had burst open as the plant clippings expanded. Then after separating the pieces, Blue took several buds and used the scissors from his desk to cut them into fine pieces. With his tongue poking out the side of his mouth, Blue tried to produce a joint identical to the sample Howard had provided. At first, he used too much weed and ended up tearing the rolling paper, and then when he thought he had the correct amount and finished rolling the joint, it did not look much like the sample. Because of the bulge in its center, it looked like a tiny, pregnant worm. Practicing with a second and third, those joints too were somewhat pregnant, but the fourth, which he rolled with his thumbs working outwards from the center, was almost perfect.

With his technique just about down, Blue rolled for almost two hours, using up one complete pack of rolling papers and completing almost a hundred joints. In the end, his thumbs were sore and he had a bad taste in his mouth from the rolling paper's glue.

Because the task of rolling the joints required almost no thinking, Blue had an abundance of time to figure out how to sell them while minimizing the risk of being caught. He certainly did not want a line of students waiting for him by his locker, so he would have to create a discreet system for placing and filling orders.

When Blue was finished rolling for the night, he considered testing his product. He needed to relax and the weed would be the best way. He held a joint in his hand for a moment and contemplated lighting it up before deciding it was not a good idea. It would certainly relax him, but he would have to smoke it outside and out of sight and then he would have to hide away so no one noticed he was high. Hiding away would certainly raise questions, and then if he were caught, there would be more questions, which would certainly risk destroying any chance of helping his father out of his debt. No, Blue figured, smoking a joint would only add to his stress.

Then to give him a change of mind, Blue decided to check up on the progress of Dwight and Lyon's hovercraft. The two had earlier finished gluing together the pieces for the craft's body, which looked like a short, rectangular box with its sides angled out, and as they waited for the glue to dry, they were constructing the balsa wood mount for the small electric motor that would go on top of the craft.

"How are you going to steer it?" asked Blue.

"We don't," answered Lyon. "We pull it along to show how it doesn't touch the floor."

"Yup," Dwight said. "I thought we could have used the parts from Av's broken plane to control it, you know remotely, and somehow use the parts for steering the plane to steer the hovercraft."

"That sounds cool, but sounds like a lot of work too," said Blue.

"Yeah," agreed Dwight as he dripped a bit of white glue on one end of a tiny balsa wood stick and stuck it in place, "but Lyon thinks that's what we should do for a grade ten project, not a grade six one."

"We don't want to overdo it and raise the bar for our next science project," said Lyon as he cut another small beam from a thicker piece of balsa wood. "What we're doing is fine for a sixth grade A-plus. And if we get a new science teacher next year, we can even use this again, maybe."

Blue smiled at the boy's cleverness and then realized he had left his own project on his desk and went to hide it.

Returning to his room, Blue noticed a skunk smell and then realized it was the smell from the weed. He opened his window and then tightly tied up the garbage bag and squeezed it in the corner of a top shelf of his walk-in closet where short Mrs. Collins would fail to notice it when she hung up his laundered clothing. She could notice the smell, thought Blue, so he moved the deodorizer from his bathroom counter and placed it too on the top shelf of his closet. Lastly, he placed the completed joints in a sandwich bag and hid it and the small packs of rolling papers at the back of his desk drawer.

The next evening Blue made his way to his classmate's Thursday night hangout. Halfway through his second beer, and with a bit of a buzz to give him courage, he pulled out three joints from his pocket and asked if anyone wanted to try some weed. Almost all did. As the joints went around, some of the older boys showed the others how to smoke them by taking small puffs and holding the smoke in their mouths for a few seconds before inhaling it, and once inhaled, holding it in their lungs for almost as long as they could. Most of the boys were soon both high and quiet and would remain that way for some time.

Having avoided taking a puff, Blue sat bored on the ground waiting for someone to say something about him having the weed, like how he got it and how they could get some too. Each minute seemed like an hour to the boy.

Finally, Cal was the first to speak, causing Blue to hold

back his laughter at his friend's slow and mellow manner. "Blue. Hey, Blue, how...how'd you get this stuff? Can you get more? I'd like to get more, to get some, some more."

"I have my connections," said Blue. "I can get more, but it'll cost you two bucks each for ones like those."

"Great, I'll take some, some more, some more of them," said Cal with others agreeing to take some too.

"Ok, but there are some rules. First, if you want to get some at school, no one comes up and asks me for some, no one. You don't talk to me about them. You just discreetly pass me a small note with your name and the amount you want, like Sampson and the number ten, or something like that. If you ask me, ever ask me out loud, you get none, never again. Second, no one meets me at my locker. I don't want a lineup there. You meet me there, and you'll get none, never again. You'll have to meet me at the beginning of lunch at the group of trees just off the school grounds. So you have to order in the morning, and you have to have the exact change too. I'm not making change. And rule three: I don't mind you spreading the word, but if I don't know the guy, he gets nothing from me. Your friends have to go through you to get some."

"Ok," agreed several of the boys.

John stood up and waved to Blue. Having Blue's attention, he asked, "Hey, man, can you get me fifty?"

"You want fifty?" asked a surprised Blue.

"Yup. I don't go to your school, so how about ya bring fifty here tomorrow...say at six?"

"That's a hundred bucks," Blue informed the boy.

"Ya guys are so full of shit!" John said to those snickering about him never being able to get a hundred dollars and he must be very high if he thinks he could. "Yeah, that's...that's not a problem. I'll have it. Shut the hell up, ya uppity momma-boy prickity pricks!"

"Ok, I'll be here. And you better have the money cause I don't do credit."

John smiled sarcastically and added a thumbs-up.

The boys had lost track of time, or had forgotten that the thing on their wrists told them the time, and they left the field an hour later than usual, with two of them arguing about whether it was their last name and the number of joints to write down or the number of joints and their last name.

On the walk home, Blue was proud of his preplanning and had new hope of being able to move a lot in a short time. He already had an order for fifty joints, and that was half of what he had been able to roll the night before. He figured that if all went well, he would have to set aside two hours each night to build up his inventory. Then the thought hit him that it would be best to do the rolling after everyone had gone to bed, after ten. At that time, he had less chance of raising Av or Lisa's suspicions by them repeatedly finding his door locked.

At school the next morning, Blue received notes from several of the boys who hung out at the park, making the total sales that day forty-two joints, or eighty-four dollars, and due to the filling of those orders, making him ten minutes late for his lunch with Karen. Blue was starting to relax with his selling of marijuana. The sales at school that day and the fifty more joints to be sold that night caused him to believe he was on his way toward paying off his father's debt in just a few months.

With the fifty joints in a sandwich bag snug in his spring jacket, Blue made his way to the park where he met up with John and two of his friends, whom Blue did not recognize and considered harmless by their contrasting sizes: One tall and thin and the other short and stout.

"Hey, Blue, ya bring them?" John asked with excited eyes.

"Sure. You bring the cash?" asked Blue, not being comfortable with John's two friends moving to stand on either side of him.

"Yes...well no, but I brought these guys to make up for it."

Before Blue could respond, the two boys had him each by an arm.

"What the hell?"

"So where are they?" asked John with a smirk.

"Screw you!"

"Hold'em still," ordered John as he began patting down a squirming Blue.

While being patted down, Blue had to resist the several times he could have easily kicked John. He knew it would escalate the situation and he could not go home with bruises on the face. The questions would lead to an explanation that would end with him not being able to help his father.

"Well, looky, looky!" said John reaching into Blue's jacket and pulling out a sandwich bag. Examining the package, he said, "Now here's how it's goin' to work: every Friday at this time, yer goin' to bring me fifty more or I'll tell the school about your dealing there. If ya don't show up, ya prob'ly shouldn't show up at school too."

Blue wanted so much to fight or go down fighting if it came to that, but he just said, "Ok...ok, it's a deal. Now call off your dumbass henchmen and let me get the hell out of here!"

The two boys shook Blue by his arms as the taller, slimmer one said, "Let's teach this guy a lesson first!"

"No, we don't want him with noticeable marks," said John as he placed the sandwich bag inside his jacket. "Hey, but that only means we can't hit him in the face."

John wound back his arm and punched Blue hard in the stomach, and then punched him in his right side. The two boys dropped him to the ground, and as he lay in the fetal position trying to catch his breath, the Laurel and Hardy look-alikes kicked him several times in the legs and back.

"Let's go!" demanded John as he started walking toward the other end of the park. With his two friends joining him, he yelled back, "Ya better be here next Friday, or else!"

Blue got himself to his feet, brushed off the dirt from his jeans and jacket and by the time he had walked home had recovered from much of the shock of being attacked, but the pain in his ribs was still there.

Entering the house, he heard voices and laughter coming from the kitchen and went in to check it out.

Sitting on stools around the kitchen's island, while Sam watched from the kitchen counter, Lisa, Av, Dwight and Lyon were playing the Mouse Trap board game. No one noticed

Blue as they focused on the contraption set up on the board and none was more focused on it than Lyon.

Av released a plastic boot that swung and hit a chrome ball. The ball rolled down what looked like a set of plastic stairs and then through a gutter to hit a lever that forced a second chrome ball waiting on a tiny diving board above to roll down it, fall through a hole at the end and land in a small plastic bathtub where it rolled to the other side and fell through another hole, landing on one end of a seesaw. There, it was supposed to launch from the other end of the seesaw a plastic figure of a diver wearing a one-piece swimsuit into a small bucket that would then cause a cage to fall and trap the player's playing piece of a plastic mouse.

The mouse was Lisa's, and when the diver missed the bucket and her mouse was safe, she screamed with joy.

Blue greeted them and sat down to watch the fun and, maybe, get his mind off of the earlier incident.

"Ok, I have to go work on an essay. Blue, can you take over for me?" asked Lisa.

"I want to, but I'm only here for a minute. I have homework, lots of it this weekend."

"Ok, guys, I'm out the next game," said Lisa.

"Awww, Mom! Blue, can't you play the next game? Just one game?" begged Dwight.

"Ok, I'll play the next one, but that's all."

Lyon, who did not seem to hear them, asked, "Can I experiment with the contraption for a second?"

With everyone agreeing, he adjusted the diver, reset the balls in their places and put the contraption in motion.

"If you stare at it any harder, Lyon, you'll go blind," joked Blue as the ball went its course.

Not taking his eyes from the contraption, Lyon said, "The cause and effect are really interesting. Just one little thing off and it fails."

Lisa laughed as the cage fell on her mouse. "That doesn't count, right?"

"It does not count," confirmed Av. "But I am rather afraid to have Lyon build the trap if I am under it."

Lyon and Dwight had another sleepover that night and instead of simply going to bed and then to sleep, as they did on their first sleepover, they stayed up until midnight playing Mouse Trap and appreciating what it meant to have a sleepover, which Lyon felt was the wrong name for it since it implied they would sleep.

"If we stay up late during sleepovers, wouldn't it be better to call them sleep-nots, or sleep-less, or something like that?" asked Lyon.

"Yeah, sleep-less is a better name for it," agreed Dwight.

From then on the boys referred to their sleepovers, to Lisa's amusement, as sleep-lesses, and Friday nights would become their regular sleep-less nights.

**

Trying not to bring attention to his sore ribs, which hurt whenever he moved or even breathed, Blue joined his family and Lyon as they drove to the field atop Cowie Hill to launch Av's rocket. From the parked car, Av handed out the parts. With him, Dwight and Blue each carrying a section of the rocket, and Lyon struggling with the launch pad and ignition box, it was only when they stopped in the center of the field that Blue noticed his piece of the rocket, the top section, had the name ROY stencilled in black lettering down its side. Dwight noticed his middle section had DIXON printed on it, and they both noticed that Av had put ROSEN on the bottom section.

As he began preparing the rocket's sections, Av was pleased that Lyon asked questions; he would have a chance to show off his new knowledge.

"These are the engines," said Av, handing Lyon a tiny cardboard tube that, except for the small hole running through the center, appeared to be filled with some kind of solid, gray chalk-like material.

As Lyon examined the tube, Lisa grew concerned. "Lyon, please give it back to Av. It could be dangerous."

"They are safe as long as there is no flame around," consoled Av. He held up a tiny, bulby like thing with two short wires extending from it. "This goes inside the hole of the engine, and we attached the longer wire's clips to these small wire ends here and then the longer wires are attached to the launch box over there. It is simply a battery in the box that causes this...this little round part to burn and then ignite the engine."

"That's cool! But how do you separate the sections and make them go even higher?" asked Lyon.

"They each have an engine, and just as the first engine burns out, it shoots a flame out from the other end, pushing out the parachute from that section and igniting the next section's engine. It is rather simple. Lyon, maybe you could put the engines in the bottom of Dwight's and Blue's sections. I already packed the chutes so all we will have to do then is push them together."

With the enthusiasm only a child can show, Lyon placed each rocket engine inside the tubes of the middle and top stages, being careful that the arrow marked on the engine pointed out of the section's bottom. Then Av pushed the three stages together and placed the three-foot rocket on the wooden-based launch pad. Asking everyone to step back, he inserted the igniter into the bottom section's engine, placed the longer wire's clips on each wire end of the igniter and then wound out the longer wire.

All followed Av as he walked about twenty feet, unrolling the wire as he went. Satisfied with his distance, he made sure the safety was on before attaching the wires to the ignition box.

"Ok, who wants to press the little, red button?" asked Av, trying to contain his excitement.

Before Dwight could get a hand up, both of Lyon's were up and then out to accept the box. Amused by the boy's excitement, Av handed the box to Lyon, who sat down with it on his lap and asked everyone to countdown from ten to zero. As they all counted down, Lyon lifted the safety cap off the switch and held his finger over the button. Reaching zero, he pushed it.

With everyone wide-eyed and staring at the rocket,

nothing seemed to happen. Then smoke began to pour slowly from the bottom, and a second later and with a hiss, it took off into the air.

All watched the rocket zoom straight up leaving a trail of smoke behind it. After about five seconds, a pop could be heard and the second stage smoked further up into the air. As the chute of the falling bottom stage caught the air and began to slowly descend, the rest of the rocket, then almost out of sight, separated again, making the last section impossible to see as it flew higher.

"I should have bought some binoculars," said Av to his fascinated friends.

As Blue ran over to retrieve the bottom stage of the rocket, which was being blown slightly toward the surrounding forest, and Dwight ran over to catch the second stage coming down even closer to the woods, the third stage came in sight, slowly descending by its parachute. It seemed to be coming down where Dwight had caught the second section, but then a gust of wind blew it closer to the woods. Another gust blew it even closer, and a third carried it over the trees, dropping it somewhere in the woods.

"I'LL GET IT!" Dwight yelled out, dropping his section and heading toward the woods.

Overwhelmed by a flashback, Av yelled in a stern tone that came only from him being unaccustomed to yelling, "DEWEY, NO!"

Unaccustomed to the tone, Dwight froze in his spot, and where he certainly would have corrected his friend on his name, he could not find the words.

As if reading Av's mind, Lisa said in a purposely gentle tone, "Av, Dwight told me you had once said the odds of finding a dead body was less than being hit by lightning twice...or something like that. What are the odds of finding another one?"

Av took a second to think about what Lisa had said and then yelled out to Dwight in the same stern tone, "OK, GO AND FIND IT."

Dwight remained frozen by the second stern tone until he

realized Av was telling him to go into the woods.

Everyone headed for the woods, and it took some time searching the ground before Blue noticed the last section of the rocket hanging by its orange chute high up on a branch of a pine tree. He wanted to climb up and give the branch a shake, but neither Lisa nor Av would allow it. They ended up leaving the smallest stage of the rocket where it was.

Before Blue left the woods, he took one more glance up at the piece of the rocket with the name ROY rotating back and forth by a breeze higher up. He told himself that when he could, he would return to retrieve it. He had to get it back. He had to join his stage with the other stages.

So ended Av's second attempt at a hobby. He would have to find one that he could not destroy or lose immediately after spending hours building it; though, building the rocket took far less effort and time than building the plane, but then they only enjoyed the rocket for a couple of minutes compared to the plane that they enjoyed for almost twenty. Av found himself working out that so far the payoff was close to one hour of labor for each thirty seconds of enjoyment they received from each.

That night at the cinema as the boys and Lisa watched the movie, Av's mind was on hobbies. He was disappointed by the three he had shown an interest in. Photography was too complicated for him. The remote controlled airplane took too much time to build only to be destroyed on its first flight, and the model rocket was much simpler to build but was lost on its first launch. He needed a hobby where he could show something for his work, something permanent. He considered stamp collecting and coin collecting but though both would take too much time searching for them. He would search for them, purchase them and put them away in some organized manner. Not much of a hobby, he thought, and the argument for doing them, that they were financial investments, did not carry any weight for him since he had no interest in that. That was his wife's thing. Then there were those matchstick creations. He had seen lamps, miniature sailing ships and small replica buildings built from them, but he thought it might require too much precision with the little pieces of wood for his larger than normal hands.

Then it occurred to him that his life must be going well. He must be rather secure with everything if his biggest concern was for something as trivial as a hobby. Life was going rather smoothly, and what a great life it was, he thought.

The laughing around him caught his attention and he decided to focus back on the first part of the double feature, though he had lost much of the plot and found the seemingly alive but inarticulate racing car of a Volkswagen Beetle a bit over the top.

**

With Dwight at Lyon's and Blue upstairs locked away in his room where he was supposed to be doing his homework but was instead rolling a record number of joints, Av, Lisa and Sam sat in three of the four recliners watching Sunday night's *Mutual of Omaha's Wild Kingdom.*

With the volume up high so it could be heard over the almost constant thunder, Lisa almost shouted over the commercials, "Av, do you want some popcorn?"

"Sure," nodded Av.

With Lisa gone to the kitchen, Av looked out the window and watched the rain drops with interest as they raced down the window pain. Pulling himself out of his trance-like state, he noticed the knitted or crocheted owl on the wall beside the window and found it interesting that the owl was made between two thin, horizontal twigs.

When Lisa came back with two bowls of popcorn, handing one to her friend, Av asked, "That flat owl on the wall behind you, is that what you call crocheting or knitting? That uses the two large needles, correct?"

Sitting down, Lisa followed where her friend was looking. "No, that's macramé. That's where you knot string together...well...really it's thicker, more like cords."

"Making knots? Not much talent needed there, no?"

"No talent?" Lisa said defensively. "That took me weeks to make! There's a lot of different kinds of knots to learn and a lot of keeping track of where they go and how many."

"Right...sorry...I just meant one does not have to learn how to use the needles, the needles one uses to knit. I could possibly do it if it does not involve them. With my lack of talent with my hands, I could possibly lose an eye or two trying to use them," Av joked.

Lisa's eyes lit up. "You want to learn macramé? I have a bunch of books and even some material packed away somewhere. I could go and find them in the basement."

"You do? You can?" asked Av, feeling he was about to be forced to commit to something he was still only considering.

"I do and can," she said, bouncing up off her recliner. "I'll get them now. This is going to be so much fun!"

Watching Lisa take off out of the living room, Av hoped he would find it as much fun as she expected.

Sitting next to each other at the dining room table with a large cardboard box to their right and several macramé design books and several partial rolls of cord scattered about the table, Lisa and Av shared a book as they searched for something simple Av could start with. While perusing a third book, Av decided on a project that was both simple and practical. He liked the bracelets and figured they were simple enough to start with. After deciding which one from the dozen designs he liked and then asking Lisa which one she liked, he began making hers first. With Lisa watching and offering encouragement and suggestions and Av wearing his reading glasses halfway down his long nose, he struggled with the weaving and then knotting of several long pieces of cord. Occasionally, he would have to undo a knot he had made in the wrong order, but it did not deter him since he found he liked the activity, if only because he was creating something that could not easily be destroyed.

Av was rather pleased when he finished Lisa's bracelet and she put it on, tying the ends so it looked like it would never come off. Standing up, she giggled as she melodramatically modeled it, posing to bring attention to her wrist by holding it out at various angles, much as the models would do in the Woolworth flyers.

By the time Dwight came home from Lyon's, Av had finished his own bracelet and had an amused Dwight choose the style of bracelet he wanted.

When Blue came downstairs to see why his smaller friend was laughing so hard, Av asked him to choose a style too. Blue did not laugh, but he did fill his face with a smile.

"That's more than enough laughing!" Lisa told her son.

Dwight forced himself to stop and then wiped an eye.

"Yeah," said Blue. "It's not like he's knitting or something like that."

Dwight broke out laughing again.

Blue pointed to an image of a thicker style bracelet and said over Dwight's laughter, "I'll take that one there. But do you have any red string? It'll match my hair."

With that, Dwight laughed even louder, before stopping himself, catching his breath, and wiping his eyes a second time. "Hey, wait! That's what I was going to choose!"

"Ok, we'll each have one of those thicker ones, the manlier ones."

"Ok," said a slightly embarrassed Av wearing his thin, dainty one. "Yours will have to match. We only have one color left, so beige it is."

An hour later, and after the boys had happily tied on their bracelets, or what Blue insisted they call wristbands, Av searched for a larger macramé project, and in a magazine containing the design for the owl that Lisa had made, Av found a design for a large frog.

The next day, Monday, he would go to the hobby store to get the materials, including several rolls of green cord.

CHAPTER 11
Dealing

Smoking in the secluded corner of the razor wire fenced-in field of dirt and weeds, he looked out toward the forest. With his thoughts distracting him, Frank failed to notice the hard footsteps and heavy breathing closing in from behind.

"Hey, ya brings more with ya?"

"Sure," said a startled Frank, turning around and handing Demp an opened pack of cigarettes.

"Thanks, man."

Demp pulled out a cigarette, handed the pack back and lit the cigarette with his book of matches. "So I did as ya asks, and ya know if it was for anyone else I wouldn't be doin' it, right?" Frank nodded. "So I calls 'im, and (Can ya believe the guy?) 'e's gots the nerve ta complain abouts the long distance charges. So, I tells 'im if the Headless gots a problem with me callin' and they's gots a problem with givin' me the real scoop, cause I knows they don't just erase money owed to 'em, then they can looks for someone else ta do their dirty work in here. Let me tell ya that got 'is attention all right. I could hear Snap gettin' all red and everythin'. So, 'e starts back-pedalin', tellin' me how much they needs me and 'e'll tell me whats I wants ta know. So, I asks 'im if they found yer hidden stash or what, and like ya asks, I tells 'im it's just between 'im and me. Ya know, I thoughts fer sure that's whats it was cause 'e was all silent for a sec. Then 'e spills the beans and tells me they're leavin' ya alones cause they got yer boy sellin' weed ta pays back the debt."

"He's selling for them?" Frank asked, dropping his half-smoked cigarette.

"Yup. Ya gots a good boy there, Frank, a good boy. Don't knows if my kids would do the same. They'd prob'ly keep the cash and let me gets a hell of a bruisin', or worser."

Frank forced a smile and handed a pack of unopened cigarettes to Demp, who placed it in his shirt pocket.

"Thanks, Demp. That's...that's great news. I knew I could count on Blue. Let's celebrate. Let's go down to the kitchen and trade a few packs to Hodge for some of his hooch."

"Yeah, good idear. Ya know, I thinks when Hodge gets out, 'e should probably starts a business with 'is shit. Hodge's Hooch —that name'll sells 'er, eh? Hey, where's ya gettin' all the money for the smokes? I thought ya had nothin'."

"Not sure a hundred percent. The money just keeps showing up in my store account."

"Well, I wishes I hads that there problem. My own cigarette fairy," laughed Demp as he followed behind Frank.

**

Making the best of a bad situation while still stinging from the beating and stinging even more from the loss of fifty joints, each morning of that fourth week of school Blue took the orders and immediately at lunch distributed his product, forcing him to arm himself with an excuse when he was consistently ten minutes late meeting up with Karen.

Karen did not mind her new boyfriend's tardiness and never gave it much concern until Wednesday afternoon. That lunchtime she decided to meet him at his locker, but as she was walking against the wave of students, she spotted Blue shoving something into his jacket pocket, locking his locker and running off before she could reach him. Ten minutes later, when Karen met up with Blue instead of him meeting up with her, Blue did not have to tell the lie that he had prepared beforehand. To Blue's curiosity, Karen showed up after him the next day too.

Every evening, Blue would set aside two hours to roll

joints, and rolling more than he was selling, he was accumulating an inventory of hundreds. Knowing little about marijuana, he began to worry if what he had could go bad before he had sold it. The remaining half bag of it was becoming dry, and though it was easier to break up with only his fingers, he was concerned it would lose its strength and become bad weed.

That Wednesday night while Dwight and Lyon finished their work on the hovercraft, Blue met Howard and Snap at the field.

Howard grinned and said, "There he is! There's our apprentice!"

"Hey," Blue stoically greeted the two as he reached into his pocket and pulled out a roll of bills held together by an elastic band.

"How much is this?" asked Howard, taking the roll while showing disappointment with its size.

"One seventy-four."

"That's it? That's all you sold? What's that...seventy-five joints or something?"

"Eighty-seven," Blue corrected the man's poor math.

"That's it? We come all the way from Spryfield for this? This is poor work, kid!"

Snap interjected, "Howard, give the kid a break. He's only starteds sellin' the end of last week. He's gots ta establish 'is business."

Howard glared at Snap as if he was preparing to aim several expletives his way, then his expression softened and he turned back to Blue. "Right. That's not bad...for a start, not bad at all. Ok, so next week we'll meet here again and you'll have three times this, right?"

Blue nodded, mocked a salute and turned to leave the way he came. He stopped and turned around. "Hey, Howard, I have a question."

Howard's face contorted in anticipation.

"When weed gets dry, does it go bad, get weaker?"

Howard grinned. "No, nothing changes, but you should

probably wet the joint by running it across your lips so it doesn't burn up so fast."

"Cool. Thanks," said Blue, turning to leave again.

"I likes the kid," said Snap.

"Obviously! But don't be defending him again, man! Don't undermine my authority! We've got to motivate the little shit to sell, and giving him excuses isn't going to do it!"

Thursday night Blue left the house with almost a hundred joints in his pocket and the anxiety of expecting John to be there. Even though he was confident John would not try to take his joints that evening, preferring to wait until they were alone Friday night, he would be uncomfortable being sociable around the boy who was blackmailing him. He would not have been going at all if not for the need to sell them.

Blue was content to find John was not at the park and he was even more so when everyone there was prepared to purchase his joints. After being introduced to the new faces, he learned that many of the boys were reselling them to their friends for a profit. One was even selling them to his uncle. Selling out quickly and with pressure from those who had yet to get theirs, Blue had to return home to get forty-six more. Discovering such a high demand, Blue considered raising the price, but then he thought it best not to mess with a good thing.

Friday morning before leaving for school, Lyon and Dwight demonstrated the hovercraft to all, including Mrs. Collins and Sam. With the electric train's control box in his hand, Dwight turned the dial until the little motor at the top of the hovercraft turned the fan fast enough to lift the balsa wood body a couple of millimeters off the floor. When Lyon gave the machine a soft push, it glided over the foyer's marble floor until it stretched out the wires connecting it to the box. All were impressed.

With the demonstration over, the boys safely packed up their science project in a larger than necessary cardboard box, Lisa gave Blue and Dwight their lunches and the boys ran through the rain and into the black Cadillac. As Av was backing out of the driveway, Blue realized he had forgotten his day's supply of joints and after lying that he had forgotten some of his homework, rushed back into the house with his schoolbag.

That afternoon after quickly filling his orders at lunch, Blue failed to find Karen at their usual spot. Expecting her to show up late, he was only disappointed when she did not show up at all.

Blue thought she might not have been at school that day, but later he spotted her down the hall. Confused, at the end of the day he met her at her locker. As she was packing her school bag with books, he said, "Hey, Karen, I missed you at lunch. Everything ok?"

Karen turned around and with fiery eyes, which forced Blue to take a step back, she said, "No, everything is not ok! I followed you at lunch! I know what you're doing, and I don't like it!"

With his jaw dropped, Blue could only watch as Karen roughly closed and locked her locker.

"Come with me," she said, grabbing him by his blazer and dragging him down the hall through the waves of exiting students. Stopping at the girls' washrooms' door, she released her hold on him. "You're selling drugs! I followed you three times after lunch and watched you hand them out. I wasn't sure until today when I *finally* got to see what you gave them. And you lied to me when you were late, lied *really, really* well."

"Weed...marijuana, just marijuana," Blue forced out.

"I don't care what it is. It's all bad, and I don't want anything to do with it...or you! We're done!" Karen said in a tone that left no room for further discussion.

"But I can explain. I have a good reason," Blue begged.

"A good reason? There's no good reason! Money's not a good reason!"

Not knowing what to say next, Blue stood dumbly in front of her.

"We're done, but don't worry, I won't tell. You'll get caught on your own!"

With that, Karen pushed past Blue and walked toward the stairs at the other end of the hall.

Dwight and Lyon met a noticeably agitated Blue at his locker where, without him saying a word, they watched him pack his homework into his schoolbag, lock his locker, and then followed him down the hall to the stairs and out of the building. Neither boy felt Blue wanted to talk, so he only found out about them getting an A-plus on their science project later at supper, when Dwight told a delighted Av and Lisa.

Blue was not in a good frame of mind. He had lost his new girlfriend and soon he was going to lose another fifty joints. Still dressed in his school clothes, he lay flat on his bed and stared up at nothing as he tried to motivate himself to change and go to the park. He had to go or his problems would only multiply. He could see himself being kicked out of school and could see himself being arrested. He could see himself in the custody of Children's Services and certainly then placed in a center for juvenile delinquents. And the worst part to him was that he could see himself losing his new family.

Getting up from the bed, he joined Dwight, Lyon and Sam in Dwight's room.

"Hey, Dwight, can I borrow your Lego for a bit?" asked Blue, before a better idea hit him. "Hey, do you have marbles? I could use them instead."

Both puzzled by the connection between Lego and marbles, Dwight and Lyon just stared at him.

"So, do you have some?"

"Uh, yeah, I have some somewhere. They have to be in the toy box," Dwight said, as he got up and lifted the curved top of the box. After a few seconds, he pulled out a large, purple cloth sack. "Here they are." Handing the clacking sack to Blue, he asked, "What're you doing?"

"I'm...I'm...it's a surprise. I'll show you when it's done."

Wearing his spring jacket with its side pockets bulging, Blue walked to the park.

The entire way there, it felt like his heart was fighting to get out of his chest. He tried calming down by singing a song in his head, but each time he started, his mind flew ahead to what he expected would happen and what he thought he should say and do. Then it struck him that instead of following the saying, *If you can't beat 'em, join 'em,* he would follow a modified version: *If you can't beat 'em, have 'em join you.*

"Good, ya showed," said John, standing with the same two boys who had assaulted him the week before. "I was wonderin' if ya'd do somethin' stupid like not show up. Ok, so, let's have 'em."

"You can put your hand down. I didn't bring the weed," said Blue with a confidence that made John and his friends look to each other and then look around them. "You can relax. I didn't bring anybody with me either, but I could've easily had some of the Thirteenth Tribe join me."

John's two friends joined eyes for a second before looking to John for direction.

"The biker gang? Yeah, right! I'm thinkin' ya get the weed from a friend in Spryfield. Ya really should've brought the joints cause now you're goin' to get the shit kicked out of ya, *and* you're in deep shit at school too. Get him guys!"

As the two boys made fists and moved toward him, Blue pulled a sock from each pocket and swung around their weighted ends. One sock clacked as it made contact with the rounder one's head, dropping him to the ground, and as the thin one threw a punch, Blue dodged it and swung the other sock at his ankle. The boy's foot slid out from under him and he fell to the ground. Blue walked between the two fallen boys, heading toward John. With one laid out cold, the other let go of his ankle to grasp at Blue's pants. Blue responded with a swing of a sock to the boy's forearm, causing the boy to release a loud but short scream.

"Calm down, man!" John demanded as he walked backward trying to keep some distance between Blue and himself. "We'll forget this happened. We'll forget the whole thing!"

"Can't do that. You're still going to rat me out," said Blue with sweat dripping down his brow. "Got to make it so you can't talk."

As John turned to run, Blue threw a sock. It hit the blackmailer in the back of his head and flattened him out on the yellowing grass. Blue walked up to him to retrieve the sock and the few marbles that had escaped it.

Rolling over, John begged, "Look, man, it's over! Ya won! We lost!"

"No, we both win," Blue said, looking down at him.

John tried to sit up. "What? How's that?"

Placing his foot on John's chest, forcing him back down to the grass, Blue said, "I'm guessing you'd be up to selling weed, right?"

"Jesus, man, relax! Huh? Me sell weed? Maybe. How?"

"The guy I sell for is looking to sell into other schools. You in? You up for selling?"

"Yeah, sure, but how?"

"You can meet him here next week, Wednesday night at eight, to find out."

"Ok. What's...what's his name?"

The moans from the previously unconscious boy added to the moans of the other still on the ground holding his forearm.

"I think I might've fractured the guy's arm. It was a pretty solid hit," Blue said, lifting his foot from off of John's chest. "You can call him Blue's friend. You'll know who they are by the way they're dressed."

John got himself off the ground and rubbed the back of his head. "Jesus! You gave me an egg! Hey, I don't got the bucks for a lot of weed."

"You don't need it. They'll give you credit, but take my advice: you want to buy the weed outright as soon as you can. You don't want to be owing these guys money."

"Ok, but how do we do it? How do I get the weed and everything?"

Turning around to leave, Blue said, "You'll get all that from them. Good luck. And just so you don't sell in my area, I don't want to see you here on Thursday's anymore."

"No...no problem. Hey, thanks, man. I'll see ya around. Guys, get the hell up!"

"You can thank me by paying me back the hundred bucks

worth you took. I'll expect to see it soon."

Blue walked home both content and confident his father's debt would be paid off even sooner by whatever percentage Howard would give him from John's sales. Then it occurred to Blue that he had better start recording his sales and keeping track of the balance of money owed to the Tribe. He better find out too what his percentage would be from John's sales and how he was going to be updated on it.

CHAPTER 12
Saving a Son

Drunk from the soda bottle of prison hooch and trying to clear his head of dark thoughts, he sat back on the bed and stared at the white ceiling that would have looked much like a blank canvas if not for the shadows from the locked, barred door mixing in with the fainter ones from the metal-railed walkway outside. The shadows appeared as a grayscale abstract painting that would be erased much like a shaken Etch-A-sketch if he were able to control his cell's light mounted on the opposite wall.

If the inmates were allowed to paint on their ceilings, he wondered, what would there be? Would there be nature scenes of pastures, fields, mountains, lakes and animals, or would there be city scenes of buildings, bridges, streets and parks? Or maybe they would go abstract and paint something more suitable to their state of mind during their stay, something chaotic with hard lines, darker colors and perhaps splashes of red. Then he thought about what he would paint. He thought and thought, and then as he was wondering if painters had such a hard time coming up with a subject, it came to him. He would paint that of which he was most proud. He would paint his son. He would paint him as he wished he would be as an adult: strong, independent, noble, passionate, empathetic, nurturing and bold. Bold enough to be all the others. Then another thought hit him: if he did paint Blue, would he be there someday to see it? Would he be there one day looking up at what his father wanted him to be, but wasn't? Certainly, he was on track to be there. Even after telling him not to go that route, Blue had gone it anyway. He was selling weed and probably selling it at school. He was certain Blue would eventually get caught and sent to juvenile detention, and from there, eventually to prison. He felt certain too that when his son was arrested, he would be abandoned by Lisa and Mr. Rosen, if only to keep his behavior at a distance from Dwight.

Appreciating the effects of the Hooch, Frank forced himself off of the bed, filled the white porcelain sink with warm water and spent the next ten minutes rubbing the bar of hand soap under hot water until it was only a small fraction of its original size. He took off his tan pants and shirt, and after removing his shoes and socks, began a plan to save his son.

The hooch would certainly help in carrying it out.

**

Even with things beginning to look up on the weed-dealing front, Blue felt like someone else, someone who could not get things in order and who was a target of misfortune. Something starts to go right and then something else almost immediately goes wrong. He had only just begun to feel he belonged with Av and the Dixons, and he had even forced himself to fit in with the new school and was for the first time applying himself, and then his mother shows up threatening to ruin everything and his father's debt was then hanging over his head like an anvil about to drop. For only the second time in his short life, things seemed out of his control, very out of control.

Blue needed routine in his life, a dull sort of routine. Where in the past he had despised it, it surprised him that he had such a craving for monotony now. The same monotony he thought was only for old people. The old folks who would get up and go through the same routine each day to the point, since each day felt like the next, they would easily forget what day it was. Mr. Cline was one of them. He lived in a house on Autumn Drive and every day from spring to fall, he would sit on his porch staring past his front yard of gravel to the road of gravel, and when Blue passed his porch and greeted him, the old man would always ask the same question, "What day is it?" He wanted both the weekday and the day of the month. It became such a routine that Blue was always prepared with both. Blue had felt bad for the old man, but now he envied him. Envied him even though he had passed away in his home the previous winter and it took almost a month for anyone to discover he had.

That Monday at school, Blue greeted Karen several times in passing, and each time, she blatantly ignored him, never even giving him a chance to suspect that she failed to hear or see him. She had looked directly at him and silently kept going. It only took Blue three times to get the hint and give up on her for the moment, and the coming news the next afternoon would further help him do that.

Returning home after school on Tuesday, Dwight and Blue couldn't help but notice the large, gray car parked behind Av's, and as they passed it, Blue noticed what looked like a CB radio between the driver and passenger seats.

"We're home," the boys said as they entered the house.

"I am...we are in the library," Av called out even more stoically than normal, causing both boys to feel something was wrong.

With Dwight assuming Blue's mother had returned and Blue assuming someone had ratted him out, both reluctantly headed into the library where, standing next to Av, was a man both boys immediately recognized, if not by his gray-suited, middle-aged body, as tall as Av's, then by his small, unique moustache taking up only half the thickness of his upper lip.

Both boys stopped at the entrance, where Blue reflexively dropped his and Dwight's schoolbags.

"Blue, Dwight, you remember Detective Greene," Av said in a strangely sympathetic tone.

"Hi, boys," greeted the man awkwardly as he walked toward them, causing each to reflexively take a step back. He held out his hand to shake. "It's been a while."

Blue forced himself to shake the man's hand. "Yes, sir."

Dwight followed Blue's lead and shook the man's hand too. "Yes, sir."

"Perhaps we should go into the living room. It will be more comfortable there," Av suggested meekly.

With the adults leaving the room, Dwight, Blue and Sam followed behind them as they turned right and walked down the hall.

"What's going on?" Dwight whispered to Blue.

"I don't know. My first thought was he was going to shoot me again. He didn't, so now I know as much as you," Blue joked through a whisper.

During the short walk, which seemed like forever to the boys, Blue tried to figure out how the detective found out about him selling weed. Did Cal rat on him? Did John change his mind? Did Karen decide to make him stop definitively? The boy's heart beat so hard it was almost painful. He then understood exactly what Poe was talking about in his short story, *The Tell-Tale Heart*, which he had recently read in class.

To the detective, the living room felt like a small jungle with its plants hanging from the ceiling, growing from pots on the floor, and sitting on various sized plant stands. And the dark brown wainscoting against the dark green walls only added to the feeling.

Av turned the first recliner at an angle so it faced the other three.

"Detective Greene, please...please sit here."

"Thank you. You have four recliners?"

"Yes, I...I had purchased them instead of a sofa...in order for each to be able to sit in their own space...and as they liked."

"That's very thoughtful of you," the detective patronized Av as he sat down on the recliner to face the three as they sat down.

Leaning forward in the chair, the detective cleared his throat. "Ok, let me start by saying I have one of those jobs...jobs where no one is ever too happy to see me. I only show up when...when something bad has occurred...and something bad *has* occurred." The man paused, not to create any anxiety from anticipation, which it was doing, but out of habit to examine the reaction of his listeners. Having to remind himself it was not an interrogation, he ignored Blue's curious expression of guilt and continued. "Bartholomew, there's been an acci...a situation with your father."

"What happened?" Blue forced out while mixed between wanting to know and not wanting to.

"Your father, we believe, committed suicide. He was found dead in his cell yesterday morning."

Having already received the news earlier, Av sat stone faced, but Dwight followed along with Blue and dropped his jaw.

Blue stared at the man for a moment.

"Dead? Frank's dead? No, no, that's not right!"

With sympathetic eyes, the detective nodded his head.

The blood rushed from Blue's head.

"No...no...this...this is crazy." Trying to fight back tears while beginning to shake as the blood rushed back to his head, his voice rose. "He killed 'imself? Yer sure no one killed 'im and tried ta makes it looks like a suicide? He can't be dead! He wouldn't kills himself! He ain't likes that! No, he didn't! This is all just a big screw up!"

Av reached across and placed his hand on Blue's shoulder.

Comforted slightly, Blue calmed down slightly.

The detective looked to Av and then to Blue.

"I'm sorry, but he is. I've seen the photos and the only way it could've been done was from inside his cell...with the doors shut and locked. He was up and about when the guard locked him in the night before. There...there will be an autopsy, but from the looks of it, we don't expect a different conclusion." The detective considered stopping there since the boy seemed no longer to be listening, but he continued anyway. "I never knew your father well enough to have an opinion of him, but from what I understand at the department, he was a respected man. He may have made some poor choices, but he was still respected. From what I know of him, he was a man who showed much respect too."

Hearing his father mentioned in the past tense was a

difficult thing for Blue to accept.

"He can't be dead," he whispered. "He just can't be." He looked over at Av and asked, "Frank's dead? Suicide?"

Av had to fight back tears as he slowly nodded his head in response to his shocked and grieving friend.

The detective shifted in his seat. "I found out this morning, and I thought the news should come...come from me instead of a stranger, another officer, an RCMP officer since it's their jurisdiction."

Blue's expression went cold as he stood up and walked over to the Detective with his hand out. "I appreciate you coming here and telling me yourself, Mr...Detective Greene. I'm sure this was difficult for you."

The detective stood up and feeling as if he was addressing an adult in a boy's body, shook the boy's hand.

As the detective released his hand, Blue grabbed the man's middle and index fingers and pulled him down so he could whisper into his ear. "I...I have you to thank for his death, right? I know about the cash from the second search. I know you're a bad cop."

With Blue releasing his fingers, Green straightened up and tried to conceal his confusion before deciding not to ask the boy what he meant. With the shock of the news, he was obviously not thinking straight.

"Well, I'll leave you alone now. I'll...I'll let myself out," Greene said. He looked to Av and added the habitual, "I'm sorry for your loss."

Av nodded, stood up, shook the man's hand and watched him leave the room. All heard him walk down the hall and then heard the front door open and close.

With Blue still standing by the chair that the detective had sat in and not caring if he had just propositioned danger, Av and Dwight joined him and placed their arms around him. Blue fought harder to fight back the tears.

"I have to go to my room," said Blue, his voice cracking as he broke their embrace.

"Right," said Av.

"Ok, I'll come too, then," said Dwight.

Av looked at Dwight. "No, I will need you to stay with me."

With Sam following, Blue left his friends standing in the living room.

"What do you need me for?" Dwight asked.

"Perhaps we can talk about what you just heard and, perhaps, we should leave Blue alone for a time. He has to take in the news."

"I didn't need to be alone when my dad died."

"Right, that is true, but we are all different. Remember when Ruthy...Mrs. Rosen, died? I hid away for days. I needed to be alone, and may have been alone even longer if you and your mother had not come by and changed my mind."

"Yeah. That was the day you got Sam."

"Right. Perhaps we could sit for a moment."

Returning to their recliners, Dwight asked, "So, Blue's half an orphan like me now, right? Did you know Frank was sad? That's why people kill themselves, right? Cause they're really, really sad, right? Blue never told me his father was sad."

"I have no idea why he did what he did. Sometimes people just give up on life. Sometimes life is just too difficult to continue. But to answer your question: no, I did not know he was sad, but how happy can one be in prison and how sad does one have to be to commit suicide? I do not know those answers."

Then it struck Av that that could have been the main reason why Frank wanted to make sure Blue was taken care of.

"What's going to happen now?" asked Dwight.

"Happen now?"

"With Frank's funeral and everything."

"Right. Well...I suppose we will...we will contact Mr. Parker...the funeral home tonight and arrange it."

"That'll be two funerals in a year," said Dwight. "Three in over a year, if you count Mrs. Rosen's. But I wasn't there for that one. Hey, that's four if you count us spreading dad's ashes in the harbor. Is all that normal?"

"No, that is not normal, not normal indeed, but then, the

more people you have in your life, the more chance of knowing someone or of someone visited by Death," Av said and then cleared his throat. "Are you upset by Francois' death?"

"Not really. I guess, I didn't really know Frank well enough. I'm more upset for Blue. His dad just died and I had the same thing happen to me, so I know how he feels. Mine was a surprise too, right?"

"Right. You can empathize...relate to how he is feeling and what he is going through."

"Yeah, I guess I can...empathize."

Av reached out and placed his large hand on the little boy's arm. "Good. He needs you to be there for him. Blue may not show it, but he does."

"Ok. So...can I go see him now?"

"Yes, but please, do not force him to talk about what has happened. I think it is best if he brings it up first. I am worried he may mistake your attention for pity, and if that is the case, knowing Blue as we do, he will not appreciate it."

Av was left alone in the living room to reflect on the details Detective Greene had earlier shared with him regarding the determined suicide —*determined* because Frank was very determined to succeed at it.

The morning before, a guard making his rounds unlocking the cells' doors had made a bizarre find. What at a quick glance looked like a bundle of white bed sheets and tan prison clothes hanging from the top crossbar of Frank's cell door turned out to be a very pale Frank held up by his neck while his bottom hung two feet from the floor and his stretched out feet rested in a pool of soapy water. After shouting an alert, the guard used some effort to slide open the iron-barred door enough to squeeze through. And then after slipping in the pool of soapy water and hurting his knee and cursing loudly as he struggled to get himself to his feet, he shouted the alert again. The guard had to do a double-take at Frank's work before he realized what he had intentionally done and how he had made it impossible to save himself if he changed his mind. Tied to the top cross bar of the door was a leg of prison pants with the other tied around his neck. His shirt had been twisted several times to make a rope that was tied around his waist with his arms forced inside it to restrain them. With the pool of soapy water on the floor around him, he had made it impossible for his bare feet to get any grip once he had slid them out from under himself.

It was only seconds after the guard's first shout when the prisoners of the unlocked cells nearby gathered on the metal walkway outside Frank's cell. Some, including Demp, elbowed their way through the others to see for a few seconds the back of a lifeless Frank before more guards arrived and ordered them down to the main level.

Demp would never understand why Frank took his own life, especially considering how proud he was of his son dealing with his debt.

Then Av thought about Frank's recent will. He had no idea when they could or should act on Lisa adopting Blue. He considered calling his lawyer, Mr. Walker, the next day, but then thought he had better let Lisa decide when it was best to do so. She would also have to decide when they should inform Blue of his father's wish for her to adopt him.

"Hey, Blue," Dwight cautiously greeted his friend through the crack of his opened bedroom door.

"Hey, Dwight," replied Blue as he lay on the bed staring up at the ceiling while trying to control his tears. He had just wiped them when he heard Dwight's little feet making their way down the hall.

"You want company?"

"Ok," said Blue, squirming to one side of the bed and moving the pillows about so both would have one.

Dwight joined Blue on the bed and both stared at the ceiling.

After a few minutes of impatiently waiting for Blue to speak, Dwight said, "I'm sorry about Frank. You know I lost my dad too, right?"

"Sure, I know."

"Then I can *amfasise* with you, you know."

"You can what?"

"I can...I can...I know what you're going through."

Blue nodded. "Right."

Not knowing what to say next, neither spoke for a couple of minutes.

Then Blue said, "I just can't get why he'd do it! This is the first time someone I know does it, and then it's Frank! I can't get my head around why he'd do it!"

"Tim committed suicide," Dwight reminded his best buddy.

Blue flushed redder than his hair. "Right...yeah, he did. I...I guess I forgots about that. Honestly, I really didn't care for Tim. Hey, can we just rest here and say nothing for a bit?" Blue asked, wishing he had not broken the silence.

"Ok."

Bored, Dwight fell asleep in only minutes, leaving Blue alone to stare at the ceiling while quietly releasing the pressure from behind his eyes.

Lisa arrived home at five and was surprised to find Av doing her cooking of spaghetti and meat sauce. Av wasted no time in informing her of Frank's death, and after recovering from the shock of the news, Lisa pushed herself to make the necessary calls with the extra time he had given her by cooking supper. First, she left a message with the school's answering machine informing them of the boys' absence for the rest of the week, then she called Mrs. Collins to give her a paid vacation for the rest of that week, and lastly, she called Mr. Parker of Parker Funeral Homes, who informed her the funeral would be that Friday at the earliest and they could meet him the next day to go over the details.

When Lisa entered Blue's room, Dwight was embarrassed to find he had fallen asleep during his mission to console Blue.

"Blue, Av told me what happened. How are you holding up?" Lisa asked Blue.

"Good," Blue replied as he sat up on the bed, not appreciating the attention and expecting more to come from every direction. He wished he could just be alone in his grief until everyone had gotten over their pity for him. He wanted to scream, curse, hit something and even cry but felt there was nowhere to do any of it without bringing on more attention. He had to hold it all in until later in the night when all were sleeping.

Dwight got himself off the bed as his mother sat down on it.

"Blue, I wish there was something I could say to make it all better. When you're ready to talk about it, we're here for you. You're not alone."

Blue wanted to tell her that that was just it —he wanted to be alone. But knowing Lisa was being supportive, he just nodded his head.

"Supper will be ready in ten minutes. Would you rather eat up here?"

Blue's eyes communicated his surprise. "Thanks...that would be better...better for now."

"Can I eat up here too?" Dwight asked.

"No, you're eating with us," Lisa said in a tone that left no room for argument. "Blue, I'll bring it up to you in a few minutes. Milk, water or Sprite?"

"Sprite," answered Blue, forcing a pathetic smile.

"Ok," said Lisa as she bent over and kissed him on the forehead. "Ok...Dwight, let's go and help Av."

"What's he doing?"

"Making Spaghetti."

"Cool! I'll throw the noodles at the wall to see if they're done!"

"No, you won't. I showed him a while back how he can tell without having to stain the walls."

Lisa stopped at the door and turned around. She looked over at Blue before deciding that the information regarding the funeral and their meeting with Mr. Parker the next morning could wait until after supper. She wiped a tear from her eye as she followed Dwight out of the room and closed the bedroom door behind her.

Blue would only have to wait a few minutes for his meal and then he could cry with little chance of being disturbed. He was doubly upset: his father had died and with that, he was certain his mother would come and take him away. With his father dead, he was sure the court would give his mother custody.

Blue had no interest in eating.

CHAPTER 13
The Perfect Funeral

In a priest's robe with a large silver cross hanging from his neck and a black yarmulke covering his head's balding spot, the rabbi / priest finished his sermon.

"Now, at this time, I would like to call upon some of François Roy's friends to say a few words. Firstly, please welcome Mr. Avriel Rosen to the podium."

Accompanied by much clapping, Av left Blue, Dwight and Lisa sitting in the front pew and walked the few steps to the stage and then to the podium. He tapped the microphone and when certain it was still on, said, "I once heard that it is better to say nothing and be thought an idiot than to speak and prove it —so let's have a great funeral." With laughter from the crowd and large smiles from the first pew, Avriel feigned leaving the podium and then returned, pulling a folded piece of paper from his pocket. As he searched his suit pockets for his reading glasses, he said, "I will be the first to admit that one of my two worst faults is reading in public. I get much too nervous and sound even more robotic than I normally do."

"What's the other one?" yelled a heckler from the back.

Failing to find his glasses, Av said, "I never learned to read," and to more laughter, crushed the paper into a ball and tossed it aside.

"Somewhere on that piece of paper was written something

about François, something about not knowing him well. I did not know him well. I may have spoken with him four or five times in all. That is not to say I did not like him, which I did not." Av paused to let the chuckles finish. "But I respected him. I disliked him for the decisions he had made (the drug dealing is number one on the list) but I respected him for the way he had brought up Blue, his legacy. Now, not knowing much about François, my eulogy is less about him and more about his legacy. Since the first day meeting Blue, the lad has made a constantly growing impression on me, a positive impression, and even at my age, I have learned things from him, we all have, and that makes Blue, I believe, the extra ingredient that strengthens even more the bond between Lisa, Dwight and myself. For that I am thankful to François. That is about all I have to say. Thank you for listening to the ramblings of an old man."

Av bowed to the applause and left the podium as the rabbi / priest returned.

"Thank you, Mr. Rosen. Wasn't that great? Short and sweet, just great. Ok, folks, our next speaker is the young and pretty Lisa Dixon. Please give her a welcoming hand."

With applause filling the room again, Lisa stood up and passed the host as she walked up to the podium.

Looking at her notes and then out to the crowd, she said, "Thank you, Prabbi Smithman. I expect mine will be even shorter but not as sweet. Folks, unlike Av, I can read, but I choose not to." She threw her notes aside and waited for the laughter to subside. "I recently got to know François and even dated him for a short period, a very short period. I never got to love him, but I liked him, though I should say that I knew nothing about his selling marijuana until his arrest. Could I have loved François while not knowing about his illegal activity? Absolutely. Any man who creates a boy such as Blue would be hard not to love. Like Av said, Blue makes us a stronger family. So much so, Dwight recently asked me to dye his hair red so he and Blue would look more like brothers."

Sitting next to a grinning Blue, Dwight shouted over the laughter, "MOM, THAT WAS A SECRET!"

The laughter grew louder.

"Sorry, honey. I forgot, but it's just too cute not to share. Ok, where was I?" Lisa eyed her notes on the floor. "Ok...well, I'm not one for giving speeches so I'll end with this: I can't nor do I want to try to imagine our life without our Blue. He's a son to me, a grandson to Av and a brother to Dwight. Thank you, Blue, for coming into our lives and thank you, Frank, for allowing it to happen, no matter how unintentional."

Lisa bent down and picked up hers and Av's notes before walking back to her seat to more applause.

The host returned. "Next but certainly not the least, (though, he is the smallest) we have Dewey Dixon with a few words."

"IT'S DWIGHT!"

"Right. My apologies, young man. We have Dwight Dixon with a few words."

With applause accompanying him too, Dwight proudly walked up to the podium.

"I don't have any notes to throw," declared the disappointed boy to the accompaniment of laughter, "But I want to say Blue's now an orphan. That's right. His mother's gone and his father's dead. So, he's an orphan, but he's my orphan, my best buddy, and if I could wish for anything, I'd wish for him to be my real brother. I learned a lot from Blue. I learned how to look cool in bad situations, looking tough on the outside when I was scared on the inside. He also taught me the difference between good and bad. He didn't have to tell me. I just had to watch him and do the opposite." Through the laughter, Dwight returned Blue's thumbs-up. "I...I also learned being bad is a lot more fun. I'm joking mom!"

With that said, Dwight left the stage to applause and whistles.

"Now wasn't that cute, just so cute?" asked the prabbi. "Kids can say the cutest things, no? Ok...now for the main act. Ladies and gentlemen, I present to you the boy behind the color, the boy behind the man, François, and the boy that makes the Dixon-Rosen-Roy family an even number, guaranteeing them less of a wait for a table at any restaurant.

Ladies and gentleman, I present to you Misterrr Bluuue Roooy."

To a standing ovation, Blue patted Dwight on the shoulder, stood up and walked to the podium.

"Thank you." After pausing for the applause to die down, Blue continued, "Thank you. I used to think Frank had a lot of friends, and after seeing you all here today, I'm sure of it, and I'm sure he'll be missed too by all who knew him. I never expected to be up here. I thought Frank would always be in my life. I never expected him to die, and because of that, I may have been...I was stingy with my telling him I loved him, and I regret that. I don't know why he killed himself, but he did. Frank may have been in prison for the third time, but he was my father, but more than that, he was my friend...or, as my new family calls it, he was my first ever best buddy. Frank and I were more friends than father and son, which I think is better because I could tell him anything, or almost anything, without feeling judged. Frank was also the *personalfication* of the saying, *Do as I say, not as I do*. He smoked but never wanted me to. He drank but never wanted me to, and he sold drugs and never wanted me to. But it wasn't all like that. He didn't steal and fight and didn't want me to either, but if I did fight, he wanted me to do it only if I had to.

"Everyone liked Frank. I don't think he had even one enemy. He was straight up honest, and when he wasn't, when he sold drugs, he only sold weed...marijuana. He even smoked it sometimes because he thought it was harmless, and if he thought it was harmless, he had no problem selling it. He never sold the harder drugs, the ones that would make you addicted and even kill you. He even used to tell me that by selling weed, he was making the world a better place. No one fought on weed, no one died on it and no one needed it so bad that they'd steal to get money for it. Anyway...enough about the weed.

"It was because of Frank that I met Dwight. Frank once told me being a bully was cowardly and sticking up for the bullied was brave, and that's how I met Dwight: he was being bullied, but he was handling himself well considering he was outnumbered and out-aged," Blue said, exchanging a thumbs-up with a smiling Dwight. "And if I didn't meet Dwight, I wouldn't have met Lisa and Av, and who knows where I'd be now." Blue looked toward Frank's opened casket to the left of the podium. "Frank...dad, if you can hear me, I love you and thank you for all you did, even selling the weed." Looking back at the audience, Blue said, "I'd also like to thank you all for coming out today to wish Frank off. Thank you."

To another standing ovation, Blue left the podium and joined Lisa, Dwight and Av who were joining in on the standing and clapping, and all shared a group hug.

"So that ends our show, folks," said the prabbi. "Thanks for coming out. Food and refreshments are at the back of the room. Frank is here only for the next hour, so if you would like more time to say your goodbyes, do so. Thank you for coming and have a blessed day. Shalom."

As the crowd left their seats to mingle, eat and drink, Av left his family to thank Frank personally.

Staring down at the face of Blue's father, Av's shoulder received the gentle touch of a woman. He turned around expecting to find Lisa standing behind him but instead found his wife in a green dress smiling at him and looking just as she did their last day together. Surprised and then delighted, he stammered, "Ru–Ruthy?"

"It's been a long time, Av —too long."

Av reached out and hugged his wife, having to control himself from squeezing her to hard.

With wet eyes, he whispered, "It...it has been far too long. I have missed you so much."

Ruth laughed into his chest, the laugh he missed too much. "I haven't missed you at all. I see you every day. I even tried, when the times were trying for you, to toss you hints that I was there, but you've never been very good at catching them. I do miss your touch, though. The hardest part about being near you was not being able to touch you."

"I did get some of your hints, but they were quite subtle," Av grinned before taking one arm away from his wife to wipe an eye. "I learned something while you were away. Actually,

I...I learned a lot, but one thing I learned was time does not make the heart grow fonder. It is impossible to grow any fonder of you."

"I found the same thing," said Ruth, squeezing her husband tighter. She then broke her hold and looked over at Frank. "They look so peaceful when they're put on display, don't they?"

"I suppose," said Av, taking his wife's hand. "I had never given it much thought. I did not see yours. You wanted the traditional funeral."

"Yes, I know. And you must know that someday, that will be you there." She looked up at her husband and added, "Someday soon."

Av was taken aback by his wife's disclosure and more taken aback that she was wrong, would be wrong. She had to be. Just recently, his doctor had informed him he was in perfect health and had many years left in him. Maybe, he thought, she's not wrong. Maybe the concept of time where Ruthy is is different from where he is.

"Mind you," said Ruth, "Your peaceful expression won't be a surprise to everyone as much as it would've been if you'd passed on before meeting Lisa and Dewey, befriending them, and then loving them."

Av blushed. "I have you to thank for that."

"Don't thank me. It was luck. I was lucky enough to leave you with something you never had. Without them, you'd have everything you already had, but me. You'd be in the negative. It was you who accepted them into your life. I had little to nothing to do with that, dear."

Then the two were interrupted by the playing of an organ, maybe by a child. It was not a tune, unless a repetitive low note could be called one.

As the repeated note continued, Ruth raised her voice over it. "I'm so very proud of you. I couldn't be prouder. I'm so glad you're getting on so well and I'm glad your only problem was finding a pastime, but I think you've got that covered now, haven't you?"

Av nodded and then looked to the person who had gently

touched his shoulder. This time, it was Lisa.

"Av, it's time," she said softly.

To show her who had made a surprise appearance, he turned back to his wife, but she was gone. Not understanding what was going on, he squeezed his eyes shut and then opened them to see Lisa in a pink bathrobe with her wet, long blonde hair hanging down around her face as she looked down at him.

"Av, it's time to get up. You've been sleeping right through your alarm," Lisa said as she reached out and pressed a button on the large, plastic electric alarm clock, stopping the repeated buzzing. "We only have an hour before we have to meet Mr. Parker."

"Right...right," Av said as he sat up, disappointed that it was a dream and then disappointed that it had ended.

"We'll meet you downstairs, ok?"

"Right, right."

CHAPTER 14
Taking Control

    Making the arrangements was somewhat therapeutic to the grieving boy: his father's death was made a reality rather than a bad dream; the boy was pulled into the moment, giving him something to do besides dwell on the death and the negative changes to come, and it would comfort him to know he did the most he could to make his father's send-off the best it possibly could be, and he knew that he had Av and the rest of his family to thank for making that possible.
    In the first floor of Parker's Funeral Home in what looked much more like a stuffy living room than an office, the four sat on two of the four Victorian-style sofas placed around a square coffee table of cast iron and wood. Sitting alone on a third sofa with his tidy, dark oak desk behind him, Mr. Parker looked on as the four perused the photos of caskets trying to decide on one to use for the funeral. Earlier, Blue had decided to cremate his father, and after that, he decided on the time slot for the funeral, the snack food and what style of urn to hold the ashes when all was done.
    It concerned Av that Blue may have only chosen to cremate his father to lower the funeral costs. When his little friend had first looked at the funeral packages and the prices associated with each, he almost immediately chose one of the cheaper packages, one with cremation. Av's concern was weakened slightly when after telling him that money was not an issue, Blue explained, "It seems wrong to bury Frank...dad.

I may only visit him a few times a year. And what happens if I move away from Halifax? Who's going to visit him then? If I have his ashes with me, I'll always be near him no matter where I am."

"That is a good point," replied Av. "And later, if you wish, you could bury the urn and place a gravestone on the spot."

Later that night, after eating at different restaurants for lunch and dinner, and while the others gave him his space by watching television together, Blue squished the garbage bag of dry weed to as small as he could get it before tying it up tight. He collected his money and placed it, the bag of weed, his inventory of joints, and the unused rolling papers into the backpack that Howard had given him and quietly walked down the stairs and out the front door.

Making his way to the park, he was surprised to find he was not nervous. He was only numb. He felt little need to give any thought to what he would say or do when he got there, nor did he have any concern for how the two men might react.

With the dry grass crunching under his feet as he made his way through the park, Blue expected the two bikers to meet him further in, where he had met them last time, but this time, he heard their voices to the left of the opening in the fence. By their loud growling whispers, Blue thought they were arguing but could not make out any of it.

"Great, you're here! I wasn't sure if you'd make it tonight," Howard called out as he turned around. Then his voice took on an angry tone. "What the hell are you doing?"

"What do you think I'm doing?" Blue responded with his tone showing his lack of concern.

"Looks like you're giving back the stuff. You think cause your old man's dead, it's over?"

"Thanks for your condolences, and yes, I do," Blue said as he reached the men.

"That's not how this shit works, kid! You sell and pay off his debt, or else!"

Blue dropped the backpack at Howard's booted feet.

"Or else what? Or else you beat me up? You have nothing

that'll make me do it anymore, nothing. Frank's dead and I don't care what you do to me. If you beat me up, you best make sure you finish me because all hell will come down on you if you don't. And if you do finish me, the note I left at home will lead the police right to you," warned Blue, who then pointed down at the backpack. "There's all the money I collected this week. The joints I made and the left over papers are in there too. You should probably give that to John. He's coming to meet you at eight. He wants to sell at his school, a public school."

"What? Another kid's comin' to sell for us?"

Blue nodded his head

"Well, I'll be damned!" said Howard. He looked back at Snap and smirked. "See, it's not difficult! We'll be in all the schools in no time!"

"Ok, I'm done here," said Blue, turning around and walking back toward the opening. "You should do fine with John. He's just up your alley. He'll be here in an hour, so smoke 'em if you got 'em."

"Hey, Blue, you better get rid of that note, eh? And hey, I'm sorry about your old man," Howard yelled.

"Go to hell!" Blue yelled back.

Howard turned to Snap and smiled. "This opens us up to another great idea I had." He tapped his head with his index finger. "I'm always thinking, you know."

"This better not gots nothin' to do with that kid there. If it does, ya cans just count me out. We gotta leaves the poor kid alone. His old man just died for Christ's sake!"

"No, it's only going to involve the old man. It's only about Blue, not involving him too. Hey, look at that! I'm a poet and I didn't even know it!" grinned Howard as he playfully pushed Snap. "Come on, lighten the hell up!"

CHAPTER 15
Losing a Father, Gaining a Family

It was the second time within six months that they were in that room, but this time, instead of being there for their friend Stevie, they were there for a man who took his life for his son, though Blue would never know for sure that that was the case, but he would have his suspicions.

Like his little friend's death, Blue felt at least partially responsible for the death of his father too, and he was beginning to believe that that room of the funeral home was more a room of guilt than mourning.

To Dwight, the room looked much as it did the last time they were there. The speakers mounted in the ceiling filled the room with the same soft mourning organ music. The walls were still covered in the same morbid wallpaper of dense blood-red flowers with dark green and brown ones scattered among them. The two rows of three chandeliers still created multiple shadows everywhere, and at the front of the room behind the casket (this time, black, closed and adult size) was the same wall of white curtains. Even the mourners, an even mix of white and black with some dressed casually in jeans while others dressed formally, were mostly the same who had attended Stevie's funeral, including Stevie's mother and his three brothers.

But there were some things different. As per Av's suggestion, there were fewer rows of chairs than there were at Stevie's funeral, creating a larger standing area. There were also, as per another of Av's suggestions, food and refreshment tables set up at each corner of the room instead of one large table by the entrance causing a congestion of mourners.

It was different too because they were holding the funeral, and as Lisa had suggested, the four had stood in line at the room's entrance for almost an hour, greeting the mourners as they arrived.

Wearing a black tuxedo he had purchased for the occasion, Av stood out more as a waiter than a mourner, just as he had hoped, and being the last in the line of greeters, if he was not passed over, he was given a simple nod of the head, which he returned. Not once was he forced to shake a hand. Later, a teenager even mistook him as the caterer and approached him to let him know a table was out of beverages. Av told the teen, "I will get right on that, sir," and he did.

With the latecomers greeting Blue as they spotted him, Dwight watched from a safe distance as Stevie's stout mother gave Blue such a strong hug that it looked like he was unable to breathe during it. It seemed she could have hugged him until he passed out and only released him so her three boys could shake his hand. At one point, a group had surrounded the boy to offer their condolences and support, causing Dwight to feel that they were harassing his best buddy.

With the opened space caused by the fewer rows of chairs, Blue could easily slip away when he needed to, which he did when his mother in a black dress and her husband in a black suit entered the room.

Having seen them come in first, Av quickly stacked two paper plates with small sandwiches and pastries, explained to Dwight where the back doors were, and then nervously handed the plates to him, asking him to give one to Blue and make sure to let him know his mother had arrived.

With Dwight doing as asked, it only took seconds for Blue to see the option Av was offering, and he took it.

Sitting on the back steps looking out at two parked hearses and three limousines, the boys wearing new and identical black suits munched on their finger foods.

Blue said, "Take your time. I'm in no hurry to go back.

You?"

With several triangular sandwiches forcing his cheeks to bubble out, Dwight tried to say, "No," but not being able to, he just shook his head.

"I can't believe she showed up here."

Dwight forced down half the food in his mouth and mumbled, "Who?"

"My mo...Cindy. She even came with the asshole."

"Who?" Dwight asked more coherently.

"Her husband. I think they're the only ones here *celebrating* he's dead. There's no way they're sad he's gone. They can only be happy!"

"Maybe they came to see you," Dwight said, preparing to engulf a pastry.

"That could be it, but it's still in bad taste."

"Maybe they came for the free food."

Dwight was pleased to see his friend put on a smile. It felt like a long time since he had seen one on him. And he was more than pleased when Blue started laughing, though it was more of a stress-induced laugh.

Blue put his free arm around Dwight.

"And you tell me I've stolen Av's humor. You said that with such a straight face."

Dwight did not get it. He was not making a joke.

Glad to see his best buddy cheered up, if only temporarily, a thought occurred to him and he said, "You know, a lot of people died in the last year or so: my dad, your dad, Mrs. Rosen, Stevie...oh, and Tim. And most of the time we take days off school when it happens. You know, if too many people die in one year, we might have to repeat it. We only had a few weeks of school so far and already one funeral. "

Blue laughed again and squeezed Dwight hard, putting him almost into a headlock and causing him to drop several pastries.

Again, Dwight did not understand what was so funny.

"You working on being a comedian, are you?" smiled Blue.

"It's gotta be by accident cause I haven't made any jokes."

Blue could not help himself from roaring so loud with laughter that Av could hear it by the room's entrance. The old man broke a grin and had to force himself from joining the boys.

After Blue had calmed down, the two ate in silence for a couple of minutes before he said, "There've been a lot of bad things, but then there've been a lot of good ones too, right? We met each other and then my dad gets taken away, and then we live together. I lose one thing only to gain another or more. I get your mother as my guardian, I guess my mother, and then I get your friend, your best buddy as mine too. You got anything else I can have?"

Hurrying to swallow his sandwich, Dwight reminded Blue, "Don't forget about Sam."

"That's true, and then there's Sam."

With Dwight's plate empty, Blue followed his friend back inside where the two separated.

Dwight joined his mother who was whispering with Stevie's, the whispering that the boy learned was common at a funeral. After Stevie's funeral, when he had asked Av why people did it, Av had told him it was so they would not wake the dead. It took the boy a bit of time reflecting on what his old friend had said before he realized it was a joke and wished the old man would smile more when he made one.

Stevie's mother left Lisa after whispering, "You are a good woman, Mrs. Dixon, a very good woman. God bless you."

While Dwight continued to stick to Lisa's side as she made her way around the room avoiding Blue's mother, Blue joined a very stiff Av standing on alert at the entrance of the room as if waiting for a bell to summon him.

"How are you making out, Av?"

"Fine, fine, but more importantly, how are you faring?" asked the old man as he placed his hand on Blue's shoulder for a moment.

"Good."

It was the umpteenth time Blue had been asked that question, but it was one of the few times where he was comfortable with it. It was sincere, not programmed.

With Av continuing to look out toward the mourners, Blue followed Av's eyes and saw Cindy and Jack talking to several members of the Thirteenth Tribe, who were wearing their patched vests and must have arrived while he and Dwight were outside.

"Dad was never a member of the biker gang...club," Blue informed Av. "He didn't like what they did. See Jack there? The one in the suit. He used to be dad's best friend. They grew up together...but grew apart when Jack joined the club...and they stopped talking altogether when he stole dad's wife."

Not seeming to have heard Blue, Av looked to him and asked, "Are you still set on the cremation? We can still have your father buried...if you wish."

"I haven't decided what to do with his ashes yet, but I'd rather have him cremated."

"Right. We will have them placed in the urn you wanted, but we will not have them seal it. We can have them do that later if you decide not to spread them somewhere."

"Sure, but we can do it ourselves with just Crazy Glue. Why pay them to seal it later when we can just do it ourselves?"

Av broke his second grin of the last several days.

Blue placed his hand on Av's arm. "Av, thanks for all this. Thanks for Stevie's too. It took me a while to figure out it was you who paid for Stevie's funeral...and burial. You spent a lot of money on people you don't know."

Startled by the disclosure, Av cleared his throat. "You are more than welcome, but I did not have to know them so well. I know you and Dwight and that is enough motivation. As to money, it means little to me. There are some who collect and hold on to it as if it is a hobby, much like collecting butterflies. Then, there are some who spend it faster than it arrives, as if they cannot stand to have it. And there are those...those that never give it a priority. If more comes in than they need, they are indifferent to it. Can you tell which of them I am?"

"The last," said Blue matter-of-factly. "Hey, it's the weirdest thing: I called him Frank forever, and now, all of a sudden it feels wrong. It feels like I've got to call him dad."

"I believe that is normal," Av said before clearing his throat again. "It is ok to cry if you want to. You can cry around us. If there was ever an appropriate place to cry, it is here. Remember, always remember, you are not going through this alone. You have us. You have a family. Just because it is not blood, makes it no less than any other family."

"I know, and it's something I really appreciate too, but I'm not sad, not sad now. I'm more angry, angry and worried. It seems like everybody close to me is dying off. It eats at me that I never got to say goodbye to dad or Stevie," admitted Blue as his eyes began to water. "And it worries me that I'll lose you, Dwight or Lisa next."

"Well...well we should not spend too much time worrying about that. It does more harm than good. What we should do is spend well the time we have with each other, spend it as if one of us will be gone tomorrow, not that we will be. I do not believe it is a secret that we all love each other greatly. We show it in all we do for each other. There is not a moment I do not feel yours, Dwight's and Lisa's love, and that is the greatest thing in my world. That is better than any amount of money one could ever have."

Before Blue could respond or wipe a tear, Lisa was hugging him. "Hi, Blue."

After Lisa broke her hug, Dwight, with a giant smile on his face, moved in and hugged his friend too. "Hi, Blue," he said trying to mimic his mother's voice, causing Blue to chuckle and some of the mourners to look over at them.

Lisa hugged Av and smiled when he seemed to melt in her arms. It was a big change from when she had first hugged him, when he had stiffened up so much he seemed to grow several inches in her arms.

Breaking her hold, she reached up to his bowtie. "This has to come off. I'm tired of seeing you looking like a servant. It's...it's real? It's not a clip-on? You know how to tie a bowtie?"

Av forced himself to smile. "No, I do not...and apparently, I do not know how to tie a necktie also."

Dwight broke out laughing, causing mourners again to look their way.

With Av distracted from what he had made it his duty to do, watching Blue's mother, she and her husband approached them without anyone noticing. "Blue, how are you holding up?" she asked pretentiously.

Caught off guard, Blue could only say, "G–good."

"That's good. You know Pat, *your* stepdad."

The man put out his hand, and as his stepson reluctantly shook it, he said, "Good to see you again. I wish it were under better circumstances. Your father was a good man."

"Thanks," Blue said, collecting himself. "Guys, this is Cindy and Jack. Cindy and Jack, this is my *mom*, my *brother*, and this here is my *grandfather*. There, I'm glad you've finally met *my* whole family."

Jack said nothing as his wife's face flashed to an uncontrollable scowl and then just as quickly changed to a pretentious smile as she hissed, "It's nice to meet you again. It's a shame, really. Twice now and both under difficult circumstances. Well, have a good day and I'm sure the third time will be under a much better one, for some of us anyway...and we *will* meet a third time."

All four watched in silence as the couple left the room.

"Well, that was just what we needed, right? Boy, am I glad they came. This place was really starting to feel like a funeral or something," Blue joked sarcastically.

Av, Lisa and Dwight could not respond. With wet eyes, they were in a state of shock from Blue's introduction —a good shock.

CHAPTER 16
Busted...Sorta

The drive to school the following Monday morning was quiet. Blue's anxiety with the expectation of the extra attention he expected to receive from his teachers silenced him, and with Dwight and Lyon noticing Blue's state, they too said almost nothing. All three watched the wipers working overtime to keep the windshield clear.

With Dwight and Lyon trying to ignore their hair getting wet as they followed behind a reluctant Blue, the three walked slowly up the stone steps of the school's main entrance where an awkward-looking Karen met them just as they entered the building.

"Hi, Blue."

"Hey, Karen. Guys, I'll meet you after school," said Blue, trying to hide his surprise.

"Ok, see you then," Dwight said as he and Lyon continued down the hall.

"I'm guessing I'm not invisible today," Blue said to Karen.

Looking more uncomfortable, which made Blue regret his remark, Karen whispered, "Blue, I'm sorry I was so cold to you. I feel so awful about your father."

"Father? How'd you know?" Blue asked in a voice that gave away his frustration to the then expected even greater pity parade to come.

"I heard it from Kim on Friday. She heard it from Cal."

"Ok, well...thanks," said Blue, who paused for a second as

he considered asking her to give him a second chance now that he had stopped selling drugs, but then he thought it would do no good since he *had* sold drugs. "I got to go. Have a great one."

With Karen looking as if she had more to say, Blue walked down the hall and took a left down the perpendicular hallway where he made his way through the students and climbed the stairs to the floor of his locker. He immediately noticed something unusual: his combination lock was missing from the locker and after opening it, instead of his finding textbooks lying flat on the top shelf as he always placed them they were standing upright.

"Welcome back, Mr. Roy."

Blue turned around to face Dean Colvin with a police officer on each side of her.

"Mr. Roy, these two officers here would like a word."

Blue may have said something sarcastic if a word could come out of his mouth.

One officer demanded, "Young man, take off your blazer and hand it to me."

Blue did as he was told.

Then the second officer demanded he empty his pockets and hand him the contents.

With an officer not finding anything of interest in Blue's blazer pockets and the other not seeing anything of importance with Blue's wallet, change and keys, one demanded he face the locker with his hands up against it.

It was when the officer began patting him down that Blue was able to finally form words. "Gettin' your jollies, ya perv? Hurry it up. I think your partner is getting impatient for his turn."

"Mr. Roy, we'll have none of that vulgar talk!" warned the dean.

With the officer finished frisking him, Blue turned around. "Really? What ya goin' ta do, call the cops?"

Making a quick attempt to burn Blue with her eyes, the dean said, "Gentlemen, he must have just hidden them in his locker or they're in his bag. Check them, please."

An officer handed Blue back his blazer and moved him to the side.

Standing there as the dean's eyes bounced from him to the officer searching his locker and then to the other searching his schoolbag, Blue noticed for the first time the crowd of students a few feet from each side of him and the several stoic teachers standing in front of them making certain no student crossed from one side to the other, though not one student seemed to have any interest in doing that. The ones further back seemed only interested in getting a better view.

"Well, Dean Colvin, there is no marijuana on him or in his locker," one of the officers said, unable to hide his condescension. "We'll be going now."

"Well, thank you, officers," the dean said with obvious disappointment before looking coldly at Blue. "Mr. Roy, come with me."

Feeling as if he was following Moses through the parted sea, Blue followed the dean through the crowd of students. He followed her down the stairs and to the administrative offices near the main entrance of the building.

"We're going to have a talk with your guardian, Mr. Roy," the dean said as she entered the reception area of her office. "You can wait here for her."

"A talk about what? That I *don't* have drugs on me? She'll be glad to hear it, but not very surprised. Hey, since I'm the only one here for not having it, does that mean you found it on everyone else?"

"Mr. Roy, do you see me laughing?"

Blue meekly shook his head as the dean entered her office.

As a very slim, gray-haired secretary sitting behind her desk watched him, Blue sat down and mumbled to himself, "I don't think you can."

Sitting on the uncomfortable wooden chair for almost forty-five minutes, Blue had dozed off several times, and it seemed to be the secretary's job to wake him up by a cough.

Between snoozes, Blue wondered how Av would react to him selling weed. Lisa would be at university, so it would only be Av at home to answer the call. Would Av believe him or the dean? And if he believed the dean, how would the old man react. He had never seen Av angry, but he had seen him slightly disappointed. Blue expected that this time he would see him very disappointed, and that began to upset him. He would rather Av be angry with him than disappointed in him.

Who had ratted him out? Someone had to have, since the dean would not have figured it out on her own, Blue thought. He was too careful about taking and filling the orders. It could not have been the boys buying it. They would not want their supply cut off. Maybe it was Howard having a final slice at him. Or, maybe, it was John carrying through on his threat for a final laugh. Blue decided against either ratting him out. They would not want him to counter punch by telling his tale and ruining it for them too. Karen! It had to be Karen, Blue decided. She had nothing to lose by turning him in. Maybe she was doing it to teach him a lesson. Then instead of being angry with her, Blue found he was disappointed with her, and he found it odd how he had no urge for revenge, but then considered that it was probably just the moment and the urge may still come, even though he could never act on it. Karen was a girl, and as Frank had taught him, real men do not do bad things to girls.

**

Having received the phone call from the dean's secretary, Av had to take a few minutes to calm down. The vagueness of the call caused him to panic, and then the cold insistence from the secretary that she had no idea what the problem was had caused him to panic further. He was only able to calm down by telling himself he may be panicking unnecessarily.

Entering the reception area, Av nodded to Blue and sat down on the wooden chair next to the then red-faced boy.

"They caught you in the girls washroom again, have they?" asked Av as he wiped his forehead.

"Yes, the third time this year," said Blue nodding his head, making Av think for a second that the boy was serious.

Av was about to ask what was going on when the secretary asked, "Who are you, sir?"

"Right. I am Mr. Rosen. We talked on the telephone

earlier," Av said, and then he lied, "I am one of Blue's legal guardians."

The secretary nodded, picked up the phone and after a second, whispered into it.

"The dean will see you now. Uh, no, just you, sir. The boy will have to wait out here."

"I think not. It is the right of the accused to hear what he has been accused of," said Av, who then marveled at his spontaneous assertiveness, which seemed to come too easy through his anxious state.

The secretary watched with an opened mouth as Av and Blue passed her and entered the office.

The dean looked up from her note writing. "Mr. Rosen, thank you for...uh, Mr. Roy, you can wait where you were, thank you."

"As I informed your secretary, Dean Colvin, it is the right of the accused to hear the charges against him."

Av sat in one of the chairs at the front of her desk and motioned for Blue to take the other one.

"Well, sir, he's certainly aware of his wrongdoing."

"Is that so? You have told him why he is here?"

"No, not in so many words, but he is aware," the dean admitted.

"Well then, I would suggest you do so in as many words as you deem necessary, perhaps more words than necessary to remove any uncertainties caused by the lack of them," Av said, feeling good about being on a roll of assertiveness.

The dean placed her hands on the desk. "Well...it's like this, a student was found smoking cannabis...marijuana in the bathroom on the second floor last Friday morning. He admitted it and admitted to buying it from Mr. Roy here. This student has never been a problem. He comes from an upstanding family and his word is good for me."

With an obvious shock, Av glanced at Blue and then stared through the dean.

Not getting a response from the old man, the dean said, "We have no other option than to expel Mr. Roy from this school."

Pushing through the initial shock to try to come up with something to say, Av missed hearing the last thing the dean had said. Then the words came to him. "Dean Colvin, so you have found this marijuana on Blue? And if you have found it, have you found evidence of his selling it, besides the confession from a student who was inebriated at the time?"

"No, we never found any, but that's not necessary. He—"

"Then how could you take the word of someone who had just smoked marijuana, even when you found no evidence to further support his claim? How do you know that the boy was not only smoking it but also selling it, sampling his own product so to speak?"

"We...we don't, but it is unimaginable, seeing where the boy is coming from."

"So he can buy it and smoke it, but he cannot be selling it...because he comes from an upstanding family?"

With large eyes, the dean said, "I...I didn't...I don't mean to imply that...that you aren't—"

"And how is it that the lack of evidence leads to a conviction?" continued Av. "Where did you check only to come up with no hard evidence? Have you searched him?"

"Well...we...we checked his locker Friday and again this morning. We also checked his pockets."

"And you found nothing?"

"That's right."

Av stood up and to the dean's confusion emptied his pockets of his wallet, change, and miscellaneous receipts and placed them on the dean's desk. As an afterthought, he pulled his keys from his right back pocket and placed them with his other items, and then sat down again.

Gesturing to his pocket's contents, he said, "There. That is about it. Do you see any marijuana among the items there?"

"No, but...but that's not relevant to the—"

"Not relevant? You had found nothing on Blue, no evidence except an accusation from some upstanding student who just so happened to be high (that is the word, correct?) on the marijuana he was smoking in your school's bathroom. So, there you have it. I appear not to be in possession of marijuana also, so, therefore, going with your logic, I must be selling it also, especially when considering I am connected to Blue." Av paused for a moment to stare at the wide-eyed woman on the other side of the desk. "Dean Colvin, I expect you are well aware that none of this would hold up in a court of law, which is where it should be brought since you are accusing him of something very contrary to the law, and I expect your reference to upstanding families is to contrast it against Blue's previous situation in Spryfield, which I expect you have a bias against and which, to me, seems rather narrow-minded for an educator whose mandate it is to widen the minds of students. If I was aware of it, I certainly would not have agreed to your suggestion last summer for a donation."

As the dean fought to find a response to the old man, Blue looked at his friend with amazement, feeling like he was looking at his guardian angel.

Red-faced with defeat, the dean stammered, "M–Mr. Rosen, I–I think you may be correct. This...this wouldn't hold up in court...and perhaps, you are correct and I'm...I'm letting myself be controlled by an...an uncontrollable bias. I should apologize to you...and...and drop this matter immediately."

Av stood up and picked his stuff up from off of her desk. "To me? No, Dean Colvin, not to me." He bent his head toward Blue as he stuffed his things back into his pockets. "To him. To Blue, whom you must have shocked with the accusation. I cannot imagine the shock he would have had if you had involved the police."

The dean forced herself up from her desk and walked stiffly around it. With her continuing red face, she put out her hand to Blue. "Mr. Roy, please accept my sincere apologizes for everything that has occurred this morning, including the involvement of the police. Y–you can go back to class now."

Shaking the dean's hand, Blue fought back his smile as he said, "No problem, and it's Blue. Everyone calls me Blue. And I'll need a new combination lock to replace the one you removed."

"Right. You can get another from the secretary."

Av shook the woman's hand. "I will be taking Blue home

now. It must come as a shock to the boy when upon returning to school after his father's death, he is accused of selling narcotics to the point where you *had* involved the police." As Av was turning to leave in disgust, he stopped and turned around. "Just for future reference, if the police find it preferable not to press charges, which it seems they did, you should probably drop the issue also."

Neither spoke until they were in the car heading home through what was then only drizzle, and Av surprised Blue by speaking first. "Blue, with all the experience you have had with the police over the last few months, perhaps you should look at the police force as a potential career path," the old man joked.

"I just may. It'll be interesting to be on the other side for once," Blue joked back and then thought that it actually did make sense. "Hey, I never told you, I met up with a cop, a police officer a little while ago who told me Dwight, you and I are up for an award from the police station some time soon. I forget when, but we're supposed to get a letter or something if we are."

"You do not say?"

"Yes, I just did," smiled Blue.

"That is great. There you have it. More reason to become a police officer or even a detective like Detective Greene. Though, I would expect you to have a better aim than him...and the award would help on an application form," said Av, then taking his initial joke seriously.

"Maybe. Hey, you handled that well back there. I was really amazed."

"Thank you, but how would you have expected me to handle it?"

"Honestly, I expected you to cave into her."

"I may have done just that before I met you. But after meeting you, I seem to have become...become more assertive."

"Really?"

"Yes."

"Thanks too for bringing me in there with you."

"You are welcome, but to be honest, I did not want to be in

there alone. Sometimes it takes another person to give the other courage. Sometimes, just the presence of a trusted person is enough to give the other courage, making the other more assertive. Ruthy's...my wife's cousin taught me that, indirectly. He used to rob banks."

"Really? I feel a funny story coming."

"It may be amusing, but it is true. All my stories are true. That is why I only have a few. Ruthy's cousin robbed banks, but we did not know it at the time. He did it with an empty revolver. He would rob a single cashier of the bank and by doing it that way, he would not go around taking up too much time trying to take all of the bank's cash. He just took the cash from one teller's station and was gone. Now here is the interesting point: he needed a second person to be with him, not as a look out or to rob another teller, but just to be there with him for courage, as support. The reason he was caught was that on the day of a robbery, his second failed to show and he decided to go it alone. And as he stood there in front of the teller waving his empty gun and taking much too long trying to get his words out, the police surrounded the bank. He ended up surrendering without a fight."

Blue smirked. "Is that really a true story?"

"It is. I cross my heart."

"That means nothing when you're Jewish, you know."

"That is true. I have to admit I do feel we may have gotten lucky. Perhaps if Dean Colvin had another person in there with her we may have lost our argument. After all, it is a private school and they can do as they feel justified."

"Luck or no luck, I'm glad that's over. Thanks, Av."

"You are very welcome."

Blue sat silent for a moment before taking a deep breath and saying, "But, I have to make a confession. I...I was selling weed...marijuana."

Looking at his elderly friend continuing to watch the road, Blue saw little change in his expression. There was only the slightest hint of surprise.

"Av, did you hear what I said?"

"I did. Can you tell me why?" asked Av in a nonchalant

tone that would have incorrectly implied to a stranger that what he had heard did not concern him.

"Dad owed the Thirteenth Tribe money and they were threatening to hurt him. They gave me a way to pay it back...by selling marijuana."

"Can I ask how much he owed?"

"About three thousand bucks."

"Why not come to me for it? You must know I would help."

"I figured I could handle it myself and didn't want to bother you with it. You do enough as it is and I didn't want you to have to help me...help me sell drugs." The second that Blue added the joke, he regretted it. Av's expression had changed. He was neither angry nor disappointed, just hurt. "I...I thought I could handle it myself. The only reason I didn't get caught with joints today is because last Wednesday night I returned all the stuff to Howard. Frank's...dad's dead, so they got nothing to make me sell."

Av took his eyes off the road to glance at Blue. "Howard? The head of the motorcycle gang? That same Howard?"

"That's right, the guy who told Cindy where I was. He's trying to get drugs into schools."

Av made a left into their driveway.

"In Schools? I would not expect that to last too long. I would expect a student to talk, much as you have just experienced. It seems to me he is building a house of cards," Av said as he put the car in park. "I do appreciate you telling me the truth, but it changes nothing of what I said to Dean Colvin. Nevertheless, I feel we should keep the incident between us for now and perhaps forever. It is over, and nothing negative has come from it that anyone need be concerned about."

"Ok, but if that's the case, I should go back to school after lunch and meet Dwight afterward. If I'm not there, he'll be worried and who knows how long he'd wait for me and what questions he'd have later. I doubt he heard about me being searched. He's on a different floor and everything."

"That is a good idea," agreed Av, turning the engine off

and removing the keys.

Over the next few days, most kids in his class kept their distance from him, and Blue was ok with that.

On Thursday, he would meet up with his friends at the park and would find John selling joints there. John gave him a nod of the head, asked if he wanted to buy any for himself and then after receiving a shake of the head, finished exchanging his joints for cash.

After Cal had made his purchase, he would refuse Blue's share of the beer fund and take him aside to offer his condolences regarding his father and to confess to ratting him out. By then, Blue had already figured out by Cal's two-week suspension from school that he was the *rat*, and in the few days since the failed bust, Blue had forgiven him.

And Blue would find out that it was John the week before who had told the boys at the park about his father's death.

CHAPTER 17
Shakedown

Av was slow at macramé, but he was ok with that. With Sam routinely curled up asleep on his lap, he might spend a couple of hours at a time hunched over the dining room table while continually pushing his reading glasses back as he knotted cords with his large, awkward hands. He found the most difficult challenge was keeping track of the knot count. He had started by counting the knots in his head and almost up until Blue's incident with Dean Colvin, he did it that way, but later decided to use a notepad, marking a small line on it after each knot and then striking through the four lines to make it a block of five. It worked well except for the few times he forgot to mark the line and ended up with more knots than the instructions directed, or when he thought he had forgotten to mark a line when he had already done so and ended up double marking it. Whenever he discovered that he made more knots than directed, instead of fumbling to undo a knot or knots, where he could, he opted just to cut the cords and continue fresh on that section.

With the loud vacuum cleaner sucking away upstairs, Av tied the knots without any thought, leaving him free to reflect on the situation between Blue and Dean Colvin. Av was proud of the way he had handled it, but what would have happened if the dean had stronger evidence? It was just down to good timing that she didn't. Av knew little about what the law would do, but that didn't stop him from guessing. Then Av had to remind himself there was little reason to give the situation any more thought since it had been dealt with, but that did not stop him from reflecting on why Blue felt uncomfortable asking for his help. Av was concerned with the boy taking on the problem himself. Blue had to have known he would have no issue with paying the debt, but then he did say that he did not want to bother him with it when he could handle it himself. Av worried that Blue's overconfidence, though infrequent, could get him into trouble again in the future, and then Av worried more when he could not see any way to stop it. It is one thing, a positive thing, to boost someone's confidence, but it is an entirely different thing to deflate it, even if it is to give the person a more realistic grounding.

Then Av's reflection was interrupted by the gong of the doorbell.

With Sam jumping down from his lap and heading to the door, Av's first thought was to leave it for Mrs. Collins, but then he realized that she could not have heard it over her vacuuming. Trying to decide whether he should bother with the door, Av looked out the window. On the left he could see a man in a black suit standing a few feet from the door, leading Av to believe there was another standing near the doorbell. Assuming they were a different set of Jehovah witnesses and by their age, a set more experienced in going door-to-door, Av decided he did not want to be greeted with another question concerning his take on the world.

Sitting back at the table, the gong sounded again.

He ignored it, marked the notepad and tied another knot.

It sounded again.

He marked the notepad and tied another.

It sounded again, and again and then again.

It fascinated the old man with how tenacious the Jehovah Witnesses were, and he wonder if they had ever come to his door when he and his wife had lived on the street only a few years before. He knew that if they had, his wife would have taken it upon herself to deal with them. Then he wondered how she would have handled it and whether she would have been successful. He could not remember her once ever mentioning they had visited, but then by consistently protecting him from that sort of thing, he believed she would never have mentioned it anyway.

Av was tying another knot when the doorbell gonged several more times.

Expecting the vacuuming to continue for the next twenty or thirty minutes, Av totaled the marks on the pad and realized he was one knot more than what was directed. Disappointed, he stood up.

"Yes?" Av asked as he opened the front door.

The vacuuming stopped.

"Mr. Rosen?"

"Yes."

"Good. My name's Howard and this here's my associate, Snap," said the smaller suited man pointing over his shoulder at the man standing further back. "We've got to talk to you about Blue."

Hearing the man's name, Av immediately thought about the biker gang, but then even with the other named Snap, the two men looked too respectable to be bikers. It had to be a different Howard.

"Ok," said Av.

"May we come in?"

"What exactly is it you want to—"

As the vacuuming started again, Howard brushed past Av, and as Snap entered, closed the door.

"Look, buddy, we don't want to get rough," Howard warned and then moved aside his suit jacket to reveal a pistol's grip sticking out from behind the pant's belt. "We're not here to hurt nobody...yet. Hey, who else is here? Who's vacuuming?"

Av tried to control his panic. "Mrs. Collins...the cleaner. Just take what you want and be gone. There is nothing of value upstairs. There is no safe in the house. Take my wallet and—"

As Av went for his wallet in his back left pocket, Howard said, "Relax, old man. We're not here to rob you."

Av nervously squeezed his wallet back into his pocket.

Howard turned to Snap. "Thought you said they all left!"

"I didn't thinks about no maid! I didn't knows they had one! Don't turn this on me, man!"

"With the size of this here house, you never thought they could have a maid? What the—"

"She will be vacuuming for some time," Av interjected. "She will not hear anything, not anything quiet."

"Good. We intend to be quiet. Where can we talk?"

"In the...in the dining room. Just this way," Av said, nervously leading the men into the room where he pulled out two chairs from the table.

Ignoring the chairs, Howard looked at the partially completed Macramé frog lying on the table, which to him looked more like a stretched out blob of green string. "Whose is that? Who's doing the...whatever the hell that is? Where is she?"

"I am. It is my Frog. It is my hobby."

"Really? That's a woman's thing. You expect me to believe that?"

"Yes...yes I do it. It is macramé. I was working on it just now when you...you rang."

"Ok, whatever. Look, let's make this shit quick," Howard said before the doorbell sounded again. "You expecting someone?"

"No," said Av, who then cautiously looked out the window. "It appears to be two Jehovah Witnesses."

"I gots this," Snap said as he left the room.

Opening the door, he found the two Jehovah Witnesses prepared for verbal battle.

"Yeah? What?"

"Uh, yes, would Mr. Rosen be in?" asked Blair.

"He's busy!"

"Ok, maybe you could help us. Would you agree that the world is in its worst state ever?"

"What? Are ya kiddin' me? Yer a...yer black. It would'a beens a lot badder fer ya a hundred and somethin' years ago. Ya'd been a slave and I'd 'ave owned yer ass! Learn yer history and screw off!"

After the door slammed on them, Blair said to Will, "This

is really, really bothering me."

"Me too. Maybe, we should just give up on this house. I'd expect that kind of response from the North End or Spryfield, but not here. That's the reason we don't go to those places."

When Snap entered the room, Howard was grinning at what he had heard and Av was silently hopeful that the Witnesses would not be returning for sometime after that encounter. Mentally escaping from the current situation, Av thought that perhaps that is all it took to dissuade them from coming back, but with much less nastiness. If he could have mustered the courage to be rude, simply telling them that he was not interested in what they had to say and then closing the door before they could respond, perhaps then they would never have come back. Suddenly he needed to know how his wife, since she would never have been rude, had dealt with the Witnesses. Then it hit him: she had most likely forced them to listen to her talk about the Jewish religion.

With the two unwanted guests high-fiving each other over the handling of the Witnesses, Av was forced back into the present bizarre situation.

Howard continued on the topic. "Ok, before we got interrupted, I was about to say we're with the Thirteenth Tribe, the motorcycle club, and Blue's dad owes us money. Now, we know you've got money, so if you pay it, we'll be done. It's that easy. If not, we'll do as we do, and Blue'll end up in a bad way. Really, it's not what we want to do, but what we have to do. We have to send a message to the others out there, you know."

"Ok," said Av with whatever fear he might have had being temporarily replaced by anger with the threat against Blue. "You'll have to excuse my initial confusion. You did not strike me as bikers, not the ones I had seen driving along Herring Cove Road."

Snap jumped in. "Really? What's a biker suppose ta looks like? Some grease ball? Is that whats yer sayin', ya old fart?"

"Uh...no...I mean the style of—"

"We dressed up just for you. You should be flattered," smiled Howard as he gestured to his partner to calm down.

"We didn't want to raise any attention on the street. It would look pretty strange if we drove up here on our bikes wearing our colors, right?"

It was then that Av noticed Snap's suit pants were too short by an inch and then noticed his longer hair was tied into what must have been a ponytail concealed under his suit jacket.

"Right. Well, I...I certainly appreciate that. Please, tell me how much. I have little here, so you will also have to tell me where and when I can deliver it to you."

"Good. You get what we're talking about. Well, with the principle, the interest over several months and the extra charges associated with collecting the debt," said Howard, pretending to calculate in his head while walking to the kitchen's entrance and looking around, "I'd say we can make it an even fifty thousand."

Av's eyes widened for a split second and he noticed Snap's registering surprise too.

"What'll ya say, Snap? Is that about right?"

Snap cleared his throat. "That's abouts it...but yer givin 'im a bit of a discount, eh?"

Av saw through Snap's poor acting, but it changed nothing for him. He wanted the men out of the house and out of his life so he would agree to pay anything he could.

"True, but I expect we gave the old man quite a scare, and that deserves a discount, eh?"

"When and where, please?" Av cut in.

"Let's say a week from today, next Friday. That'll give you more than enough time to collect that much. You can bring us the cash in front of Blue's school at two. We'll be in a brown pickup. You just pass the envelope from your car and it's done. Everyone's happy. I don't know what you know about the Thirteenth Tribe, but there's a lot of us. If you call the cops, there'll always be someone to finish the job."

"I will not involve them," Av assured the two while hoping to end the visit. "Now if you do not mind. I will...I will need to address this immediately. I must change and make a run down to the bank to—"

"Good. Ok, let's go, Snap," said Howard gesturing toward the door with his head. "We'll see you at the front of Blue's school no later than two next Friday. No cops and everything'll be fine."

Av watched the two men leave and then watched from the window as they got into the pickup truck and backed out down the driveway.

"Fifty thousand!" Snap laughed. "I thoughts ya were goin' ta asks fer the real thing."

"I know, me too, but when I saw the place, and they had a maid, it just came to me. The old guy didn't even flinch on the fifty thousand. Now, I'm thinking I should've asked for more. Still, you see that there? That was some negotiation skill on my part. You gotta learn to do that."

"I hears ya. And we're splittin' 'er, right?"

"What? No! It's going to set us up with the schools. When that John kid gets us more dealers, we can set up ten right away with stuff. Well...maybe we'll take out five grand each when the old guy hands it over. That's more than you ever got for doing almost nothing, right?"

Snap smiled as his eyes lit up. "Yeah, that sounds good!"

Av's anxiety was much weaker than he would have expected for that situation. But then, all he had to do was go get the cash and deliver it. There would be no complications with it, and there was even some consolation with being able to deal with the problem while keeping it a secret from Lisa, saving her some unnecessary stress.

By the time Av got to the bank, his anxiety had grown to its appropriate size.

**

Av walked through the door with a large McDonald's restaurant bag. "Hi, all. I am home," he called out.

"Hi, Av!" Dwight responded from the floating stairs. "Where'd ya go? What you got? Hey, when did you start wearing sunglasses? When'd you get them?"

"It is *what have you got*, and I bought them today," Av said, taking them off and sliding them into his suit jacket pocket. "I thought we would eat McDonald's tonight. It has been a long time since we have eaten it. Sorry to make it back so late. There was a long line. I trust you got in ok."

"Yeah, Blue had his keys. Hey, you wore a suit?"

"I forgot it was not that kind of restaurant. You know, not the sort that...that...that takes tips," Av lied badly.

Joining Av as he removed his shoes, Dwight asked, "What's in that other thing?"

"Oh, just some stuff I had to pick up from the bank. I forgot your mother would not be here for a bit. Do you think the food would be ok if we left it to warm in the oven?"

"Sure," said Dwight. "That's what they do there, right? They make a bunch and then stick them under those lights, and they're still great."

"Right. Where is Blue?"

"In his room doing homework. He still hasn't caught up yet. Hey, can I have a fry now?" Dwight asked as he followed his friend into the kitchen. His stomach growled as he watched Av place the large bag on the counter and then pull from it two envelopes of fries.

"These should hold you two over until supper. I will be up in a moment."

CHAPTER 18
A Win-Win

Over the next few days, Av pondered the situation with the Thirteenth Tribe, and it was while working on his macramé frog that an idea came to him, an idea that could possibly solve two problems at once.

Av's pacing back and forth in the library only added to the sweat dripping off his forehead. In several minutes, he expected the doorbell to announce the arrival of an invited but unwanted guest. After removing his large sunglasses to wipe the sweat from his brow and then drying his palm on his slacks, the thought struck him that perhaps the library was not the place to receive guests. Perhaps that was partially why Blue and his mother's meeting went so badly. Perhaps it was too formal. Av thought for a second, trying to decide which room was the proper venue for the conversation: the dining room, the living room, or the kitchen. He decided the living room and kitchen would be too informal and moved to the dining room where he placed most of the chairs against the walls, leaving a chair on each of the longer sides of the table. After wiping his forehead again and fearing his sweating could lose him some negotiation power, he opened one of the three windows to cool the room down.

It was ten minutes later than the agreed time when Av heard the sound of a car coming up his driveway, and seconds later the gong of the doorbell sounded. Instinctively, Av went to straighten his tie and then remembered he was not wearing one. He had decided against it since it could say something he did not want it to say. As his wife would say, "If you want the best price on an automobile don't dress to the nines."

Av opened the door and found his guest dressed in jeans with his black T-shirt covered by an opened, leather jacket, which Av would soon notice had the patches of the Headless Norsemen on the back. "Hello, Pat. Thank you for coming. I am...I am Mr. Rosen. Please, come in."

Walking into the foyer, Jack gave Av a strange look before shaking the old man's extended hand. "I answer better to Jack. And yes, I remember you from Frank's funeral. This is quite the large house you have here, Rosen."

"Uh...right. We moved here a couple months back. It is a bit large, but I...I like the privacy of the area. Please, come into the dining room. Would you like a coffee or tea?"

Jack sat himself down at the table and grinned. "Tea? I'll take a beer."

"Right...we do not keep beer in the house. We...we do not drink it. There is wine. I could use wine. Would you...would you like wine?"

"Sure, wine's cool."

"Red or white?"

"You decide."

"Right. I will be back in a moment."

Av soon came back with a bottle of red. He would have preferred white, but he could not be bothered taking the time to chill it. In the kitchen after grabbing two wine glasses from the kitchen cupboard, he pulled off the bottle's cork and almost filled each glass. He removed his sunglasses to wipe his brow again and then guzzled down the contents of one glass. He refilled it, asking himself how Blue might handle the situation. Av shook his head, deciding against spitting in the other's glass.

"Thanks," said Jack, taking a glass as Av sat down across from him. "So, why am I here? I'm guessing you're going to try to convince me, man to man, to leave Blue with you. Let me tell you how it is. Blue's Cindy's kid. She wants him with her, and I'll admit I'm really not into someone else's kid living with me, but now that we're married and I'm going to be busier, much busier, it's good for her. She won't be getting lonely and all that."

Av cleared his throat. "Right. It is partially about that, but more so about the other thing. I must say I...I find it rather confusing that you would allow Howard to do as he is doing, especially with what you have just said. The two seem to conflict, no? It seems strange that he would expect me to pay when you are expecting to be able to take Blue with you. The threat against the boy seems rather empty, no?" Seeing what seemed to be impatience on Jack's face, Av added, "I mean to say, the threat seems contrary when I expect your wife would not allow any harm to come to Blue, the harm Howard has threatened?"

The impatience in Jack's face leaked out through his voice. "Rosen, what the hell are you talking about? What threats?"

As he stared at the man, Av became enlightened.

"Rosen, hello?"

"Sorry...I...I apologize. It makes more sense now. I thought you knew what was going on." Av stopped to gulp a mouthful of wine. "Frank owes...owed some money to the biker gang and Howard has threatened to harm Blue unless he receives it in full."

"Ok, just a sec. First, it's a biker club, and second, this is news to me. I'm sure Frank's debt is cleared up, and I'm sure Howard knows that. Maybe, Howard saw you as easy money or something. Still, threatening Blue is not (what do you folks say?) kosher. But then, why bring this to me? Why not just pay the...what is it, three or four grand? I wouldn't expect that's much money for you. Look at this house. Look at the Cadillac out there. Let me tell you, Rosen, you seem worth a lot of money, so why not just pay it and leave me out of it? Is it a Jewish thing?"

Av's anger overrode his nervousness.

"No, it is not a Jewish thing, and it is not four or five grand. It should be less than that, but he wants fifty thousand dollars in cash, and if he does not receive it, he says that he will harm Blue."

"Say what? Fifty?" Jack laughed. "I'll be damned! So, he's *seriously* extorting money from you. I'll be damned! I bet he's tryin' to get himself a little nest egg. Maybe some seed money for his dealing," Jack said and then catching himself saying too much, took a more serious tone. "Well, that doesn't matter. The bastard is threatening Blue for fifty grand. Leaving out the fact that it's Blue, extortion using kids isn't our sort of business. It can raise attention with the cops, just like kidnapping. Speaking of cops, you haven't gone to them, right?"

"No," Av said. "But I do have the money. I was thinking I would rather give it to you to have you stop Howard with his threats...and to have your wife allow Blue to stay here as long as he wants to. I expect that if Howard gets the money easily...this easy, he may just be tempted to come back for more. I also expect that even if you are able to take Blue, knowing Blue as I do, he will only run away, run back to here."

"Right, I get where you're coming from. You have a good idea there, Rosen. I could do both, one easier than the other (you already experienced Cindy) but what's to stop me from asking for more than fifty? Maybe I should ask for two or three times that."

"That would be difficult for me. I was able to obtain the fifty thousand in cash while avoiding questions, but it will be almost impossible to do that again. It raises too many alarms, and I may not be able to persuade certain people to ignore it next time. We could always setup some sort of scheduled monthly payment to you...perhaps five hundred dollars a month. Please, do not mistake my intentions. I am not saying I do not want his mother, your wife, in Blue's life. I certainly would not want to stand between a boy and his mother. By all means, I would like them to get to know each other again through visits, if you will, as long as Blue agrees of course."

"Ok," smiled Jack, "But let's make it a grand a month."

"Right, one thousand a month. I can do that...until Blue is

eighteen. It seems...I suppose, wrong to continue paying into his adulthood, no?"

"Right. Ok, I think we have a deal, Rosen. I'll call you with my bank info and you can deposit it monthly. Now, let's see the fifty grand. You just said you got it, right?"

"Well...seeing that these transactions are not exactly legal, I would be more...more comfortable paying when I have confirmation directly from Howard that he is dropping his threats."

Jack rose from his seat, putting Av on the defense. "When are you supposed to give him it?"

"Tomorrow at two,"

"Ok, let me deal with it, and you can expect his confirmation tomorrow by noon. I'll be by the day after next, this Saturday, for the cash and with my bank info. Let's say the same time as today, at two."

Av joined Jack in standing. "We will have to make it Monday. That would be more agreeable. Do you need my number?"

"I got it. You gave it to me when you called. So, why Monday?" Jack asked with suspicion.

"Others will be here Saturday, and I would rather they not be aware of what we are doing."

"Ok, fine, Monday at two then. I'll show myself to the door. Hey, no games, Rosen. If you're messing with me, you're...well, let's just say people have been hurt for much less."

Av stiffly nodded his head and shook Jack's hand, then a thought occurred to him and he said, "I would like to ask too that no one gets hurt over this...this matter."

With his face registering disgust, Jack dried his then wet palm on his jeans.

"Right. To be upfront with you, I couldn't hurt Howard if I wanted to. He's untouchable while he's the president of the thirteenth. It wouldn't go over well." Leaving the room, he added, "Rosen, you know those are women's sunglasses, right?"

As the man left the house, Av removed and examined his

glasses, wondering how someone could distinguish the men's from the women's. They both have two eyes, two ears and a nose, so why have different designs for the two sexes?

Hearing the door close, Av exhaled a portion of his stress before becoming very proud to the point where it would be impossible to be any more so. His pride was quickly smothered in disappointment when he realized he would have to keep it to himself.

CHAPTER 19
The Results

Howard, Snap and Numbers had been at the secluded ranch style house, their clubhouse, for two hours before Jack showed up with his wife an hour before noon. With a simple nod of their heads in response to the greetings from the three sitting at the bar, the two entered the church and sat down at the far end of the table. Sitting beside her husband, Cindy pulled a pistol from her large purse and placed it on the table between them. After whispering to each other, Jack got up and met the three at the bar.

"Numbers, Snap, go do something outside. Howard and I have to talk."

Howard whispered to Snap, "Hey, don't go far. We got to be you know where at two."

Snap nodded and followed Numbers out the front door.

Gesturing for Howard to follow, Jack returned to the church and sat down next to his wife.

"Howard, you're a jackass!" Cindy hissed, "A dumbass!"

Standing at the other end of the table, Howard's eyebrows rose to both the woman's words and the pistol lying on the table.

"Cindy, please," Jack begged, placing his hand on his wife's knee. "Howard, I talked to Blue's friend, the old Jew, and you know what he told me?"

Fighting to hide his surprise, Howard said, "No."

"You know damn well what he told me! You threatened to

hurt Blue unless he gave you fifty grand! Have you lost your damn mind? What the hell were you thinking threatening my wife's kid? You really thought I'd never find out, really? You told him not to call the cops, but you should have told him not to call me too, you dumb idiot! It's over! You're done!" Jack said, placing his hands over the pistol. "You're lucky I don't finish you here and now! You want to mess with the stepson...the son of a Headless Norseman? Really, man? Cindy here thinks I should just finish you now. She thinks you're going to be more trouble down the road." Placing his elbows on the table, he wrapped his left hand around his right fist and said in a calmer voice, "But seeing how you got things rolling with the patch-over, I'm letting you go on your way. In the end, it's my choice. You can forget about selling for us. The little respect I had for you is gone." Jack glanced at his wife and then glared back at Howard. Pulling a piece of paper out of his pocket, he flicked it at Howard. "But first, you have to call the Jew and tell him you won't be needing his money. His number's there. Come back after you've called him."

"Sure, ok. I...I appreciate that. I...I might have jumped too fast on an opportunity. Give me a minute," Howard said humbly as he picked up the paper.

Howard went behind the bar, picked up the phone and was about to dial the number when he took a deep breath and fought to control his growing anger.

After dialing the number with his shaking hand, the call was answered after the first ring.

"Yeah, old man...Mr. Rosen? Right. This is Howard. Right. I...I just met with our *mutual* friend. Yeah Jack, and he says to...to tell you not to worry about the...about Frank's money. It's fine, all fine. Yeah, you're welcome. Yeah...you too."

Hanging up the phone, it occurred to Howard that Jack could do little to him before the patch-over, but he certainly could once it was completed, and Howard was certain Jack would, if only to please his wife.

Howard succumbed to his growing anger but successfully held off his need to scream out in a rage. He reached beneath the counter of the bar and grabbed something heavy before walking stiffly back into church.

Cindy stopped whispering and looked to Howard. Her eyes widened.

Seeing his wife's expression, Jack turned to Howard too. "That was a fast phone ca—" Jack reached for the pistol as the deafening sound of gunshot filled the room. He fell back in his chair, his body jerking with the next two slugs entering his chest.

"WHAT ARE YOU DOING?" screamed Cindy, who grabbed her neck with the next blast.

The next two shots knocked her off of the chair.

"Bitch," said Howard as he walked casually over to the quietly dying couple.

"What happened? What the hell happened?" demanded Numbers as he and Snap rushed in.

"What the hell ya do?" asked Snap just as dumbfounded as Numbers.

"What did I do?" Howard asked, placing his pistol in his vest pocket and picking up Jack's. "What did *you two* do?"

"Wha...?" both asked.

"Step back by the door," demanded Howard, pointing the dead man's pistol at the two. "I'm sorry this got to happen, but things just took a turn for the worse, which could just take a turn for the better. Not for you two, but for me."

The two men knocked down several framed pictures as they fell from the repeated shots.

Howard walked over to where Numbers was lying dead with his back against the wall and Snap was lying flat on his back clutching his stomach as he gasped for air.

"Nothing personal, dumbass. A man's got to do what a man's got to do," said Howard before firing a slug into the Snap's head. "Survival of the strongest, you know."

At the bar, Howard pulled out his wallet and searched through it until he found a business card. He picked up the phone's receiver and referring to the card, passed his shaking finger along the rotary phone. As it rang, he took a deep breath.

Yeah?

"Leo, I don't know what he said to him! I wasn't there! I don't know what he said to him!" Howard blurted out, faking his panic well.

What? Who is this?

"Howard, Howard from the Tribe. They're all dead!"

Howard Swanson? Calm down! Who's dead?

Howard took two long and loud breaths. "Jack, Cindy...Numbers and Snap. They shot each other! I guess Numbers and Cindy were caught in the crossfire cause only Snap and Jack had pistols out."

Tabernac! You're sure they're dead?

"They are now! I don't know when it all happened, exactly," said Howard. "I just got here a couple of minutes ago. I should never have left Jack alone with Snap. That guy can take things too too damn personal, but he's never done anything like this with us, to another Tribe member? Did Jack tell you if he had some problem with Snap as VP?"

Taberbac! I don't know. Jack...he can be a bit harsh sometimes. Where did it happen? Did anyone hear it, see it?

"In the church. No, no one would have noticed the shots. We're deep in the woods off Herring Cove Road. What...what should I do?"

Merde! I don't know! I can't believe this! Ok...ok, I'll send someone down as soon as I can.

"What should I do with...with them in the...in the meantime?"

Tabarnac! Let me call you back. Give me the number again. Listen, we may need you to stay onboard as president. Colisse! Maybe...maybe, we'll get you up here to see how we deal with the business side...or send someone down there to help you out. Sorry, man, I'm trying to figure two things out at once. Give me the number, and I'll have answers on both. I can't believe this! Merde!

After giving the French-Canadian the number, Howard hung up the receiver and released the smile he was holding back: there was no hint from Leo that he had heard anything from Jack regarding his using Blue for extortion.

Then after pausing to think for a moment, he picked up the phone and dialed again.

"Tiny? Hey, it's Howard. We've got a situation. I'll be holding church Monday morning to go over it. No, I can't say anything, yet. There's still shit to be worked out. I'll bring everyone up to speed then. Hey, I need you to spread the word for me. Right, at eight on the dot. I'll see you then. Thanks, man."

Howard was proud of himself. Monday, he would make a case for the Tribe to back out of the patch-over. All he felt he needed to do was to simply describe the fight between Jack and Snap and then let them know that not all the Tribe members would be accepted as Headless Norsemen. With the shock of the fight combined with not knowing who would and would not be patched over, he was confident the deal would fall through. His only question was how the Headless would react to it.

CHAPTER 20
Shakedown 2.0

"Hey, Blue," Howard called out while leaning over to the rolled-down passenger window.

Blue's heart skipped a beat as the three boys stopped and looked at the driver of the pickup truck.

"Blue, come here. I've got to talk to you. Come here. It's cool. Everything's cool."

Blue looked to Dwight. "You two keep going. I'll meet you at home."

"Again? No, we'll wait," said Dwight trying to sound forceful.

"No, you'll go!" Blue demanded as he set their schoolbags on the sidewalk.

"Fine, but I may just tell mom and Av this guy keeps meeting you on the street!" Dwight emptily threatened as he and Lyon picked up their bags and began walking on. "Why doesn't the man just come to the house if he wants to talk to Blue? He seems strange...like Tim."

"Maybe he's shy around people," offered Lyon.

"He doesn't seem shy. He seems strange, in a strange way."

As Blue watched to make sure the two walked away, Howard gestured with his arm. "Come on in. Everything's cool."

With the boy reluctantly getting into the truck, Howard told him to close the door. Nervous, Blue had to close it twice before it closed all the way.

"You're alone? What's....what's going on? Where's Snap?"

"Right, Snap...he's preoccupied. I was just driving by and noticed you there. Small world, no?" Howard lied.

"I guess?" Blue said with suspicion.

"Hey, you see that house there, over on your right there?"

"Which one? The white brick or the one with the three car gara...?"

The palm strike to the back of his head stunned him. Then a tug on his hair pulled his head back while a wet cloth was forced over his face. The ether-like fumes of the sweet-tasting chemical immediately made the boy's head spin even more.

The ringing of the bar's phone woke him. Realizing he was lying flat on a hard, felt-covered surface and hearing someone walking around and then the clinking of empty glass bottles, Blue pretended to still be unconscious in hopes of discovering what was going on.

Howard gave a loud sigh, ensuring the caller heard it. "Leo? Thank God, man! I've been dying here trying to figure out what to do! What? Yeah, yeah, I heard the call. I was puking up in the bathroom when ya called. Yeah, I saw a dead body before, but not so many of my friends' all at once! And the blood! Jesus, there's a lot of blood!"

Blue's eyes opened as they tried to escape his head.

"No, I can't do that. There's one freezer here and it's not big enough for even one. Ok, I can do that, but it seems pretty cold, man. Right, not a great way to start the chapter. Right, we don't need that. Monday? If they're coming to Halifax on Sunday, why don't I just meet them at the motel? Ok, Monday it is. It's off Herring Cove Road, about two miles past the city limits. Once they pass a pond on the right, we're the next road after that...on the right too. We're at the very end, about a thousand feet in. Not the best road for bikes, but no one can go down it without us knowing about it. Tell them not to mind the dogs chained near the front. They're our warning system. Ok, right, thanks for everything."

Blue knew exactly where he was. He had never been in the clubhouse, but he had accompanied his father there. He remembered the dogs that had ferociously barked when their car turned onto the dirt road, and he figured then that their barks were what had triggered the person to come out and meet their car in the carport, which looked as if it was purposely designed to hide any transactions from any *official* eyes possibly hidden in the woods around the house.

It was not until he decided to sit up that he realized he was on a pool table, his head hurt and a handcuff had been clamped around one of his ankles. The handcuff's mate was clamped through the link of a chain that he followed and found its other end fastened down around the pool table's leg by another pair of handcuffs. Taking his attention away from the chain, Blue looked around and, because of the many opened beer bottles and dirty glasses spread out among the room's tables, wondered if a bunch of people had just left the place. Through the windows to the church, Blue saw red splatter on the wall of photographs at the far end of the room and guessed it was the blood Howard had just mentioned.

"Good, you're awake! You were out longer than I expected. Almost worried me for a bit there. I thought you might have overdosed. That Chloroform is tricky shit. You never know how long to hold it over the face, never know how much it'll affect someone," said Howard from behind the bar. "Hey, how's your head?"

"It hurts. What the hell's goin' on? Chloroform? What are ya doin'? Why'm I here and why the hell am I chained to this pool table?"

"Kid, I'm raising the stakes. I tried to work with the old guy, I really did, but he messed it up."

"The old guy? What old guy?"

"Your old guy. Your Jew," Howard answered while opening a bottle of beer.

"Av?"

Howard took a gulp of his beer. "I forget his first name, but he agreed to hand over fifty grand to leave you alone —but then he goes and tells Jack! What a dumbass! Hey, sorry about the cuffs and chain, but I'm not in the habit of tying someone up. That's usually someone else's job, eh?"

"What fifty grand? What're ya talkin' about?" Blue asked as the gravity of the situation sank in.

"I went over there to ask for what Frank owed, but it looked like the old guy has lots of cash, and he didn't even flinch with the amount. He was supposed to hand it over today, but no, he has to mess it up! I should really be asking for more now, but there's no time."

Having a hard time accepting the situation, Blue asked "So, I'm...I'm kidnapped? Really? Ya really lost yer mind, didn't ya!"

"Yeah, maybe I did. Anyway, this time he's going to do as I say, for sure. I have to tell you, the old guy seemed to care for you, but then he tells Jack and all that shit breaks out in there," said Howard, gesturing with his head toward the church and then finishing off the bottle of beer.

"He told Jack? What did he do?" Blue looked back to the church. "Is that his blood? You killed him?"

Howard poured some water into a small, dirty glass. He walked out from behind the bar and offered the glass and two Aspirins to Blue, who used the water to swallow the pills.

"Yeah. I'll get you to clean that up after you help me bury the bodies out back. It's just temporary until I figure out what to do with them. Can't leave them smelling the place up, can we?"

"Bodies?" Blue asked, starting to sweat. "How many bodies?"

"Yes, *bodies*. Listen, kid, my patience with this whole thing is pretty much gone. I don't want to have to hurt you, so you best do as I say or I may just have to add to the body count. Really, what's the difference between four and five, anyway?"

"One," Blue reflexively answered sardonically and then wished he had said nothing.

"Don't be a smartass, kid, or you'll be that *one*!" hissed Howard. "Now, I need you to shut up for a sec while I call the old man."

Blue watched Howard walked back to the bar, take another beer from the fridge, open it, take a drink and then pick up the phone's receiver. He was about to dial when he hesitated. "I don't have the number. I don't know why I thought I did." He shook his head and yelled, "SNAP, GIVE ME THE NUMBER FOR THE OLD FART. SNAP?" Getting no response, Howard laughed. "Jesus, I forgot he's dead too! Can ya believe that? I put three or four slugs in him and then forgot about it! Maybe I *am* losing it. You just don't know how much you rely on someone until they're gone, eh? Ok, ok, what's your phone number? Oh, wait, I got it here. The irony, eh? Jack gave me it just before I did him and his old lady in."

"What? You killed his wife...my mother?" asked Blue not wanting to believe he had heard Howard correctly.

"Oh, right. Sorry, kid. My condolences. Uh...you want a beer?"

Blue's mind was having a hard time processing the news of his mother death and accepting that the man who had killed her was casually offering him a beer. He found himself going numb as the blood rushed from his head. He was sure he was going to pass out, but he didn't. Instead, he vomited what was left of his lunch over the edge of the pool table.

"Jesus, kid! Just ask me for a damn bucket!" Howard demanded before he took a drink of the beer, placed the receiver on the counter and dialed the number on the paper.

Blue tried to collect himself while searching for an emotion. He felt no fear, grief or anger. Guessing he was experiencing what he had once heard described as shock, he tried to shake himself out of it and was suddenly overcome with rage. Cursing, he began pulling at the chain with hard jerks.

"Good, it's ringing. Hey! Calm the hell down, kid!" Howard demanded. He tossed the paper aside and began laughing again. "I can't believe I forgot I killed him. Damn, that's funny, eh? Is this...is this..." Howard paused to look to Blue.

"IT'S MR. ROSEN TA YA, YA FREAK!" Blue yelled as he gave up on trying to free himself.

Off Herring Cove Road: The Problem Being Blue

"Is this Rosen? Good. Guess who this is. That's right, me again. Let's cut to the chase. I want the money again and *you* need to give it to me cause, guess what, I got Blue with me. That's right. He's making himself comfortable, as comfortable as he can be. You've the cash, right? Good."

"AV, DON'T DO WHAT THE FREAK SAYS! YA CAN'T TRUST 'IM! HE'LL KILL US BOTH! WE'RE ATS THEIR CLUBHOUSE! CALL THE COPS!"

"Just a sec, old man."

Howard switched the receiver to his left hand and grabbed one of the many empty beer bottles from the counter.

Blue tried ducking it, but it still managed to nick the back of his head, flattening him out on the pool table. Calming down, he put his hands to his head and cursed under his breath.

"You hear that? That was Blue, trying to give you bad advice. If you call the police, you'll never see the kid again, no one will. You got that? Ok, here's what's going to happen. We'll meet at noon at Cochran's Lookout. It's just past the city limits. You'll see a white house with red shingles on your left. That's it, on Herring Cove Road. The road up to the lookout's at the corner of that house. Bring the cash. Good...and, old man, if there are cops, it'll be really easy for me to know. Yes, he's fine...for now. Be there at noon or he'll be in heaven with his mother. We just do the exchange and go our separate ways. It'll be as simple as that. Remember, if something happens to me, there are others here who'll get payback. I'm not doing this on my own, you know."

Hanging up the phone, Howard said, "Shit! I probably shouldn't have said that part about your mother, eh? Oh well, what's done's done. Ok, kid, let's go dig us a hole. Now where the hell are the shovels? SNAP, WHERE ARE...shit." Howard smiled. "I did it again." Then his face went dead serious. "Hey, idiot, how's your head? You need a Band-Aid?"

With the back porch light lighting up one side of his face as he sat in the lawn chair drinking a beer and while watching a sweat-soaked Blue spreading the last of the loose dirt on the high mound, Howard said, "That's a mighty fine job you did there, mighty fine. You should look into being a gravedigger when you grow up. That's quite a neat hump of dirt there too. Were you as surprised as me to get as deep as we did? I'd have thought we'd have hit rock before we did. Ok, toss the shovel by the trash cans over there and rest up."

Saying nothing, Blue threw the shovel out of reach, wiped the sweat from his forehead and then stood there watching Howard search his front pocket for a key. Finding it, Howard unlocked the handcuff from his own wrist and placed the key back into his pocket. He picked up his end of the chain with one handcuff locked through its last link and used it to lead Blue into the house.

Blue followed Howard in, disappointed that Howard did not carry a gun in the back of his pants. He would have a better chance going for that then trying to jump the man, which he so much wanted to do. Physically he was no match for Howard, but he would be with a gun. He had discovered months before that it took almost no effort to pull a trigger and he would have had no problem firing one that evening. Blue hungered so much to shoot Howard dead, to pull the trigger and have the situation end, that he found himself fantasizing about putting a bullet in Howard's forehead, unlocking his handcuff and making a phone call to Av to see if he could pick him up.

Inside the clubhouse, Howard cuffed his end of the chain around the leg of the pool table.

"It's tough losing a mom, eh? I lost mine a few years back. It hurt. It really, really hurt. I didn't know you still had feelings for yours until I saw your eyes water back there when you saw her. I didn't think you'd even be able to roll her up in that plastic sheet, but you did. Boy, it sure shut you up, eh? Not even the bottle to the head did that."

Howard walked into a room to the left of the bar and came back with some bedding. Tossing a pillow and some sheets to Blue, he said, "Make yourself comfortable. Hey, I'm going to get some McDonald's. What do you want me to bring you back?"

Blue shook his head.

"Come on! What kid doesn't like McDonald's?" asked

Howard as he went behind the bar and grabbed another bottle of beer.

"I'd like ta be able ta eat it again after tonight."

"Oh look, he talks! What are you saying? If you eat it tonight, you won't be able to stomach it again? It'll have too many bad memories attached to it or something like that? You're one complicated little shit. You sure you're Cindy's kid?"

"Yer goin' ta kill'im aren't ya? Yer goin' ta kill Av...and me too, right?"

"What? No, that's not the plan. I get the money and everyone goes their way," said Howard, obviously trying hard to sound sincere while opening the bottle of beer. "Kid...Blue, you have to learn to trust people."

With Howard's snoring escaping from the opened door of the room to the left of the bar, Blue finally gave up on his tired and hungry body being able to lift the pool table to slide the chain out from around its leg. Expecting that the table was somehow bolted to the floor, he laid himself on top of it. Placing his head on the dirty pillow and pulling the stained sheets up to his neck, he tried to come up with a plan to counter Howard's, but it would be almost impossible to counter a plan without knowing it or the full intentions of the person carrying it out. All Howard had told Av was to meet him at the lookout. Having been there before, Blue knew the straight, half-kilometer of potholed-ridden dirt road leading up to it, which only a truck could navigate, had forest on both sides. It was an isolated spot, being perfect for Howard, but not for them. And to make it even better for him and worse for them, before arriving Howard would be able to spot any police already there by their parked cars at the entrance to the road. Once up there, he would be able to spot any on their way. Then Blue struggled in his exhaustion to figure out Howards plan. Was he planning to leave him there at the clubhouse so he could kill Av after getting the cash, and then come back and kill him? Blue did not think so. If that was the plan, why not just kill him now? Maybe, Blue thought, Howard was keeping him alive in case Av had hid the money somewhere, refusing to disclose the location until he saw him safe, which would be a good idea, or maybe Howard would bring him along to kill them together. He had already killed four people and was hardly disturbed by it, making Blue think that he could easily kill more. Blue figured Howard pretty much had to kill them. He would have to since he knew Howard had seen the bodies and knew where they were buried, and Av had seen Howard's face and knew his name. Blue could not see any other ending but death for them both. Then a thought hit him and he had a rush of hope. If Av agreed to Howard's vague instructions, leaving out any questions on how the transaction would work, Av must have a plan too! But Blue lost that hope just as fast as he had found it. Av was probably too shocked by the call to think straight, and not knowing how to contact Howard to clarify the details after they had sunk in, he was forced to follow along with the vague instructions.

It seemed to the boy that a bit of good luck was the most he could hope for, and if there was ever a time he felt helpless and useless it was at that moment.

CHAPTER 21
Kids Think Differently Than Adults

With sweat running into his already wet eyes and his heart slamming against his chest, Av tried to control his shaking hands as he hung up the phone.

"Was that Blue?" Dwight asked as he popped into the kitchen, surprising the stressed old man. "Where is he?"

To Dwight, it seemed like forever before Av answered, "Yes, he...he is with his mother?"

To Av, it seemed like forever before a watery-eyed Dwight digested what he had heard and almost begged, "When's he coming back? He's coming back home, right? He's not staying there, right? He's not, right?"

"Right, he will be home tomorrow, tomorrow afternoon. I am to...to pick him up then."

"I just knew that guy was trouble!" Dwight declared as he left the kitchen with the hope that things would be back to normal the next day.

Av would have asked whom Dwight was talking about, but he was not prepared to lie if asked more questions. The more lies he told, the greater the chance the boy would see through one.

Walking into the library, Av sat in a leather armchair, laid his elbows on his knees, placed his head in his hands and allowed his body to shake. His fear for Blue was soon mixed with anger at himself. Then an enormous guilt covered him as he blamed himself for the bizarre twist the situation had taken.

If I had just gone along with Howard's plan, just gone along with it instead of trying to better it, it would be over with by now, he scolded himself.

Av had no choice but to tell Lisa what had happened and what was happening. With his continuing guilty shame, he sat the young mother down at the kitchen's island and told her everything.

With both believing Dwight was upstairs trying to finish his homework before supper, which he had been doing, and neither hearing him come downstairs for a drink, Dwight picked up a strange tone in his mother's excited whisper and stopped near the kitchen's entrance. Her voice contained a mix of anger and fear; a mix he had never heard coming from her before then.

Av, you should have told me! I understand you thought you'd kill two birds with one stone, with thousands of dollars, but you should've told me!

Normally, Dwight would have gone into the kitchen to find out what was going on, but Av's whispering stopped him. When he whispered, which was rare, it was usually because Av did not want him to know what was going on. Knowing that, Dwight stayed where he was and listened. He failed again to make out what Av had whispered, but he had no problem hearing his upset mother.

We only have until noon tomorrow? We should call the police, right? What did he mean about his mother? Jack never called you? Do you think he...ok, so...so no police? It would've been better to meet in a mall or someplace somewhere more public. He's bringing Blue with him, right? How can you not know? Ok, let's call him. What? Ok...I...I guess it would've been stupid on his part to leave it. So, we can only show up tomorrow with your money and hope to see Blue? That's right, we. No, Av, I'm coming too. It's not open for discussion! We're in this together! Here's what I think: I can hide in the woods. Av, it's off Herring Cove Road —there's always woods. So I hide in the woods and if it looks like this...this guy is going to hurt you after giving him the money, then I'll cause a distraction. I'll be further in so I'll have a head start if he comes after me. He'll have to rethink hurting anyone then, right? Good, then that's what we'll do. Right, if everything goes as planned, I'll just stay there until he's gone.

Dwight could not believe what he was hearing. Av had lied to him!

Frustrated and worried, Dwight was about to walk boldly into the kitchen for more details when he heard his mother again.

Ok, let's just treat tonight like any other, ok? Dwight will have Lyon over for a sleepover and then I'll have Lyon's mother watch them tomorrow.

Dwight's worry was overridden by anger as he took off in a huff up the stairs to his room.

"Did you hear that?" Lisa asked as she wiped an eye with a finger. She got up from her stool to check if Dwight was eavesdropping outside the kitchen. Relieved in not finding him, she sat back down at the kitchen's island, composed herself for a moment and then whispered, "Ok. So, let's send Dwight over to Lyons after a late breakfast. We should probably leave here by eleven. Should we hide the money somewhere just in case this Howard tries playing any more games?"

"I do not know," whispered Av, who rested his elbows on the island, laid his forehead in his palms and looked down in shame. "I would expect that the faster it is over, the better, and what could happen when he discovers we do not have it with us and then does not believe we hid it? It would be an added risk." He sighed as he straightened up, dropped his arms to his sides and looked into Lisa's stressed eyes. "I-I should have asked for details. I do hope he calls back to confirm that I understood him...but then the instructions were easy enough to follow. I am...I am so sorry I caused this...this situation."

"You caused? You did no such thing! This is all that Howard's fault, not yours! You tried to fix someone else's problem, and you still are. I'm just sorry you tried to put it all on your own shoulders," whispered a sympathetic Lisa. "Ok, I think we need some wine. Would you like a glass...or two?"

Through supper, all quietly ate their hamburgers and fries. Nobody was in the mood to talk and neither Lisa nor Av noticed Dwight was unusually quiet too. Dwight was still steaming with anger and was hardly looking forward to Lyon showing up. If Lisa and Av were not so distracted by the situation, Dwight would have vented his feelings. All it would have taken was one question to him and he would have exploded into a napalm bomb of sarcasm.

With Dwight being the first to finish forcing down his food, placing his dish in the sink and leaving without a word, neither Lisa nor Av seemed to notice his mood, and that angered him even more.

Lisa met Lyon at the door, where she put him off by her obviously forced smile as she directed him upstairs.

Lyon entered the bedroom, joined his lackluster friend and Sam on the edge of the bed and after offering a few excited suggestions of what they could do and getting only negative responses, asked his friend if he was still up for a sleep-not.

"No, yes, I don't know. Maybe not. My mind's somewhere else," Dwight's voice cracked as he tried to speak in a whisper. "There's something bad happening...and you're only here to make me think there's not!"

"What?" asked a surprised and then offended Lyon. "I'm only here to do what?"

"To make everything seem normal. Something's happened to Blue. That strange guy in the truck took him, and now Av has to pay him money to get him back," answered Dwight who thought it strange that just saying the words made his eyes water. "That guy's a bad guy, and he could hurt Blue!"

"Took him? Really? They told you this?" Lyon asked in a disbelieving tone.

"No, they're keeping it a secret from me...or they think they are! I overheard them before supper!" Dwight said, fighting to whisper. "They're always keeping things from me!"

"Seriously?" asked Lyon still in disbelief.

"Yes, seriously!"

"Ok, when are they giving him the money?"

Irritated by Lyon's questions and with a better understanding of why Blue would get frustrated with the boy, Dwight's voice rose as he said, "Next Easter! Tomorrow! It's happening tomorrow at lunch!" Dwight fought to control his irritation with his friend and his frustration with the situation. "After we go to your place, they're going to meet them somewhere. And this guy must be really, really bad because they're scared, really, really scared. They're not even calling the police! They're that scared!"

"Where are they doing it, giving it to him...giving the bad guy the money?" Lyon asked, his voice rising in his excitement, which only irritated Dwight further.

"On the Moon! I don't know! All I know is it's not a mall! That's all I know!"

Fighting hard to control his boyish excitement with the surreal situation, Lyon said, "Probably some place private, right? Do you think it's serious...like he has a gun or something?"

"If they're that scared, he must. Blue's dad had two (I saw them) and he was a good guy."

"Then they'll need our help. They don't know it but they do, right? They'll need something for a distraction. Something that'll make it hard for the bad guy to use it, at least for a little bit, so we have time to all jump him and get it. There's five of us and one of him, right? Or...or we can just get away quickly."

Dwight stared at his friend for a moment before huffing. "We? Mom and Av aren't going to let us come with them. I just told you they're keeping it a secret!"

"But we can sneak there," offered Lyon, and then his eyes lit up and he added, "We can hide in the car's trunk. It's big enough."

"No, we'll never get in. Av locks the car and keeps his keys in his back pocket."

"There has to be a way. Do you trust a bad guy to hand over Blue and let them go after they saw his face? Remember, we saw his face too. What if he does something bad to them and then comes back to do something bad to us? Don't you think he'd be scared we'd talk? They don't know it, but they need our help. They don't know you know, right? So they won't think we have a plan, just like the bad guy won't. We have to get in that trunk! We have to go too!"

Dwight thought for a moment, weighing the being bad part with the doing good part.

"I guess I could wait until Av is sleeping and then borrow his keys to unlock the car so it's ready tomorrow morning," he conceded.

"Ok, that's a plan. Now we have to figure out what to use. Something to surprise and confuse him, like a police siren. You got anything that makes a noise like that?" Dwight shook his head. "Ok, maybe something that makes a loud bang. A loud bang always surprises people and freezes them for a second. When he's stunned, we won't be because we'll know it's coming. Then we push everyone to get away."

"Something like...like a firecracker?" asked an apprehensive Dwight.

"Right. You have one?" asked Lyon, his eyes widening with the excitement of the adventure.

"No."

"Well, what do you have? I had some things in my chemistry set I could use to make a loud bang...but my mom took those away when I used them to make a loud bang."

"A cap gun. That's all I got, if it still works and if I still have some caps."

"Too little of a bang," said Lyon as he shook his head. He scrunched up his mouth and thought for a second. "I got it! We could make a gas bomb, something like...like a hydrogen bomb!"

"Shhh!" Dewey warned his friend. "What? An atom bomb? Seriously?"

"Not that kind of hydrogen bomb. The kind that *makes* hydrogen, makes enough to create so much pressure that it'll burst something with a loud bang. Does your mom use Drano for unclogging drains?"

"Drano? I don't know. My dad used to use

something...some liquid to fix the showers' slow drain. He used to get mad about mom's hair clogging it up. He just poured it in and it was fixed."

"That's probably it!"

"Maybe, Mrs. Collins uses—"

"Great!" shouted Lyon as he jumped up from the edge of the bed. Catching himself, he lowered his voice. "We can make a hydrogen bomb with the Drano. It'll be even better than a loud noise. When the top pops off, it'll spray Drano all over the bad guy. It's acid, so it'll burn the bad man, giving us even more time to get away!"

"Ok, but where do we get a...a Drano bomb?" Dwight asked, not sure if he should be taking Lyon seriously.

"We make it. I'll need a piece of paper and a pencil."

Dwight grabbed some paper and a pencil from his top desk drawer, handed them to his friend and sat back on the edge of the bed to watch him sit down at the small desk. Dwight and a curious Sam stared for almost a minute at Lyon as he tapped the desk's top with the pencil's eraser while his brain worked overtime to come up with a design.

"I think I got it! Yes!" Lyon exclaimed more to himself than Dwight and then began sketching excitedly on the paper. "We need a big jar, like a peanut butter jar. Inside it, we use a battery, a double 'A' battery, and a thin piece of rolled up aluminum foil. We wrap tissue paper...toilette paper around the rolled up foil and put it through the hole in one of those rocket engines we know he still has. Then we attach the ends of the foil to each end of the battery and when the battery heats up the foil, it burns the paper that'll ignite the rocket engine. The engine'll burn a hole in a little plastic container full of Drano, something like a pill bottle. Then the Drano pours out onto the aluminum foil at the bottom...the balls of aluminum foil," said Lyon, who then threw up his small arms in victory. "This'll work!"

Dwight asked with impatience, "What'll work? What are you talking about?"

Lyon looked to Dwight as if he was an idiot.

"The bomb. We mix the Drano with aluminum foil and

that'll create the hydrogen. With the jar sealed, the hydrogen'll build up to the point where it'll explode the top off the jar, making a loud bang and spraying Drano all over the bad man." Lyon began tapping the desk again as he thought out loud. "But how to turn it on later? How do we make the connection when it's needed?" He stopped tapping and shouted, "Right!" He began sketching again. "We attach the aluminum strip to the battery with an elastic band and we have two strings attached to the top of the jar. The end of one's stuck to one end of the battery but the other has a piece of plastic attached to its end. We put the plastic end between the battery and the foil and when we shake it, the plastic's pulled away from under the elastic band and the connection's made! That's it! Then the rocket engine's ignited by the tissue and that burns a hole in the small bottle holding the Drano. The Drano pours out, mixes with the aluminum balls in the jar, the gas builds up and *bang*, the top bursts off and the man's stunned!" Lyon said, his voice rising again.

"Shhh!" Dwight warned again. "If they hear you, they'll know what we're doing! Ok, so...so we mix the Drano with aluminum balls? But where do we get the balls?"

"Aluminum foil. We make them from aluminum foil. The balls have more surface area to melt and, therefore, make more hydrogen. This'll work. It'll work great! It's just like the Mouse Trap contraption, but this is real! We just have to figure out how much of the rocket engine to cut down so it doesn't burn too long, and then we have to figure out how to make sure the engine burns only the bottle holding the Drano."

"Hey," said Dwight, uncertain if what he was about to say would make him look stupid, "Instead of all that stuff, couldn't we just mix the aluminum foil with the Drano and have it explode that way?" With Lyon again looking at him as if he was an idiot, Dwight added, "We could glue the foil balls to the inside of the jar's top, fill it with Drano and just turn it over when we're ready. They'd mix together easier, wouldn't they? I mean, it'll be easier to glue the balls to the top than to the bottom, wouldn't it?"

With a disappointed face, Lyon nodded, "Yes, but it won't

be as interesting."

Dwight's eyebrows turned in and he whispered sternly, "Blue's in trouble! That's interesting enough! Let's make it a grade six science project, not a grade ten one!"

"Ok, ok, let's make a boring bomb," Lyon conceded. "I guess we'll just need the Drano, a package of aluminum foil, glue and a jar...one we can't see through. I'm not sure how long it'll take to burst the top off, so try to find a plastic one. Oh, and we'll need glue to seal the top on tight so the bad guy can't get it off before it pops off."

"Hey," asked Dwight as the thought suddenly occurred to him, "Why would the bad guy even bother with the jar?"

"Because...because...because we tell him the money's in it. Yes! That's perfect, right?" Lyon asked with his excited eyes showing his age.

With the verbal list, Dwight tipped toed around the morbidly quiet house grabbing a roll of foil from the kitchen, a half bottle of Liquid Drano from the second-floor closet, and a small tube of Crazy Glue from Blue's room. After dropping the items off to Lyon, he returned to the kitchen for the jar he had forgotten and found his lunch thermos, which seemed large enough to him.

Neither Av nor Lisa heard Dwight. In the living room with the televisions' volume down low, each was quietly trying to relax with a glass of wine in hand. They wanted to be fully awake when meeting up with Howard and Blue, and neither felt they could sleep unless they calmed their minds. Neither said it, but both were concerned about what Blue was going through, what thoughts would be going through his mind, what emotions he was feeling, and both hoped he knew they would be there for him.

After the boys had rolled many small balls from many small pieces of aluminum foil, Lyon, who had never used Crazy Glue before and was fascinated by how fast it dried and how strong it was, slowly glued each ball securely to the inside portion of the child-sized thermos' screw on top. When he was done, the small balls formed a much larger half sphere of aluminum foil, which had no chance of falling on their own into the Drano at the bottom. Lyon was also certain that when the thermos was upside-down, the Drano would dissolve the glue, dropping the small aluminum balls into the bottom once the thermos was turned right-side up again

"Ok, we'll finish the rest when the car stops. If we put it together now, it could explode with the car's shaking and spray us instead," warned Lyon. "We'll take the Crazy Glue and the bottle of Drano with us, and when we get there, we'll pour in the Drano and glue the top on tight. We'll give the bad guy the thermos upside down to start the chemical reaction, and as he fights to open it, he'll soak the aluminum with the Drano even more. And then, *boom,* he's stunned and sprayed with Drano, and we're all running away...running away with Blue. Oh, but we'll need a flashlight to see what we're doing in the trunk."

"That's easy, I have one here we can use," said Dwight, who felt good for the first time since coming home from school that day. "This is going to be too cool! We'll be heroes!"

Later that night, with the boys' items packed in Dwight's backpack, Lisa and Av wished the two a goodnight and went off to try to sleep.

Less than half an hour later, Dwight, whose heart pounded in his chest, was standing by Av's door. With the loud snoring making the boy confident the old man was sound asleep, he used the light from the hallway to guide him to the pants folded on Av's dresser. The snoring stopped and Dwight froze. He knew his friend well enough to know that no snoring meant no deep sleep, so he waited until Av began to snore again before grabbing the keys from the back pocket of the pants. The wait was only seconds but it felt like minutes to the boy, who had to freeze once more before he was able to exit the room undetected.

It wasn't until returning the keys when Dwight figured out his friend was having a difficult time sleeping. He had to freeze three more times while returning them.

With the anticipation of the next day's events, neither boy could sleep and were up at three in the morning. They passed the first couple of hours playing Mouse Trap, and later, as they were playing Trouble, Lisa and Av joined them and the four started a fresh game, though none got into it to the point where they were competitive.

That morning's breakfast of eggs and bacon was one of the few breakfasts that Dwight was glad was over when it was — the other times being when it was porridge. With the anticipation of the events to come, Dwight was anxious to have everyone safe and their lives back to normal, and that morning's breakfast only seemed to amplify his anxious state. No one, including Lyon, finished their breakfast that morning.

When the boys were ready to go to Lyon's, Sam followed them to the door.

"Mom, Av, we're going now. I'll see you at supper," Dwight called out while zipping up his spring jacket.

"Ok, we'll see you then. Lyon, please tell your mother I said thank you."

"Will do, Mrs. Dixon. Thanks, it was fun," said Lyon, who then winked at Dwight.

With Lyon holding the backpack, Dwight opened the driver's side door and reached down to pull the trunk's release lever as he had seen Av do. Locking and then closing the door, he joined his smaller friend in the trunk. With both boys fitting easily into the space, Lyon reached up and slowly pulled the hood down over them, using his weight to slam it the last few inches so it would be sure to shut securely.

Lying on his back in the dark, Dwight asked, "Lyon, is that you?"

"Is what me?"

"Are you tapping my foot?"

"No."

"Sam! Lyon, Sam's here! Now he's lying on my legs!"

"Shhh! Ok, then let him out," Lyon whispered.

"You're closer. Can you find the latch? It has to be where the key goes."

Lyon felt around the trunk.

"There's no latch or anything. Gross! There's grease, lots of it! I–I think it only opens from the outside."

"Ok, I guess we'll have to take him with us," said Dwight as he grabbed Sam and placed him on his chest. "Hey, Lyon."

"What?"

"Are you scared?"

"Not really. I'm more excited about our bomb...our plan, but I will be when we get there, I think."

"Me too," lied Dwight, who was scared of the coming scare.

Waiting in the trunk for almost twenty minutes, both boys fell asleep before being jolted awake by the car turning out of the driveway.

CHAPTER 22
Dead End -October 22, 1977

Through his sunglasses, Av looked at his watch, but without his reading glasses, he failed to make out the position of its small, thin arms.

"How are we doing for time?" he asked as he fought to keep down his protective shell.

Lisa looked at her watch.

"It's twenty to. We have plenty of time," she said in a controlled voice and then patted Av's arm hoping to calm the man she knew only appeared to be calm.

With the patting, Av's heart began breaking for the mother who was as upset as himself and yet was still trying to console him, making him think of his wife who would also put his feelings before her own.

Spotting the house with the red roof, he slowed down and signaled to make the left turn. He pulled onto the steep dirt road beside the house, stopped and backed out onto the gravel side of the road next to the ditch.

"Are we there yet?" Dwight whispered as he held on to a purring Sam.

"I think so," replied Lyon, feeling around in the dark for the zipper of the backpack. "We better finish the bomb. Here, take the flashlight."

With Dwight lighting up the trunk, Lyon poured the Drano into the thermos.

The car's engine turned off.

Lyon rushed to drip Crazy Glue around the threads of the thermos' aluminum-balled top and quickly screwed it on tight.

The car's doors opened and then closed.

With Lyon packing the Drano and Crazy Glue back into the backpack, Dwight turned off the flashlight, dropped it onto the floor of the trunk and then knocked hard on the inside of the hood.

Av and Lisa looked to each other, and then Av, with even more apprehension than he had a second before, opened the trunk with his key.

"TA DAAA!" yelled Dwight as he and Lyon sat up.

Lyon tossed Dwight a confused look.

"What? I didn't know what to say. It just came to me."

Both Lisa and Av had to take a step back to take in what they were seeing. After a second, Lisa scolded, "Dwight! Lyon! Wh–what are you doing here? You're supposed to be...supposed to be...well, you know where you're supposed to be...and it isn't here!"

"Bloody hell," whispered Av.

All heard him and all looked surprised.

"Excuse me, but this is not good, not good at all."

"You two, out of the trunk now!" Lisa demanded.

With Lyon being careful with the thermos hiding under his jacket and Dwight being careful with Sam, the two boys left the trunk.

"I can only guess that you eavesdropped on our conversation yesterday, and you thought you could help, but why in the world would you bring Sam?" asked Lisa.

Av put his hand on her shoulder. "He must have snuck in with the boys, I am guessing."

"Yeah," said Dwight. "We didn't know he followed us until we closed the trunk...which there is no way to open from the inside, by the way!"

"Can we leave him here?" asked Lyon.

"Right, that would be best," said Av as he took Sam, opened the front passenger door, placed him on the seat and then after closing the door, stared for a moment at the animal standing with his front paws against the window protesting his confinement. Something told Av it was a sign, a sign that something bad was going to happen. Trying to shake off the extra fear, he opened the back door of the car and said, "And you two can wait in the back seat."

"What? No way! My best buddy is in trouble and you want me to wait in the car?" protested Dwight.

"Yes," Av said, the stress causing his voice to rise.

"No way! I'm coming with—"

Lisa cut in, "Av, we can't leave them in the car. We've got to bring them with us and hide them until we make the exchange. What would this Howard do if he finds them sitting in the backseat, ransom them too?"

"That is a good point."

Av reluctantly closed the door just as Sam jumped over the front seat's backrest.

With Sam then protesting at the back window, Av cleared his throat. "We will have to be quiet as we walk up the road. They may be up there waiting." He looked toward Dwight and Lyon. "Walk some distance behind us, and if we see them, I will wave my palm behind me as a signal for you two to hide in the woods, very quietly...just as you did when you snuck into the trunk."

"No," said Lisa. "I'll take them in the woods with me. We'll walk up and hide at the edge. If there's a problem, like we planned, I'll make some noise to distract Howard and then we'll run down to the house over there for help. The windows are opened, so there's probably someone there. If this Howard knows what's good for him, he'll run off without hurting anyone and getting himself in even more trouble. If everything goes ok, we'll come out after he leaves, just like we agreed. Ok, let's...Lyon, what's in your jacket?"

Lyon's face went guilty as he pulled out the thermos.

"I thought we might get...get thirsty?"

With Lisa and Av both thinking the idea strange but considerate, Av said, "Right...I'll put that in the car, for now."

"No, Av. We'll take it with us. There isn't time and...and we just may get thirsty," Lisa smirked.

After watching the three enter the woods, Av forced

himself to walk slowly up the potholed road. He could hear the three struggling to make their way through the trees on his left and slowed his anxious walking to keep pace with their progress.

After ten minutes, he came up to a clearing of rock and weeds, which extended to the edge of a cliff. Walking to the edge, he could see the horizon of dark-blue water meeting lighter-blue sky. He gazed down past the almost smooth drop-off to the waves slapping at the shore of boulders some thirty meters below and thought it strange how he was unaffected by the height.

Just inside the woods bordering the clearing, Dwight and Lyon joined Lisa behind a large boulder.

Squeezing together while crouching down, Dwight whispered to Lyon, "I'm in so much trouble!"

"Not as much as I'm going to be in," Lyon whispered back. "When this is all over, your mom's going to be relieved, and you'll get off easy. My mom's waiting for us right now, and she's not going to be happy when we don't show up, and then finds out why."

"Shhh, you two!" demanded Lisa.

Looking out in the opposite direction of the water, Av could see Herring Cove Road snaking its way through the forest landscape down in the distance. Then he saw, coming from the opposite direction than they had come, a pickup truck much like the one Howard had used the morning he came to their house. His heart slammed against his ribcage.

Howard had been quiet the short drive to the lookout, but as that morning's five to seven beers helped him hit each pothole on the way up the hill, he began cursing under his breath.

During the drive, Blue could say nothing since Howard had duck taped his mouth before leaving the clubhouse. But if Blue could have spoken, he may have annoyed Howard during the short drive by repeatedly telling him he was being stupid. As it was, the boy could do nothing but think, and the way he figured it, he had only two options: one, run off the edge of the cliff, removing Howard's bargaining power, or two, go for

Howard's gun, which would be difficult since his wrists were handcuffed behind him. Option one could only make things worse. If Blue did send himself over the edge, Howard would have even more reason to kill Av since he would still want the money. Option two seemed to the boy to be the only feasible thing to do. Though it had little chance of success, he expected Howard could do little if the attempt failed. He still needed him for the exchange.

It seemed like forever to Av when the pickup finally pulled up to the clearing, stopped a couple of dozen feet or so from him and its engine turned off.

Howard stepped out holding a pistol. "Hey, old man, sorry for the delay. I had to make sure there was no one else coming, like the cops I mean. Kid, come out through my door. Hurry up!"

Not being able to form words, Av began walking toward the truck.

"Just stay where you are!" Howard demanded, pointing the pistol at Av. "No, better yet, back up by the edge back there. Get going!"

As Av moved back a half-dozen steps, Blue squirmed his way out of the driver's side to stand next to Howard. He shook his head at Av and moaned something through the duck tape.

"Blue, are you...are you ok?" asked Av.

Blue nodded his head.

"Ok, kid, go wait there," Howard said, lowering the gun and pointing with his other hand to the right side of the cliff.

Blue did the only thing he could. He swung his body around and with his arms behind his back, hit Howard hard in the side.

The attack failed to move Howard, who said, "Fuck!" and slammed the side of the pistol against the side of Blue's head, knocking the boy to the ground.

Av had to halt his rush toward the two when Howard pointed the gun down at Blue's head and said, "Really, old man...really? Get back there! And you, dumbass, get up!"

Dazed, Blue struggled to get to his feet. Just as he was about to stand, Howard pushed him back down with his foot.

Lisa, Av and Dwight had to use every bit of self-control they could muster to stay where they were.

"I said get up!" demanded Howard.

Again, Blue struggled to get to his feet, and again, Howard knocked him down.

"Get up!"

Blue was knocked down again.

"I could do this all day, kid. Ok, get up and go wait over there!" Blue just looked up at Howard. "Really, kid, you can get up." Howard let Blue stand and as the boy began walking toward the old man, he said, "Did I point there? No, I pointed over there on the other side. You can join him when we're done. For now, stand at the edge over there, on the far side."

Leaning back against the front of his truck, Howard smirked and ejected the pistol's clip. He eyed the thin slot in the clip, counted the rounds packed into it and inserted it back into the grip. Looking to his right at Blue, he said, "Stand closer to the edge. What the hell is wrong with you? Stand at the edge just like the old man's doing. If either of you move, it'll only be forward into a bullet. Old man, you can walk a few more feet to your right there."

Av did as he was told, glancing between Blue about six meters to his immediate left and Howard about seven meters in front of him.

Howard walked a couple steps toward the nervous old man, pointing the pistol from him to Blue.

"Ok, old man, you have the money, right?"

Av nodded stiffly.

"Good. Throw it over to me."

Before Av could reach for the bundles of cash he had earlier shoved through the small rips he had made to the inside of his spring jacket that morning, Lyon caused Lisa to gasp by jumping out from behind the boulder, rushing through the few trees and yelling out, "Ihaveithere." Holding up the thermos, he took a breath. "I have it here. They gave it to me so if you hurt them first, you'd get nothing."

As Lisa stayed in the woods holding on to Dwight's jacket with one hand while holding a finger up to her lips with the other, Blue stood by the edge of the cliff shaking his head violently while moaning and stamping a foot in frustration.

Howard pulled his eyes from Lyon to look at a confused Av and then to the woods.

"Who else is in there? Get your asses over here, now!"

Before Lisa could respond, she lost her grip on her son. In seconds, he was standing next to Lyon. Lisa soon joined them with her fear for the boys far outweighing her anger at them.

"Blue, did he hurt you?" she asked, her heart breaking for the bound boy.

Blue just shook his head.

With disgust on his face, Howard said, "Well, I didn't see that coming. So you decided to make it a family outing, did you? What the hell were you people thinking? Who the hell would bring kids to this thing? What the hell is wrong with you all? You know, I should just shoot you now for being the worst parents of the year, instead of...anyway, kid, where is it?"

"It's in here. In this thermos. We thought no one would think of searching here, right?" Lyon said.

Lisa and Av looked to each other, their eyes asking the other if they knew what was going on. Both subtly shook their heads.

"Really? Ok, whatever. Open it up and hand me the cash."

"Ok," said Lyon, who then pretended to try to work the top off. "It's too tight."

"Christ! Just bring it here!"

Lyon turned the thermos upside-down, looked to Dwight and then back at Howard.

"Don't make me repeat myself, kid. And, you two, go stand beside the old man at the edge. What are you waiting for? Go! You, kid, bring it here! What the hell are you waiting for, a formal invitation?"

With Dwight standing between them, Lisa and Av looked to him with the same question mark on their faces. Dwight gave a cocky wink and placed his finger over his lips, leaving Lisa and Av more confused as they each took his hand.

With the thermos purposely shaking in his hands, Lyon

slowly walked over to hand it to Howard, who turned it upright and examined it.

"Ok, kid, go and stand by the others. Hey, how the hell can you fit fifty grand in here? Are you honestly messin' with me? I know no hundreds of hundred dollar bills are going to fit in here!"

As Lyon stood beside Lisa, his eyes widened. "Uh...it's...it'sinthousanddollarbills. It's in thousand dollar bills. It's only fifty of them, right? It's not a big pile, right?"

"You saw him put them in, did you?"

Lyon nodded.

"What color are they?"

"Red," Lyon said without having to give it any thought and thankful for his mother's *Currencies of the World* coffee table book.

"Right...ok," said Howard. "Hey! Stop holding hands! What are you guys doing, posing for a picture? Let go of each other! Even better, put your hands behind your backs. If I see a hand, you feel a bullet. Now just stand there and no funny stuff!" With the gun in one hand, Howard shook the thermos in the other. "Is there liquid in here? This better not be some kind of bullshit game or I swear I'll be doing target practice with you!"

"We put water in it so nobody'd think there was money in it," Lyon lied. "You can never be too careful, right?"

"That's a bit...a bit extreme, but ok," Howard smirked as he knelt down, laid the pistol to his right and with both hands struggled to remove the top. He turned the thermos upside-down and beat its top against the ground to loosen it.

With impatient eyes, Dwight looked to Lyon who only shrugged back at him.

Howard tapped the lid with the butt of his pistol, laid the weapon back down and tried turning it again. "This thing is on here tight! You put this on, old man?" He picked up his pistol, stood up and extended his arms toward the group, one pointing the pistol and one holding the thermos. "Come here and give it a try. You best be able to open 'er up or—"

The loud, ear-ringing pop stunned them all.

At the same instant, something tore at Dwight's shoulder, causing him to lose his balance and stepped back off the edge. Falling back, he yelled, "MOM!"

Lisa and Av both grabbed for Dwight's wrists —both missed.

As Av crouched down and grabbed for his little friend's ankle, his shoes slipped, knees smashed against the edge of the cliff, and he dropped straight down. With the fingertips of his free hand scraping the cliff wall, Av's mind raced at a speed he was not use to, a speed that seemed to slow time as he hoped to grab onto something before he was falling too fast.

"DEWEY! AV!" Lisa yelled out as she threw herself on the ground and hung her arms over the cliff's edge.

To her relief, Av, who had just watched his sunglasses fall to the rocks below, was hanging on to a small protrusion in the cliff wall with one hand. With his other hand, he was holding on to the ankle of an upside-down Dwight looking at the boulders below and fighting his urge to scream.

It took a second for a stunned Lyon to pull his eyes away from the white vapors surrounding an unconscious Howard and then realized from the partial Superman logo on a piece of plastic at his feet that the thermos had exploded rather than its top simply popping off. Joining Lisa on the ground, he too looked over the edge at the two.

Lisa stretched down her arms. "Av, you're too far down!"

Av grunted. "Right. I–I think I am going to have to swing Dewey up to you first. Dewey, do not look down," Av said before grunting again.

"It's...oh, never mind," sobbed Dwight.

"Blue, I need you here!" Lisa yelled. "Av, hang on!"

Blue said something incoherent from behind the tape as he knelt with his back to an unconscious Howard, who he failed to notice had lost his left hand and if not for the attached little pinky his right hand would have been fingerless. With his cuffed hands behind him, Blue strained to look over his shoulder as he searched the man's pockets for the key. Finding it, he unlocked them, chucked them at the bloody-faced man and only then noticed that a piece of the thermos has sliced off a portion of the skin on the left side of the man's face. Pulling back the tape from his mouth, he ran to join Lisa.

"Good. Blue, you're ok," said Av.

"Are you guys ok?" Blue asked before feeling stupid for asking the question.

"I think I dislocated my shoulder, but that is not the main problem. Dewey, are you listening?"

"Yes," Dwight sobbed.

"Ok, Blue, Lisa, I have to swing him up to you. Dewey, this is what we are going to have to do. You know when you are on a swing and you want to get higher, you use your legs to throw your weight into it."

"Y–yeah."

"Right. I need you to do that each time I swing you back and forth. I need you to swing your arms as you would swing your legs...and bend your body into it. Now, when you get high enough on one side or the other, your mother or Blue will grab you."

"Blue?" asked Dwight, afraid to look anywhere but straight out to the upside down horizon.

"I'm here, Dwight. You just think about the...about the Chinese food Av's going to order when this is all over, and we'll have you up here before you know it."

"Ok, and...and whoever grabs me first gets my dessert," offered Dwight.

Lyon moved out of the way so Lisa and Blue could lie down a couple of meters on each side of Av. With their arms hanging over the edge, they anxiously waited.

"Ok, here we go," grunted Av, who began slowly swinging Dwight from one side to the other.

With Lisa and Blue offering words of encouragement to the old man grunting while hanging out to his side by only his fingertips, a teary-eyed Dwight bent his body and swung his arms into the swings. The swings started out small with Dwight's body movement being more of jerks than a flowing motion, but soon he was swinging wider and his movements became smoother as he began gaining height, making him more terrified than he was when he was hanging straight down by his ankle. He may have been even more terrified, if that was possible, had he known of Av's weakening grip, though he might have worried less about himself and more about his old friend then.

Av was focused so much on swinging Dwight that he failed to notice his fingers growing numb as the protrusion's jagged edge cut through their skin and compressed their thin muscles to the point where it would have seemed, if Av thought about it, that the cliff was holding on to him.

As Dwight gained height, Lisa and Blue took their turns stretching their arms down to grab at his wrists. Soon Blue was able to grab one, and he and Lisa pulled up the terrified boy.

Partially relieved, both Lisa and Blue took a few seconds to check Dwight's shoulder and then hug him.

"That was incredible!" exclaimed Lyon, standing up and holding out his hand to help Dwight stand.

Taking his friend's hand, Dwight winced from a shooting pain in his calf and sat back down. "Av has a super strong grip. I guess that's a good thing."

Lisa peered again over the edge. "Ok, Av, now we have to get you up." She looked to Blue who was examining Dwight's ankle. "Blue, I need you to run down to the house at the bottom of the road to get some rope...something to pull him up with."

"And I'll go look for a long branch," said Lyon, who took off into the woods.

With Blue taking off down the road as fast as he could while avoiding the potholes, Dwight crawled over to the edge and peered down at Av. Seeing his friend's predicament from a different angle, tears began again to build up in his blue eyes.

"How are you?" Av asked Dwight.

"I'm...I'm ok. I...I didn't know you have a G.I. Joe kung-fu action grip," replied Dwight with his tears dripping down around the old man.

"I did not know either," said Av.

"Av, his shoulder's fine. His jacket's a little torn from whatever hit him, but he's only scratched at the most," said Lisa, who then began to give in to her crying. "Av, you have to hang on for just a few more minutes."

Av forced his fingers along the bit of rock as he tried to get a better grip.

"I will certainly try."

"You have to do better than try!" Lisa demanded, her tears dripping down on to him. "You better not fall! You can't leave us. It's too soon!"

"It's all relative, Lisa," Av said, forcing a smile through his fear as he tried to calm the young mother. "I have lived more in the four hundred and twenty-two days with you and the boys than I have in the last thirty years. If I must go today, I will have no regrets. I would rather...I would rather appreciate the time we had rather than to dwell on the time we could have had."

"You sound like it's the end!" Lisa scolded. Then her tone changed. "You counted the days?" she asked with the slightest smile, which was all she could form at that moment.

"I counted the days of my new life. I would have counted the hours, but I-I can...I can always struggle with the math...if I have a need to know them."

Lisa wiped her eyes. "Look at me. My tears are raining down on you."

Av did not mind the tears hitting his head but worried about the few that landed on his fingers. They could only make his grip worse.

Looking down at the patiently waiting boulders and then back up at the two, he said, "While I am hanging around, I have never thanked you both for forcing yourselves into my life. I do not expect my life would have been much without either of you. It...it would not have been anything to be...to be proud."

"You're welcome," Dwight blurted out and then immediately regretted it.

"You can thank us when you're up here safe!" said Lisa. "Though, it's really us who should be thanking you."

"Right. We...we will have to argue that point when I am up there."

"Well...since we're thanking each other, I'll...I'll thank

you for being there for us." Lisa's voice cracked and her tears flowed faster as she added, "When everything was going from bad to worse, you hung in there. You never gave up on us, never got scared away. And now look where that's got you! This is all my fault! Three times you've been in danger because of me!"

"I certainly do not agree with that," said Av. "You are as much at fault for this, or any of that, as you are for the weather. It is a matter of circumstances, no more. The Autumn Drive thing was a wrong place at the wrong time situation. This...well, this was me acting on a false feeling of control. This is pretty much my fault. As for thanking me, there is no reason to thank me for anything. I enjoy being there for you, being useful when I can...being needed. It is the first time in over thirty years that I felt I was."

With Lisa not knowing how to respond since it felt as though they were about to have their first ever argument, Av glanced down at the boulders. The tide was rising, but it would still be some time before the water covered them, though he was certain it would still do little to break his fall. With the two's tears dripping down on him, Av forced a consoling smile and was about to say something when he found himself struggling with his fingers' bloody grip. He tried desperately to change hands but could not lift his other arm high enough.

"Hey, if Blue was here, I'm sure he'd be thanking you too," said Dwight with a cracking voice. "He learned lots of stuff from you. He told me once that...he told me that besides his dad, you're the man he respects the most. You're the smartest man he knows. He says you know a lot about people for someone who doesn't know a lot of people."

Av's face formed a genuine smile and his eyes began to water. "Well...well, that is nice...nice to know," he said as blood slowly began dripping from the protrusion he was desperately clinging to.

"How's your hand? How's your fingers?" asked Lisa.

"I cannot say for certain. I seem to have lost feeling in them."

"Av, you just need to hang on for a bit longer," Lisa

begged. "Don't let go! Blue'll be here soon!"

"I can hear him coming up the road," Dwight lied as tears began pouring faster from his eyes. "He'll be here any second."

Av hoped to hold on a bit longer. He wished to give Blue some encouraging words on moving on from all that had happened, was happening. Trying again to adjust his bloody fingers, his smallest finger slipped, and then the next finger did the same. With the middle finger slipping, Av said only, "I am sorry." He closed his eyes as his body went horizontal and his wife's perfume filled his nostrils. For the first time, there was no questioning the scent's existence.

Lisa's scream followed her friend as he fell toward the boulders. It was the longest and most painful three seconds of the Dixons' lives.

For the second time in his short life, Dwight had experienced everything in slow motion. Av had made his dramatic entrance into the boy's life in slow motion and now had dramatically exited his life in the same way. The boy needed to scream but he could not make a sound. Rolling onto his back he tried to convince himself that what he had just seen did not happen, could not have happened. It was something out of a nightmare, and he wished he could wake up at that very moment and hear Av snoring down the hall.

Lisa rolled away from the edge, sat up and released a scream so loud and so high pitched that, because of their elevation, it may have been heard for miles.

Dwight sat up and both he and his mother hugged and cried together as they had never done so profoundly before.

Hearing the scream, Lyon returned from the woods empty handed, ran over and sat down with the mother and son, and was swallowed up by their embrace.

Hearing the scream too, Blue, holding firmly onto the rope wound over his shoulder, ran even faster up the dirt road. Passing Howard's truck, he froze, let the rope fall and stared dumbly at the three sitting and tightly hugging each other as they shared their grief.

Blue did not need to ask what had happened. His sorrow,

which had replaced his fear, then morphed into an intense anger. Standing there with his fists clenched at his sides, he shook uncontrollably before Howard's moaning caught his attention. With the growing sounds of sirens in the distance, Blue stiffly walked over to the wounded man lying on his back and shouting, "I can't see! I can't see!" Without uttering a word and with all the energy he could find, Blue kicked and kicked and kicked the bleeding man, silencing him.

A white-haired man who had been trying to keep up with Blue stopped at the front of the truck to catch his breath. He looked in disbelief toward the three sitting huddled together crying and then watched in wonder as the redheaded boy cried and kicked the unconscious man.

Blue was about to let loose a furious stomp on Howard's head when he felt a hand firmly but gently placed on his shoulder. He looked to his left but there was no one there. When he looked to his right, there was no one there either. Defeated, he forced himself to walk over to the three, where he collapsed in grief and was immediately engulfed in their arms.

Blue shook in the others' arms, allowing the tears running down his cheeks to mix with theirs.

CHAPTER 23
Moving On

I had as quick and painless a death as I could have. I do not know if during the fall everything had appeared in slow motion or if my life had flashed before my eyes, since I could not help but keep them closed.

I believe, yet again, that Ruthy was right. Because it was a Jewish burial, my pine box was closed. But if it had been open, I think my family would not have been surprised by the peaceful look on my face, though I expect the other mourners, the members of the synagogue I had attended much fewer times than I should have, may not have been able to recognize me, perhaps even requesting a fingerprint check to confirm the peaceful man's identity.

Some days after laying me in the plot next to Ruthy's, all three returned to school. With the boys quickly losing their motivation for it and their marks soon dropping, Lisa struggled to finish the remaining few weeks of her first semester but ended up dropping her studies to give the boys more attention, which the two denied needing. Blue was confident he could look after Dwight and himself, and Dwight was confident he could look after Blue and himself. Neither mentioned that the postponing of her goal to become a teacher caused them additional guilt.

It would be great to say that everyone lived happily ever after, but that would not be true. The three had experienced so much in the last year and a bit, including having this old man pass away, that it left them with issues, which they would have to come to terms with, including each blaming themselves for my death. Lisa blamed it on her befriending me. Blue blamed it on his befriending me, and Dwight blamed it on his falling off the cliff's edge. "If I didn't fall, Av would still be here!" the boy often thought to himself. Personally, I blame my death on life. If I had not lived my life as fully as I had those fourteen months, I may have lived to be ninety, but then I would have lived a sad, pathetic and lonely life for those extra twenty-four years. A life I would have preferred not to have lived.

As I had told Lisa, I have no regrets. I could say I regret leaving them, not being able to spend more time with them, but that regret would be wiped out by my appreciation for the time I did spend with them. I was not lying to Lisa when I told her I would rather appreciate what I did have than to dwell on what I could have had.

There is one rather small regret that I may have had if I forced myself to come up with one and that would be not finishing my macramé frog. Finally, I had found a hobby worth the energy, and I was good at it, or so I like to think, but I failed to complete my biggest project. A short time after leaving university, Lisa would end up finishing it for me, also giving her something to do to pass the time. A few weeks after my death, she came across my unfinished frog while dusting my bedroom. It would take that long before she could again bring herself to enter the room, which she would not allow Mrs. Collins to clean, taking it upon herself to do it when she was ready. And she would not clear my things out of the room; in fact, she moved some in. Along the mostly bare walls of my bedroom, she hung candid pictures of the family. There were pictures of us during our trip to Disney World the first week of summer break, pictures of us on Halifax's waterfront and pictures of us at my previous home and at theirs on Gilmore Street. There were many, many pictures —too many pictures. There were even some Lisa had to search hard and long for. Pictures of Ruthy and me before we left England, before the war, before I decided to practice introversion, when I could smile without being self-conscious of it. She did not stop at my bedroom but continued putting pictures of me all through the house: in the other bedrooms, in the library, the living room, along the walls of the halls, and even in the kitchen. Thankfully, she left me out of the washrooms. To anyone entering the house for the first time, it could appear as a multi-roomed shrine to their old friend.

Besides finding my unfinished frog, Lisa also found under my bed the top section of the rocket with ROY stenciled onto it. She was rather surprised by the discovery, and when she asked the boys if they knew anything about its recovery, neither did. Blue realized then why, when he had gone back three days later to recover it from the tree top, it was gone. I did not know he had gone back to get it, so I did not know that he left empty-handed and heartbroken. Why did I recover it? I went back and got it for the same reason Blue needed to get it back. With his name on the piece, it had to be joined back with the others. Why did I keep it to myself? Well...being afraid of heights, I had a rather terrifying time climbing the tree, and if my family knew I had recovered the missing section, they might have wanted to launch the rocket again, and that could require making a second climb that I would prefer not to do.

I would like to think that all the pictures of me around the house were hung only out of love, but there was some guilt mixed in. Instead of doing as a sociopath may do, creating far-out, illogical excuses to cover their feelings of guilt, Lisa and the boys did the opposite. They created more and more reasons to feel a strong guilt over my death, and living with all that guilt, no matter how unrealistic, was both mentally painful and exhausting. With hers taking its toll on her, Lisa recognized her need to talk to someone, a professional, and after her first meeting with a psychologist, she arranged weekly family sessions and then weekly individual sessions for each. Initially, neither Blue nor Dwight thought the family meetings or individual ones would be useful, but after several weeks, both started to trust and open up to the psychologist, with Blue even bringing up his continuing guilt over both his father's and Stevie's deaths. Both boys eventually gained from it. It took a while, but over time they blamed themselves less and began blaming my death more on unfortunate circumstances beyond their control, which is what it was, and they eventually stopped asking themselves what would have happened if they had done this, that or some other thing differently.

Soon after the sessions began, Lisa started proceedings to adopt Blue, and after almost a year and a half, Lisa, Dwight and Blue were legally a family, but they still had different last names. Perhaps as an act of posthumously adopting me, Lisa and an agreeable Dwight had their last names changed to Rosen. It pleases me that Blue, to honor his father, kept his last name of Roy.

It would take almost two years before all three felt they no longer needed the help of a psychologist, and by that time, things were going well for them. Lisa returned to university and the boy's marks were back up to where they were before my death (higher in Blue's case,) and both would head to university, with Blue studying Criminology and Dwight following two years later to study Commerce and then Law.

That day at the lookout everyone was a victim, including little Lyon, who also blamed himself for my death, figuring their improvised bomb had started the chain of events that ended with my death. There would be no psychologist for him, and to make his situation worse, his mother forbid him from hanging out with Dwight.

For a short time and without Lyon's mother knowing, the two hung out together at school, but with Dwight making more friends and hanging out with them too, and then Lyon being moved up a grade that coming January, Lyon had little to keep himself connected to Dwight and soon found himself alone at school again. That next summer, Lyon would spend some of it within the thick line of trees separating his home from Dwight's, watching his one-time friend hanging out around the pool with his new friends. Several times that summer when Dwight and Blue caught him and called out to him to come and join them, he quietly and quickly returned to his home to lose himself in a textbook.

The next three years were very lonely years for Lyon.

Three years because over that time, Lyon was moved ahead twice more, spending a year in Blue's class and still taking bids for the position of his science project partner. Blue paid almost six hundred dollars for the opportunity of an easy 'A', and of course, he got it, but he did not fully understand what the project was about and would never have asked Lyon to explain it to him.

Dwight and Lyon would not cross paths at university. Dewey went to Saint Mary's University and Lyon went to Dalhousie University. By the time Dwight entered university, Lisa had earned her teaching degree and was teaching grade four at Chebucto Heights Elementary School at the top of Cowie Hill and Lyon had finished his three-year bachelor degree and was just finishing his masters in physics. He was then only eighteen years old and still not old enough to enter Dalhousie University's pub. The next year he was, and he would visit it alone while earning his PhD, which he would receive in Molecular Physics. With his PhD, he moved to Palo Alto, California, to teach at Stanford University. After that, he would seldom visit his mother, father and two younger sisters, preferring instead to spend his vacations in the company and comfort of a bottle of Jack Daniels.

As for Howard, the man who never failed to pass on an opportunity, when he was well enough to leave the hospital and wait in prison for his murder and kidnapping trial, on the third night of his stay he was found in his cell stabbed to death. The murderer was never found. The prison guards certainly had their suspicions, but without any evidence or a non-reluctant witness, nothing could be proven.

Oh...and about those Halifax Police Department's Citizen's Awards for Bravery medals: the boys did receive them. Two months after my death, the boys accepted them with Lisa accepting mine on my behalf, which she hung in my bedroom. Sadly, the boys accepted their awards as stoically as I would have done had I been there.

With all that said, I would like to tell you more about Dwight and Blue's story, but that is not for me to tell. Perhaps, the last story is how a wonderful, intelligent and compassionate woman stumbled into love with a nincompoop of above-average height and under-average looks, but that would be before Herring Cove Road, forty-something years before.

The End of Book Three

Author's Notes

i. Though the characters and their situations and events are fictitious, the named streets, except for Gilmore Street, are true for the period of the story.

ii. With the exception of the school, the location of Thirteenth Tribe's clubhouse and the lookout, all the places mentioned, including the prison, are real as of the period of the story

iii. The Headless Norsemen Motorcycle "Club" is fictitious but a chapter of the Thirteenth Tribe existed in Halifax up until the early eighties, when it was patched over by the Quebec chapter of an international "club." The name of that group was not used in the story to avoid any undo "stress" on the author.

ABOUT THE AUTHOR

Michael Kroft is an eclectic reader and an accidental novelist. Being a writer of short stories of various genres, his first novel began as a short story, but because of his love for the characters, it quickly bloomed to a full-length novel. With his newfound interest in writing novels, Michael turned his first novel, *On Herring Cove Road: Mr. Rosen and His 43Lb Anxiety*, into the family saga series, *Herring Cove Road*, with each additional novel in the sub-genres of a murder mystery, a crime and a romance.

With the series *Herring Cove Road* completed, Michael is now working on the first novel of an amusing, heart-warming and historically-accurate family saga that begins with an English immigrant, William Lovely, and his younger brother, Oscar, coming to America in 1715 through indentured servitude, and then follows the next nine generations, reaching 1905. The series is tentatively called *The Lovely American Family Tree*, and the first novel in the series is tentatively titled *Indentured Bonds*.

Originally from Halifax, Nova Scotia, Michael Kroft is single and, apparently, with too much time on his hands.

For more information on Michael Kroft and his works, please visit his website at http://www.michaelkroft.com

Michael Kroft's current works:

The not-so-nuclear family saga series, Herring Cove Road:

1 – On Herring Cove Road: Mr. Rosen and His 43Lb Anxiety
2 – Still on Herring Cove Road: Hickory, Dickory, Death
3 – Off Herring Cove Road: The Problem Being Blue
4 – Before Herring Cove Road: Ruth Goldman and the Nincompoop

CPSIA information can be obtained
at www.ICGtesting.com
Printed in the USA
LVHW042350010719
622953LV00010B/274/P